Faith Found in Frisco

Robin L. Scott

PublishAmerica
Baltimore

First printing

Hardcover 978-1-4626-3072-1
Softcover 978-1-4626-3073-8
PUBLISHED BY PUBLISHAMERICA, LLLP
www.publishamerica.com
Baltimore

Printed in the United States of America

Dedication

To Jim—my love, my life, my best friend…

Acknowledgement

My inspiration for writing love stories comes from the greatest Love Story of them all—the Bible. Thank you Lord for another opportunity to share the secret of the Scriptures…Your Word speaks to my heart and reminds me there's a story to be told…

Chapter One

"I know why you're smiling so much today," Patricia teased, "Liam's due back from Texas today isn't he?"

Amelia opened her lunch and grinned at her friend. "We have a date tonight to finalize the wedding plans." Amelia turned the engagement ring on her finger slowly. "I've missed him so much. I can't wait for him to get home."

Patricia rolled her eyes. "You two have been together since high school. I can't believe you've waited this long to get married!"

Amelia laughed. "I had to finish college and Liam was building a career in the Air Force. We couldn't get married until now. In just eight weeks I'll be Mrs. Liam Nelson."

Patricia glanced at her watch. "Uh Oh, my little monsters will get back to the classroom before me if I don't get a move on." Patricia tossed her lunch bag into the trash can and headed back to the fourth grade class.

The cell phone in Amelia's pocket was vibrating and she answered it grinning. "Hi sweetheart, where are you?"

"I'm home. We need to talk." Liam's voice sounded odd.

"I've got a classroom full of third graders that I can't leave alone Liam; is something wrong?" Amelia asked.

Liam cleared his throat. "No, I'll just talk to you tonight. I've got to go."

Amelia felt a chill run down her spine. "Ok. I love you."

Liam paused. "Yeah, love you too, see you tonight."

The bell rang as Amelia closed her phone. The hall was filled with elementary students and she hurried to her classroom.

When the final bell rang, Amelia hurried to gather her things and headed for her car. She put the top down on her convertible and headed into Orlando traffic. On a good day she could make it home in twenty minutes. Today was not a good day. As the traffic crawled, Amelia allowed her thoughts to wander.

Liam was a sophomore and the quarterback for the high school football team when Amelia met him. The marching band practiced in the field next to the football team and Amelia loved watching Liam play the game while she played her flute in the band.

Amelia remembered prom and graduation. Liam had proposed the day he left for boot camp in the air force and Amelia had worn his engagement ring ever since. It was hard to believe five years had passed and the wedding was just two months away. Their time together was based on email, letters, phone calls, short holiday visits, and military leaves. Their relationship was comfortable more than romantic and Amelia hoped that marriage would change that.

Amelia pulled into the driveway of her parents' home. She loved this house. The ranch style house looked cool and inviting and Amelia walked from the heat of the Florida sun into the coolness of the air conditioning. Amelia had just poured herself a glass of lemonade when the doorbell rang.

Liam stood at the door still in his uniform. He wanted to get this over with.

"Liam!" Amelia flung herself into his arms and hugged him. "I've missed you so much, come on in the house."

Liam followed her inside and shut the door. "Amelia, we need to talk."

"What's wrong? Are you ill? Has something happened?" Amelia had never seen Liam this serious.

"It's over Amelia," Liam spoke without remorse.

Amelia didn't understand. "What's over? Liam, I don't understand what you're talking about."

Liam took Amelia's hands and spoke softly. "I'm breaking our engagement. I can't marry you."

Amelia felt the blood drain from her face. "What? Why? Did I do something to make you not love me anymore?"

"You didn't do anything. I'm in love with someone else." Liam explained.

Amelia was shocked and angry. "How could you be in love with someone else? How or should I say who, is she?"

"It's Courtney Williams." Liam hung his head.

"Courtney? You're in love with Courtney?" Amelia felt the tears and wiped at them in frustration. "When did this happen? You've been in Texas for six months."

Liam ran his hand through his hair. "Courtney and I went out a couple of times about a year ago and she has been with me in Texas for the past six months. I'm going to marry her this weekend."

Amelia was shocked. "You dated her while we were engaged? Why did you wait until now to tell me that you were involved with someone else?"

"I wasn't sure if it would last with me and Courtney. If our relationship had failed, I had every intention of marrying you," Liam explained nonchalantly.

"Get out of this house," Amelia held the door as she spoke. "I never want to see you again." She was angry and hurt.

"I need my ring back, Amelia," Liam spoke firmly.

Amelia took the ring off and threw it at him. "Take your ring and get out of my house and out of my life."

Liam left the house, tucking the engagement ring in the shirt pocket of his uniform. He was whistling as he walked towards his car. Liam grinned as he backed out of the driveway, getting out of the engagement was easier than he thought. Amelia would still be there if the relationship with Courtney failed, he was sure of it.

Amelia walked in a daze to her room and quickly changed into her swim suit. She grabbed a towel and headed for the pool in the backyard. She had always found comfort in swimming laps. The sound of Liam's voice telling her that he would have married her if his other relationship hadn't worked out drove her harder and faster across the pool. The coolness of the water felt good to Amelia's heated body. She swam back and forth until she was exhausted. The tears had stopped and the anger had replaced them.

"Amelia, where are you honey? Your daddy and I have some catering samples for you to try." Cecilia sat the trays on the counter and walked down the hallway towards Amelia's room. "Amelia?"

Amelia spoke through the closed door. "I'll be there in a minute mom, I'm changing clothes."

Cecilia opened up the trays of samples as Reggie poured glasses of iced tea.

Amelia walked into the kitchen. "Hi daddy," she spoke softly.

Reggie hugged his daughter. "What's wrong honey? You've been crying."

Cecilia looked up quickly. "Baby, what's wrong?" she asked in concern.

Amelia pulled out a chair. "The wedding is off. Liam came by today to get his engagement ring back. He's marrying Courtney Williams this weekend."

"What?" Cecilia sat down in the chair across from Amelia and took her hand. "Oh honey I am so sorry. Are you ok?" she asked.

"I think I'm still in shock mom." Amelia sipped the tea in front of her. "I've got to cancel all the arrangements and I've got two more weeks of school till summer vacation. I don't have time to not be ok."

Reggie pulled out the chair next to Amelia and sat down. "Why don't you let your mother and I take care of cancelling the arrangements. We don't mind doing that."

Amelia felt the tears start. "Thank daddy, I think I'll take you up on that."

Cecilia squeezed Amelia's hand. "Honey, can you tell us what happened?"

Amelia sighed deeply as she began, "Liam told me he has been involved with Courtney since last year." Amelia felt hollow inside. "He told me he kept the relationship a secret so that if it didn't work out, he would still marry me."

Reggie spoke quietly. "Amelia, I know this is painful and I don't understand what happened to that young man. However, it's best to find out now that he isn't trustworthy than to marry him and then find out."

"I know daddy, I just feel so betrayed." Amelia excused herself and spent the rest of the evening in her room.

The next morning, Amelia was up and out of the house early. She was in her classroom when Patricia arrived.

"Ok so how was the reunion last night?" Patricia teased.

"Patricia, there was no reunion. The wedding is off." Amelia spoke matter-of-factly.

"What?" Patricia was speechless.

Amelia leaned back in her chair. "Do you remember Courtney Williams from high school?"

Patricia thought for a moment. "Courtney Williams, wasn't she the head cheer leader?"

"Yes. She has been dating Liam for over a year and she moved to Texas for the past six months and they've been together. They are getting married Saturday," Amelia said.

Patricia was shocked. "I am so sorry Amelia. Are you ok?"

"I'm angry. First I was hurt, now I'm just angry." Amelia shifted the papers on her desk and looked at her friend. "I've wasted the past five years of my life waiting for Liam and now I'm ready to make a change in my life."

"What kind of a change?" Patricia asked.

"I don't know but I promise you that it won't involve a man!"

Patricia smiled at her friend. "Don't judge all men on what Liam did to you Amelia. The right man is out there, you just haven't met him yet."

Amelia, Cecilia and Reggie arrived at church on Sunday just as morning worship was starting. They slipped into their pew as the Pastor addressed the congregation.

The praise team led the congregation in worship and the Pastor began his message.

"This morning I'd like you to open your Bibles to Hebrews chapter eleven. '*NOW faith is the substance of things hoped for and the evidence of things not seen…*' if I were giving this message a title, I'd call it NOW Faith. This is a very familiar scripture to all of us. However, today I'd like you to pay special attention to the word NOW. If you'll look closely at this scripture in your Bibles you'll see that NOW is in all caps. God meant for this word to be emphasized with the word Faith. I want you to think about how faith operates; is your faith based on things that will happen in the future? Or is your faith active and ready for action now? We set priorities in our lives and goals that we strive to achieve. Our faith must be Christ based and ready for His leading and His direction. We must be willing to act on that NOW Faith when God says act."

Pastor moved from the pulpit to the floor and continued his message among the congregation. "The book of James chapter one and verse three tells us '*Knowing this, that the trying of your faith worketh patience.*' Perhaps you've been faced with a situation in your life that has made you question your beliefs or values. This scripture reminds us that our faith will be tried."

Pastor paused and turned the pages of his Bible. "In the book of first Peter chapter one and verse seven we are told, '*That the trial of your faith, being much more precious that of gold that perisheth, though it be tried with fire, might be found unto praise and honor and glory at the appearing of Jesus Christ.*' Yes we are tested and tried and sometimes it shakes our faith to the very foundation of our beings. Through the trials, NOW faith will give you the courage to keep moving forward and believing what you cannot see."

Amelia listened to the message with a heavy heart. Her faith had been sorely tested by loving a man for five years and finding out that he was unfaithful.

The praise team sang a song during the altar service and Amelia felt the words deep in her soul. *"I need You more, more than yesterday; I need You more, more than words can say; I need You more, than ever before; I need You Lord, I need You Lord."*

Cecilia and Reggie went to lunch with another couple from the church after dropping Amelia at home. Amelia had declined the invitation preferring to spend some time alone.

Amelia poured herself a glass of lemonade and opened the Sunday paper. The front page of the living section had a full story of the wedding of Courtney Williams to Liam Nelson. The photo showed a beautiful bride looking up into the face of her adoring groom. Liam wore his dress uniform and Courtney's gown was breathtaking. Amelia closed the paper and walked slowly to her room.

Amelia knelt beside her bed. “Lord, I don’t think I have the words to pray.” She felt the tears falling and wiped at them with a tissue. “I just know that I need you more than I ever have before Lord. If there’s a purpose in my life, could you show me what that purpose is? I’m ready to make a change Lord. Give me the now faith that pastor preached this morning and lead me where you would have me to go.”

Chapter Two

Field day at the elementary school was full of fun and excitement for the students. Lessons were over and the last two days of the school year consisted of races, games, and just physical activity to prepare students for their summer vacation. Field day also gave teachers time to prepare final report cards and to clean out their desks for the summer.

Amelia was sitting at her desk listening to the children's laughter drifting through the window when Patricia walked in.

"Another year bites the dust!" Patricia teased.

Amelia smiled as she asked, "Now what?"

Patricia sat on the corner of her desk. "I've got an idea, want to hear it?"

"You have an idea that sounds dangerous." Amelia and Patricia had grown up together and were more like sisters than friends. "Do I really have a choice?" she teased.

Patricia laughed out loud. "You need a change, that's what you said, right?" she asked.

"Right," Amelia agreed.

"I've booked a trip for the first week in July and I want you to come with me," Patricia offered.

Amelia looked skeptical. "That's just three weeks away. Where exactly are you going?"

Patricia pulled out a letter from her handbag and unfolded it. "I've got a week reserved in a condo in Frisco, Colorado."

"Colorado? Who do you know in Colorado?" Amelia asked surprised.

"Absolutely no one," Patricia grinned. "That's the beauty of it. My mom and dad have a time share and they had a week that was going to expire this year and they gave it to me. I've wanted to go to Colorado for a long time."

"I'm not very good company right now," Amelia explained. "I'd hate to ruin your vacation with a bad attitude."

Patricia leaned across the desk and tipped Amelia's chin up. "Listen, we've been friends since kindergarten. I know you're still angry and hurt over Liam's betrayal, but you need a change of scenery. This is a chance to get away for a week and just have some fun."

"Can I think about it?" Amelia asked.

Patricia grinned. "Yep, just let me know if you want to go."

Amelia smiled at her friend. "So how are you getting to Colorado?"

Patricia stood and twirled around the room with her arms extended making motor sounds like an airplane. "I'm flying of course!"

Amelia laughed out loud. "You are crazy. I'll think about it, I promise."

Amelia stopped by the grocery store on her way home from the school. She had volunteered to pick up some fresh fruit and vegetables for the family cookout. Amelia placed the last item on the list into her cart and turned towards the cashiers as she came face-to-face with Courtney.

"Hello Amelia."

"Courtney..." Amelia wasn't ready to see the reality of Liam's betrayal.

"We didn't see you at the wedding; Liam was sure you'd want to be there to wish us well," Courtney spoke cruelly.

"Excuse me Courtney; I don't have any desire to see you or Liam." Amelia turned her cart to go around Courtney.

"Really Amelia, don't you think you're being childish? I know you are jealous, but did you really think a band geek like you could keep a man like Liam satisfied?" Courtney asked laughing.

Amelia felt her temper flare. "I'm not jealous. I'm actually grateful that Liam showed his infidelity before we got married. You did me a favor Courtney."

Courtney was stunned. "How did I do you a favor?" she asked.

"If Liam would cheat on me with you, he'll cheat on you with someone else." Amelia smiled. "I wish you both, happiness."

Courtney was angry. "We will have happiness, the head cheer leader and the quarterback from the football team are always meant to be together."

Amelia smiled as she spoke. "Courtney high school was a long time ago, you need to get over yourself." She pushed her cart towards the cashier and paid for her groceries. Amelia drove home smiling. She unloaded the groceries and then slipped into her room to call Patricia.

"Hello?" Patricia answered on the first ring.

"Am I still invited on your vacation?" Amelia had a pad and paper in her hand waiting for Patricia's answer.

"Of course! Are you coming?" Patricia asked.

Amelia laughed. "I'd love to go to Colorado with you. Give me the flight details and I'll book my ticket."

Patricia was giggling. "I can give you the details but I've already got your ticket."

"You what? How did you know I'd say yes?" Amelia asked laughing.

"Amelia, we've been friends for too long. I know you as well as I know myself. I was determined to get you out of this town and on vacation even if I had to kidnap you!" Patricia assured her.

Amelia smiled. "Patricia you are the best friend I've ever known. How can I thank you?"

Patricia laughed. "You don't have to thank me. I'll come by tomorrow and we'll get online and lay out an itinerary for our little adventure."

"That sounds great! Bring your swimsuit and we'll take a swim." Amelia hung the phone up grinning.

"Aunt Mia, where are you?" Hilary's three year old voice could be heard all over the house.

Amelia threw open her bedroom door and scooped us her niece. "Here I am sweetie, did you bring your swim suit?"

Hilary threw her little arms around Amelia's neck and hugged her tightly. "Aunt Mia, I'm wearing my swim suit. Can we swim now?"

"We can swim while papaw and daddy are grilling." Amelia grabbed some beach towels and placed them over Hilary's head causing her to giggle. "So do you think your brothers want to swim with us?" she asked.

Hilary scrunched up her nose in distaste. "Do we hafta let them swim? They're boys."

"Well if we don't let them swim with us, who will play ball with us?" Amelia explained.

Hilary released a large sigh and crossed her little arms. "Well, all right, they can swim too."

"Go tell your brothers we're going to swim now and then we'll eat." Amelia sat Hilary down and watched her run for the porch to get Henry and Harmon.

Myron stood in the kitchen doorway. "Hey sis thanks for entertaining my kids in the pool."

Amelia hugged him. "Big brother, my nephews and niece are the best gift you've ever given me."

"They certainly love their aunt Mia." Myron grinned. "I personally don't know what they see in you."

Amelia swatted him with a towel. "They love me because I'm the fun one." Amelia hurried to the pool laughing as she went.

Henry and Harmon were waiting beside the diving board anxious to get into the water.

"Gosh Aunt Mia we thought you'd never get out here. Daddy says we can't get into the pool until you're with us." Henry was the oldest of the three children and had just turned seven. "Can we get in now?" he asked impatiently.

Amelia smiled. "Yes sir!" She laughed as Henry ran and did a cannonball from the diving board into the deep end.

Harmon stood on the diving board waiting for Henry to resurface. "Aunt Mia, watch this!" Harmon was five and had no fear of the water. He pointed his little arms above his head and did a perfect dive from the board into the water.

Amelia and Hilary were clapping and cheering for him when he came up out of the water.

Myron and Reggie had started the grill and were preparing the hamburgers and hotdogs. Myron grinned as he watched his children in the pool. "Dad, I don't think I ever told you how much I appreciated you and mom giving us that swimming pool."

Reggie smiled at his grandchildren's antics. "Son, that pool was the best investment your mother and I ever made."

"When I see them in the pool, it reminds me of Amelia and me growing up." Myron watched Amelia as she worked with Hilary in the shallow end. "Dad, how is Amelia doing?"

Reggie started placing the meat on the grill as he spoke. "She's a brave girl, but I know she's hurting."

Myron's wife Anne and Cecilia had joined the men. "I'm worried about her." Anne spoke softly. "She loved Liam very much and he broke her heart."

"My baby girl is tough." Cecilia watched Amelia with the children. "She's been hurt by Liam but I'm grateful that it happened before she married him."

"I never cared for Liam." Myron spoke with conviction. "He always acted like he was doing Amelia a favor dating her. I'm glad they're not getting married."

"Myron! She loved him!" Anne scolded.

Myron wrapped Anne in his arms. "Honey, I know my sister loved that man with her whole heart. I also know that Liam wasn't true to her, even in high school."

"Are you sure you aren't just over protective? She is your only sister." Anne questioned.

Myron glanced over at the pool. "I probably am overprotective but I promise you that when Amelia finds the right man, she'll have her big brother's support one hundred percent."

"What if she had married Liam? I don't think you ever told her how you felt." Cecilia asked; she had no idea that Myron had disliked Liam.

"Mom, I wouldn't do anything to hurt Amelia. If she had married Liam, I would have kept quiet but I also would have kept watch over her," Myron promised.

Reggie smiled as he turned the meat on the grill. "Son, I'm proud of you. Not only are you a great father, you've always been a great brother."

Anne hugged him tightly. "I am praying that Amelia finds a man to love that's as good to her as Myron is to me."

"Mommy, look what Aunt Mia taught me!" Hilary was standing on the diving board. "Mommy, daddy, watch me!"

"Ok Hilary, just like I showed you," Amelia was in the water waiting for Hilary to jump.

Hilary giggled and jumped from the diving board tucking her knees in her arms and making a large splash in the deep water below.

Amelia was waiting as Hilary swam back to the surface giggling. "Woo hoo that was excellent Hilary!" Amelia encouraged.

Hilary hugged Amelia and swam quickly for the side of the pool to dive again.

Henry and Harmon quickly joined Hilary and the three children jumped from the diving board over and over; each trying to outdo the other for Amelia's attention and praise.

Dinner was eaten in the sun room off the back of the house. The children were ravenous from their swimming and ate quickly. By the end of the meal, all three children were yawning. Hilary slipped into the hammock beside Harmon and the gently swaying soon rocked them both to sleep.

Anne covered them with a light blanket.

Henry sat next to his mamaw Cecilia on the glider and fell asleep with his head against her shoulder. Cecilia gently stood and eased Henry onto the glider and covered him.

Myron sipped his iced tea. "Sis, you wore them out."

Amelia laughed softly. "How do you think I've survived the past two years as an elementary teacher?"

"I watch my grandchildren and see the two of you all over again." Reggie paused remembering. "The two of you were constantly trying to outdo the other."

"So what are your plans for the summer?" Anne asked Amelia.

"Patricia and I are going on vacation the first week of July."

Myron looked surprised. "Where are you going?"

Amelia grinned. "We are going to Frisco, Colorado for a week."

"Colorado?" Anne leaned back in her chair. "That sounds exciting. Does Patricia have family there?"

"No and that's the best part. We are spending a week in the Rocky Mountains and exploring Colorado like typical tourists." Amelia smiled at the thought.

Myron winked at Anne. "I think my baby sister needs a really great camera for this vacation, what do you think?" he asked slyly.

"Myron, that's a great idea!" Anne excused herself and slipped out of the house returning with a camera bag. "Myron and I bought a new camera this year and our old one isn't being used. We'd like you to have it Amelia," she offered.

Amelia slipped the digital camera from the bag. "Let me pay you all for this."

"No way sis. We aren't using this one anymore and you don't have a digital camera do you?" Myron asked.

Amelia grinned. "I do now!"

Chapter Three

Patricia arrived at Amelia's early Saturday morning. She carried her laptop and gym bags into the house and dropped them off in Amelia's room. "So what's on the agenda today?" she asked.

Amelia grinned. "It's a balmy 104º this morning in beautiful Orlando, so let's take a swim before it's too hot to enjoy the pool."

Patricia grabbed her beach towel and headed for the pool with Amelia. They laughed and swam for over an hour.

"Whew, Amelia I'm ready for a snack; you did plan to feed me right?" Patricia teased.

Amelia laughed as she wrapped her hair in a towel and slipped on her flip flops. "When have I not had snacks for my best friend?"

Patricia's stomach growled and she grinned. "I think the natives are restless. I didn't eat breakfast this morning and I'm starved!"

Amelia sat bagels, cream cheese, ham, and fresh fruit on the table. "Iced tea?" she asked.

Patricia snagged a strawberry. "Iced tea would be great. This is the perfect snack. How do you always know what I like?"

"I have two nephews and a niece; they like the same food you always have." Amelia sat down and offered the blessing over their food.

"That was so good." Patricia carried their dishes to the sink and put them in the dishwasher while Amelia placed the food back in the refrigerator.

"Okay so what did you bring for our vacation plans?" Amelia asked.

Patricia sat up her laptop and pulled out pads of paper and pens. "Here's the condo we'll be staying at," Patricia slid the computer in front of Amelia. "I thought we'd look up some of the local activities and see what we want to do that week."

Amelia leaned back in her chair. "Would you consider going to Rocky Mountain National Park? I'm not sure how far that is from Frisco but I've heard that it's pretty amazing."

Patricia typed in the search engine and grinned. "According to MapQuest, the park is only two and one half hours from Frisco so that's a day trip!"

"That's not bad. What else have you found for us to do?" Amelia asked.

Patricia grinned. "I registered for the concert schedule at Red Rocks Park and Amphitheater, it's a beautiful place and even if there isn't a concert while we're there, we can visit the park."

"That sounds great. I'm up for whatever you want to do," Amelia agreed.

Patricia closed the laptop and sipped her iced tea. "So how are you? I was kind of surprised that you agreed to go without any influence by me."

Amelia smiled softly. "I paid close attention to Pastor's message last Sunday. I've been giving it a lot of thought."

"Care to share?" Patricia was curious.

"NOW faith, those two little words have been spinning in my head since Sunday," Amelia spoke softly.

"I'll agree that message was wonderful, but Amelia when you called me, there was a tone to your voice that tells me something else is going on," Patricia prompted.

"I ran into Courtney at the grocery store." Amelia frowned before she continued. "I wasn't ready to see her face-to-face and I should be able to handle it."

Patricia straightened in her chair. "You were engaged to Liam for five years and you were two months from your wedding. How do you think you are supposed to feel to find out he betrayed your trust? As for Courtney; I probably would have smacked her. It's a good thing it was you and not me."

Amelia laughed out loud. "Oh Patricia, you are so good for my ego." Amelia's laughter brought tears of mirth to her eyes. "Whew, sorry," Amelia took a deep breath to control her laughter. "I laid awake last night thinking about Pastor's message and about Courtney and Liam living in such close proximity and I realized that my life has been on hold for five years now." Amelia took a deep breath. "I'm in need of change in my life."

"Well I'm sorry you had to deal with Courtney, however, I'm glad you're coming on vacation with me. The change of scenery will do you good." Patricia was sure this trip would cheer Amelia up.

"I agree. So what time is our flight to Denver?" Amelia asked.

"Our flight leaves at 10:30 a.m. and we have to check in an hour early. We arrive in Denver at 12:40 p.m. their time." Patricia opened the flight itinerary on the laptop for Amelia to view.

Amelia grinned. "I am getting more excited the more you share the details. Do you know how long it's been since you and I took a vacation?" she asked laughing.

"Hmmmm, I think it was our high school graduation trip to the Bahamas right?" Patricia asked.

"Exactly and that was six years ago!" Amelia looked at her notepad before asking. "So what about a rental car?"

Patricia pulled up the confirmation page on her laptop and grinned. "How does a mustang convertible sound?"

Amelia grinned. "That sounds perfect! We are going to have a blast."

Amelia and Patricia spent the remainder of the afternoon planning their trip and looking up tourist attractions on the Internet.

Cecilia entered the house carrying two bags of groceries. "Hey girls, how are the vacation plans coming?" she asked.

Amelia took one of the bags and carried it to the kitchen. "We've got it all planned."

"Cece do you need me to help carry anything in from the car?" Patricia asked.

"Thanks sweetie, there are more in the trunk and I'm exhausted." Cecilia placed her bag on the counter and smiled. "Patricia is the only person that calls me Cece and I have to admit I love it."

Amelia smiled. "She couldn't say Cecilia when we were little and the nickname just stuck." Amelia headed outside to help Patricia with the other bags.

"That's all of it." Patricia pulled up a barstool at the counter. "Any cookies in that bag?" she asked innocently.

Cecilia laughed. "When have you known me not to buy your favorite snack?" Cecilia pulled a bakery package out and opened the box of Oatmeal, craisin and pecan cookies.

Patricia took a bite and sighed. "Mmmm now these are heavenly."

Amelia filled three glasses with iced tea and picked up a cookie. "Mom, can you drive Patricia and I to the airport so we don't have to pay to park the car for a week?"

"Of course honey. So what made you pick Frisco, Colorado as your vacation destination Patricia?" Cecilia asked.

Patricia snatched another cookie and leaned back in her seat. "I've always loved the Rocky Mountains and wanted to visit. I was surfing the net one night and found a link called '*Main Street to the Rockies*' and the town was Frisco. This town looks like the perfect spot for someone who wants the true western experience."

"I think it's exciting and I'm glad you girls are going together." Cecilia picked up a cookie and sat down. "Did Amelia show you what Myron and Anne gave her last night?" she asked.

"Oh, I almost forgot!" Amelia ran to her bedroom and returned with the camera bag. "Check out this digital camera."

Patricia picked up the camera and looked through the viewfinder. "Wow! I've seen them use this on the kids. They gave you this?"

"Yep, Anne said they bought a new one and they wanted me to have this one. How cool is that?" Amelia giggled.

"That is amazing. We can download the pictures in our condo; I'm taking my laptop." Patricia looked at the camera ports. "Do you have a USB cable to pull the pictures to the computer?"

Amelia looked through the camera bag and pulled out a gray cable and a black power cord. "I believe this is what you're looking for."

"Smile Cece," Patricia snapped the photo quickly before turning the camera towards Amelia and taking a picture of her friend. "Let's practice downloading."

Amelia watched as Patricia hooked up the digital camera with the USB cable and downloaded the two photos to her laptop. "Wow that was quick!" Amelia exclaimed.

Patricia disconnected the camera and handed it to Amelia. "We'll keep the camera charged at night and we'll download the pictures you take each night." Patricia closed the laptop and stood. "So let's take another swim; we've earned it!"

Cecilia stood watching the girls in the pool as Reggie slipped his arms around her waist from behind and kissed her cheek. "So how's our baby today?"

Cecilia smiled and wrapped her arms over Reggie's. "She's very excited about this trip with Patricia. I think this vacation is just what the doctor ordered."

Reggie watched his daughter with her best friend. "I hope so. When I think of what Liam did to her it makes me pretty angry."

"I know, makes me angry too. We will just have to be supportive and help Amelia any way we can," Cecilia agreed.

Reggie sighed and hugged Cecilia close. "I hope that this experience doesn't turn Amelia away from marriage. She's so good with children that she needs a family of her own."

Cecilia turned in Reggie's arms and hugged him close. "You are a hopeless romantic at heart. That must be why I married you."

"I thought you married me for my gorgeous body." Reggie teased.

Chapter Four

"We are now making our final descent into Denver; the flight attendants will be walking through the cabin and picking up any remaining trash you may have. Please return your seats to their upright position and stow your trays."

Amelia snapped a photo of the Rocky Mountains and the landscape from the window. "Patricia, I feel bad taking the window seat. You haven't seen anything!"

"Oh yes I have. I've seen a couple of very handsome cowboys in first class that look promising." Patricia wiggled her eyebrows up and down suggestively.

"You are incorrigible!" Amelia tucked her camera back into the bag and tucked it under the seat for landing. "We are here for vacation not to find a man for you!"

Patricia giggled. "We are here for vacation; if I find a man in the process that's just an added perk."

After picking up their luggage from baggage claim and securing their rental car, Amelia and Patricia pulled out into traffic and on their way to Frisco.

Amelia was driving while Patricia read the directions to their destination. "How long will it take us to drive to Frisco?" Amelia asked.

"Approximately two hours. Our check-in is any time after 4:00 p.m. so we'll have an hour for lunch before we go to the condo."

Amelia's stomach growled. "Perfect timing; that snack on the plane didn't last and I didn't eat breakfast this morning."

Patricia dug into her handbag and pulled out a chewy granola bar. "I planned ahead. We've got over an hour to drive and I didn't eat breakfast either."

The sun shining overhead felt warm as Amelia and Patricia drove towards Frisco with the top down on their rental car.

"Ok, take the Main Street Exit 201," Patricia instructed. "Turn left on West Main Street and then right onto South Fourth Avenue."

Amelia loved the sign at the entrance to Frisco as she turned onto the main street she smiled at what she saw. The downtown main street was picturesque and colorful. Old fashioned black iron street lamps with frosted globes held hanging baskets of multi-colored flowers.

Amelia drove slowly down Main Street, absorbing the lovely view of the Rocky Mountains framing the landscape beyond the town. She parked the car in front Butterhorn Bakery and Café. The smell of cinnamon floated from the restaurant beckoning diners to enter.

"Do you smell that cinnamon?" Patricia leaned her head back and breathed deeply. "That smells heavenly!"

Amelia laughed. "That settles it, we're eating here."

Patricia and Amelia were greeted by a friendly waitress. "Hello ladies, my name is Dori and I'll be your waitress today." Dori seated them at a table in the corner.

"Is this your first visit to the Butterhorn?" Dori asked.

Patricia laughed. "This is our first visit to Colorado. Whatever you're baking smells wonderful!"

"We hear that quite often." Dori had worked here since she was sixteen. "The cinnamon you smell comes from our cinnamon fruit bread. We also have fresh poppy raspberry muffins and cheese Danish."

Amelia laid the menu aside. "I think I'm going to try your lunch special."

"I'll have the same." Patricia handed their menus to Dori.

Dori wrote their orders on her pad. "What would you ladies like to drink?"

"I would love a Coke," Patricia grinned.

Amelia nodded in agreement. "Coke sounds good to me too."

Dori excused herself and placed their orders with the kitchen. She brought their cokes and moved to take care of other patrons.

"Patricia, let's buy some of their homemade pastry for breakfast."

Patricia grinned. "We'll have to get several; I don't think one will suffice."

Amelia was still laughing when Dori brought their lunch.

"Ladies, here are your chicken salad croissants and kettle chips. Can I get you anything else?"

"Dori, this looks wonderful." Amelia breathed deeply. "Could we also have a cup of your tomato basil soup?"

Dori smiled. "Absolutely, I'll be right back."

"I'll offer the blessing, Amelia." Patricia bowed her head. "Heavenly Father, we thank you for our safe journey and this wonderful food that has been set before us. Bless us on this vacation and bless the hands of those who have prepared this meal. We give you all the praise, honor and glory, Amen."

Dori waited quietly until Patricia ended her prayer. "Here you go ladies." Dori placed their soup on the table. "It's so nice to see someone say grace over their food."

"Everyone used to pray before they ate." Amelia commented. "I can't imagine eating without offering thanks first."

"Enjoy your lunch, ladies. I'll bring you each a refill on your cokes in just a few minutes." Dori moved away whistling softly under her breath.

Patricia bit into her croissant and chewed thoughtfully. "This is divine!"

"We are going to have to eat here again." Amelia tasted her soup. "You have to try this soup."

"If the rest of our vacation is anything like this lunch, I am going to have a blast." Patricia teased.

The diner filled quickly with patrons as the girls ate their lunch. Four firefighters came in and took the table across the restaurant from Amelia and Patricia.

Patricia gasped. "Wow, now that's what I call a good looking man."

"Who?" Amelia asked.

"That fireman with the blond hair and blue eyes just took my breath away!" Patricia's cheeks were flushed.

Amelia looked across the room and locked eyes with one of the fireman. He had black hair and deep blue eyes. His expression was solemn and although he never smiled, Amelia could not tear her eyes away. Amelia felt a chill run up her spine and she shivered.

"What do you think?" Patricia whispered.

"About what?" Amelia answered absently.

"Hello! Did you not see that gorgeous fireman sitting across the room?" Patricia stole a glance and blushed crimson when she realized that the object of her attention was staring at her. "He's coming over here," she giggled.

Amelia looked up just as Geoff approached the table.

"Good afternoon ladies, welcome to Frisco." Geoff smiled as he spoke. "I don't think I've seen you here before."

Patricia smiled up at Geoff as she answered. "We are here on vacation. This is our first visit to Colorado."

Geoff pulled out a chair at their table. "Can I join you for a minute?" he asked.

"Please join us," Patricia slid her dishes to the other side of the table and offered Geoff her hand. "I'm Patricia, and this is my best friend, Amelia."

"It's very nice to meet you Patricia," Geoff grinned as Patricia's cheeks filled with color. "Amelia, it's nice to meet you too." Geoff turned his attention back to Patricia. "I'm Geoff."

"It's nice to meet you too, Geoff." Patricia could not stop smiling; her pulse was racing.

"So where are you ladies from?" Geoff asked.

"Orlando, Florida." Patricia offered.

"You are certainly a long way from home." Geoff settled back in his chair comfortably. "So what brings you to Colorado?"

Amelia watched Patricia's interaction with Geoff and smiled softly. Her best friend was smitten with this young firefighter and Amelia was happy for her.

"I've always wanted to visit Colorado. Amelia and I just wanted to see the Rocky Mountains and take in this beautiful scenery," Patricia explained.

Geoff grinned. "Are you staying here in Frisco?"

"Yes." Patricia winked at Amelia. "Today is our first day."

"Do you have plans for tonight?" Geoff asked.

"Not really, what did you have in mind?" Patricia's eyes were sparkling with excitement.

"We are having a barbecue at the firehouse to raise money for a local elementary school. There's going to be food, a band, and you'll get to meet a lot of great local people." Geoff wanted a chance to get to know this young lady.

Patricia turned to Amelia. "What do you think Amelia? Do you want to go?"

Amelia saw the look of longing on Patricia's face. "That sounds like fun. Where is the firehouse and what time is the barbeque?" she asked.

Geoff turned the paper placemat over and quickly drew a map and directions. "The festivities start at 6:00 p.m." Geoff stood to join his fellow firefighters. "Patricia, Amelia, it was great to meet you both and I'll see you tonight."

"See you tonight, Geoff." Patricia was grinning as she turned back to Amelia. "I told you this would be a GREAT vacation!"

Amelia laughed out loud. "Patricia, you are forever an optimist. Come on, let's pay this lunch ticket and go check into our condo."

Patricia waved at Geoff as she walked out the door to the convertible.

Amelia and Patricia checked in at registration and drove to their unit.

The unit had two floors with a bathroom, kitchen, dining area, and living room on the first floor. The living room opened up to a private balcony with a hot tub overlooking a wooded area full of birch trees. The second floor had a master bedroom with a huge master bath and a second bedroom that had two single beds and a desk with a full bathroom in the hallway.

Amelia placed her suitcase on the bed in the small bedroom. "I love this place! Patricia, I can't believe you booked such a gorgeous room."

Patricia walked into the master bedroom and giggled. "Amelia, I can't take this room. I want to be able to talk before we go to sleep like we used to do at camp and our college dorm room."

Amelia laughed out loud. "Tell you what, since that master bedroom has a large flat screen TV, we can veg out in there and we'll sleep in here when we get tired."

"Now that sounds more like it!" Patricia walked to the window and looked out at the view. "Amelia, I think I'm falling in love with Colorado. Have you seen this view?"

Amelia joined her at the window. The window overlooked a walking trail that wound through a field of wildflowers in brilliant red, purple, yellow and blues. A stream crossed under the path, caught the sunlight and reflected beams of light like a mirror. The Rocky Mountains in the distance lent an air of grace and beauty to the scene. "It certainly is different from Florida."

Patricia sighed deeply. "I think I could live here."

"Have you forgotten about the winters?" Amelia cautioned. "They get snow in feet, not inches and it is cold in these mountains."

Patricia turned away from the window and sat down on the bed. "Do you remember when you told me that you needed a change in your life?"

Amelia looked closely at her friend. "Yes, right after Liam jilted me for Courtney. Why do you ask?"

"I've felt the same way for a very long time." Patricia drew in a deep breath and continued. "I love teaching and I love my family, but I feel like there is something missing in my life. I'm twenty-four years old and I have no personal life."

Amelia sat down on the bed and faced her friend. "Because you're not in a relationship?" she questioned.

"Not exactly, I've dated but I can't find anyone that I want to get serious about. I've always envied your relationship with Liam." Patricia admitted.

"Why?" Amelia was stunned.

"Because you knew exactly what you wanted and you made a plan and followed through," Patricia explained.

"Some plan, look at me now," Amelia whispered.

Patricia regretted her words. "I'm sorry, Amelia, I didn't mean to hurt you. I just meant that you've always been able to see what you want and go get it. I've never found what I want and I'm ready for a change."

Amelia grinned. "No need to apologize. I do understand what you're feeling and I feel like I've been living in a fairy tale since high school. I think my desire to have this perfect relationship, kept me from seeing the truth about Liam." Amelia squared her shoulders. "I'm ready for a change in my life too, but I think moving to Colorado is a bit more drastic then I had in mind."

"I had an ulterior motive for coming here on vacation." Patricia watched Amelia for a reaction. "I'm seriously thinking of moving from Florida and I want to see what Colorado has to offer."

Amelia gasped. "Wow, now that's news I wasn't expecting. You're really serious about changing your life."

"I've never been more serious about anything in my life," Patricia spoke with conviction.

"So this vacation is a test of sorts, to see if you like this area?" Amelia asked trying to understand.

Patricia smiled knowingly. "Call me crazy, but the minute you drove past that 'Welcome to Frisco' sign, I felt like this was home."

"Well, I guess we better get unpacked and start exploring to see exactly what your new home is all about," Amelia teased.

Chapter Five

The fire station was filled with music, laughter and the aroma of barbeque permeating the air. Amelia sniffed appreciatively as Patricia scanned the crowd for Geoff.

"Hi ladies, I'm so glad you came!" Geoff had joined them from behind and was smiling; but his eyes were on Patricia.

"Thanks for the invitation," Patricia felt her cheeks heating up. "I've been looking forward to this."

Geoff grinned. "Would you like a tour of the fire station?"

"I'd love that." Patricia turned to Amelia. "Are you going to join us?"

Amelia smiled softly. "I think I'm going to check out the crafts. I'll catch up with you two later."

Geoff winked at Amelia and took Patricia by the arm leading her to the fire station.

Amelia watched them walk away grinning to herself. She turned towards the large tent at the edge of the parking lot.

Dozens of tables were lined up on either side of the tent with a walkway open down the middle. Homemade jams, jellies, and salsa filled the first table. The next table held homemade breads, cookies, and baked goods. The tables that followed were filled with candles, flower arrangements, and paintings.

Amelia loved the community spirit that she felt within the bazaar. Children ran to and from the tent giggling, playing and enjoying the freedom of the wide open space. Amelia was looking at the handmade jewelry when a little girl tugged on the hem of her shorts.

Amelia knelt down on one knee in front of the little girl. "Hello there, what's your name?"

"I want to hold you," she whispered.

"Excuse me?" Amelia wasn't sure what the little girl wanted. "Can you tell me your name?"

"I want to hold you," the little girl repeated. She reached out her tiny arms for Amelia to pick her up.

Amelia's heart melted and she picked the little girl up into her arms.

"Lovella, where are you?"

The little girl in Amelia's arms wrapped her tiny arms around Amelia's neck and laid her head on Amelia's shoulder snuggling close.

Amelia hugged her gently and patted her back as another little girl approached.

"Lovella, daddy's looking for you."

Amelia looked down into the eyes of a beautiful little four-year-old. Her hair was jet black and her complexion was dark with her American Indian heritage. Her eyes were a piercing blue.

"Is this Lovella?" Amelia asked the little girl.

"Yes ma'am. That's my baby sister, she's two," she spoke convincingly.

"Ahh and what is your name?" Amelia asked.

"I'm Topanga and I'm four. Why are you holding my sister?" she asked curiously.

Amelia smiled. "She came up to me and said she wanted to hold me."

Topanga turned her head sideways and looked at Amelia closely. "She says that a lot." Her four-year-old wisdom was evident. "My daddy was looking for her and she got away from me."

"Well I'd be happy to carry her back to your daddy if you'd like." Amelia offered.

"Daddy is here," a deep baritone voice spoke from behind Amelia.

Amelia turned to face the girls' daddy and came face-to-face with the fireman from the café.

"Lovella, you know better than to run away from you sister," Chogan gently chided.

Lovella cuddled closer to Amelia and smiled at her daddy. "I want to hold her," she whispered.

Chogan smiled at his daughter. "Ma'am, I hope my daughter hasn't been a nuisance."

Amelia smiled. “She hasn’t been a nuisance at all. I’m Amelia. I think I saw you at the Butterhorn Bakery today.”

“Yes ma’am.” Chogan felt a tug at his sleeve. “I’m Chogan; it’s nice to meet you.”

“Daddy!” Topanga whispered loudly. “Ask her to eat with us.”

Chogan grinned at his eldest daughter. “My daughter is correcting my rudeness, would you like to join us for dinner?”

Amelia smiled. “I’d love to.”

Chogan heard his name being called. “I’ve got to help finish setting up the tables. We will be eating in about fifteen minutes.”

“I’ll keep the girls with me, if that’s alright with you?” Amelia asked.

Chogan looked down at Topanga who had slipped her hand into Amelia’s. “I think my daughters would like that.”

Amelia watched him walk away and gently squeezed Topanga’s hand. “Topanga is there something you’d like to look at?”

Topanga looked up at Amelia. “Could we look at that table?” she pointed to the table filled with Native American jewelry.

“That’s a lovely idea.” Amelia allowed Topanga to lead the way.

The table was filled with silver, turquoise and precious hand polished stones. There were belts, combs, and jewelry for men and women. Topanga touched a hair comb gently and pulled her hand back.

“Do you like that one?” Amelia asked.

“It’s pretty, like mama’s.” Topanga’s eyes filled with tears.

Amelia knelt down in front of Topanga. “Your mama has one like this?”

Topanga felt the tears fall. “She did. She was pretty like you.”

Amelia gently wiped the tear from Topanga’s cheek. She had seen this grief before. “Your mama had to be beautiful; she had two beautiful little girls.”

Topanga looked directly into Amelia’s eyes. “Mama went to heaven.” Topanga spoke softly. “I look like daddy and Lovella looks like mama.”

Amelia felt the tears prick her eyes and she took a deep breath to compose herself for the little broken heart standing before her. "I bet your mama is watching from heaven and is very proud of both of her daughters."

Topanga smiled and wiped the tears with the back of her hand. "I like you. I can't say your name though."

Amelia laughed softly. "Tell you what, my niece calls me Mia, you can call me that too if you like."

"Mia," Topanga grinned. "That's easy, I like that. I'll call you Mia."

The announcement for dinner was heard across the loud speaker and Topanga took Amelia's hand and led her to the table where Chogan was waiting.

Chogan reached for Lovella and she turned her face and buried it in Amelia's neck, clinging tightly.

"Daddy, I can fix Mia a plate." Topanga offered.

Chogan looked at Amelia confused. "I'm sorry. I've never seen Lovella act like this."

Amelia grinned. "I have a three-year-old niece; I don't mind at all," she assured him.

Chogan looked relieved. "What would you like to eat?"

"I'm pretty easy to please," Amelia sat down with Lovella in her arms. "I'll eat whatever you bring."

Topanga grinned and took her daddy's hand. "Come on daddy; let's go get them some food."

Chogan walked away with Topanga leading the way.

Patricia and Geoff joined Amelia at her table.

"You've been here less than an hour and you've already made a new friend." Patricia teased. "Who is this lovely little girl that's attached herself to you?" she asked.

Geoff answered for her. "This little darlin' is Lovella. She's two-years-old and her daddy is a fireman here with me."

Lovella turned and grinned at Geoff.

"Is she always so taken with strangers?" Patricia asked.

Geoff's look turned serious. "Actually, she's usually very shy around new people." Geoff winked at Lovella. "How did you meet her, Amelia?"

Lovella spoke before Amelia could answer. "I wanted to hold her."

Geoff's eyes turned glassy and he laughed to lighten the mood. "You're doing a great job Lovella."

Patricia looked questioningly at Geoff and he whispered. "I'll explain in a bit."

Chogan returned with Topanga and a tray filled with plates of barbeque, kettle chips, brownies, and sodas.

"Patricia, I'd like you to meet Chogan." Geoff grinned at Topanga. "This is his oldest daughter Topanga; and you've already met Lovella, his youngest."

Patricia grinned. "It's nice to meet you Chogan. I think I saw you at the café today, didn't I?"

Chogan smiled. "Yes, I was there. It's a good thing you came tonight."

Patricia was intrigued. "And why is it a good thing I came?" she asked.

"Because Geoff has talked about you non-stop since he met you this afternoon," Chogan explained.

Amelia and Patricia joined the laughter as Geoff's face turned crimson.

The meal was delicious and the sun was setting as the band started playing under the lights.

Lovella had walked to the bandstand with Topanga and was dancing under the lights with the other children.

Amelia excused herself and walked to the craft tent to make a few purchases before they closed up for the night. She placed one bag in the trunk of her car and two small boxes into her handbag. Amelia walked back to the bandstand to join Patricia.

Geoff had spread a large quilt on the grass, with others. Patricia sat beside Geoff and Amelia sat next to Chogan watching the children laughing and dancing to the music.

One-by-one the children tired of the music and found their way to their parents.

Lovella walked to the blanket and crawled into Amelia's arms. Amelia cradled her close.

Topanga crawled into her daddy's arms and cuddled close.

As the darkness fell the stars appeared and the air turned cool. Couples moved to the area the children had vacated and waltzed slowly to the music.

Patricia and Geoff joined the other couples, getting to know one another with whispered conversation and smiles.

Chogan pulled two children's blankets from his duffle bag and wrapped one around Topanga who had fallen asleep in his arms. He placed Topanga on the blanket and kissed her forehead softly. Chogan took the other blanket and wrapped it around Lovella who was sound asleep in Amelia's arms.

Amelia felt her senses heighten as Chogan tucked the blanket around his daughter. The smell of his aftershave teased her with a masculine appeal.

"I can take her so you can rest your arms." Chogan offered.

Amelia smiled. "She's so sweet; I don't want to disturb her sleep," she whispered.

Chogan laughed softly. "Trust me; once she is asleep, she rarely wakes up." He gently moved Lovella from Amelia's arms and placed her on the blanket next to her sister.

Amelia shivered and Chogan pulled another blanket from the duffle and wrapped it around her shoulders. "You look cold."

"I am a little." Amelia loved the warmth of the quilt and stroked it lovingly. "This is beautiful, is it hand-made?"

Chogan sobered. "Yes. My wife made it."

Amelia saw the hurt in Chogan's eyes. "How long ago did she die?" she asked softly.

Chogan looked puzzled.

"I'm sorry, I didn't mean to pry. Topanga told me her mama was in heaven." Amelia didn't want to inflict any additional pain.

Chogan smiled sadly. “You don’t need to apologize.” He drew in a deep breath and continued. “Samantha was a wonderful wife and mother. She was healthy and happy and the day after she gave birth to Lovella she developed a headache. Within four hours, she was gone.”

Amelia couldn’t stop the tears. “I’m so sorry for your loss. What happened?” she prompted.

“Aneurysm; she was apparently born with it. The doctors tried everything but there was nothing they could do.”

“Topanga told me that Lovella looks like her mama,” Amelia said.

Chogan smiled as he watched his daughters sleep. “The blond hair, bronze skin, and green eyes; she looks just like her mother,” Chogan replied.

Amelia grew quiet.

Chogan spoke softly interrupting her thoughts. “When I saw you today at the café, I was shocked.”

“Why is that?” Amelia asked.

“You resemble Samantha with the color of your hair and eyes.” Chogan cleared his throat. “Although Lovella doesn’t remember her mama, she had an instant reaction to you; I’ve never seen her do that.”

Amelia smiled. “I am an elementary school teacher. I also have two nephews and a niece so I’m very comfortable around children.”

“It’s more than that.” Chogan offered. “Why did Topanga call you Mia instead of Amelia?”

Amelia laughed softly. “Topanga couldn’t say Amelia; I told her my niece calls me Mia.”

“Thank you, for making my girls smile, today,” Chogan spoke appreciatively.

“It was my pleasure.” Amelia looked closely at Chogan. “Your name is very unusual; can I ask its origin?”

“Chogan means black bird. My father is Ute Indian; Ute meaning, land of the sun,” he explained.

“That’s beautiful. Are the girls’ names also Native American?” Amelia asked.

“Yes, Topanga means a place above; Lovella means soft spirit.”

Amelia smiled. “That’s lovely. Samantha must have been an amazing woman.”

“She was amazing. We met when we were children, and we married at eighteen.” Chogan laughed. “Our parents were not happy that we chose marriage over college.”

“I think that’s wonderful.” Amelia’s expression turned sad. “Finding someone you love and sharing your life together as a family is the best choice.”

Chogan watched her closely. “So why haven’t you married? You obviously love children.”

Amelia’s eyes filled with tears and she dashed them away with the back of her hand. “I was going to be married, it just didn’t work out,” she answered quickly. Amelia didn’t elaborate that she had wasted too many years on that relationship.

“I’m sorry, Amelia,” Chogan said softly.

Amelia smiled. “No need to apologize. I’m a great teacher and I will always have children to love, even if they’re not my own.”

Patricia and Geoff returned to the blanket.

“Chogan, I think your girls are worn out.” Geoff teased.

Chogan gently picked up Topanga and stood up. “I’m going to carry her to the truck, can you get Lovella?”

Geoff picked Lovella up and she opened her eyes and reached for Amelia. “Wow, she’s really taken with you,” Geoff teased.

Amelia grinned and cradled Lovella in her arms. “I’ll take her and you two gather our stuff, ok?”

Patricia laughed. “We can do that.”

Amelia followed Chogan, softly singing a lullaby until Lovella was sound asleep once again.

Chogan tucked Topanga in her car seat and buckled her in gently. He motioned for Amelia to follow him and he moved to the other side of the truck.

Amelia tucked Lovella in her car seat and kissed her softly on the forehead. “Goodnight sweetie.”

Chogan closed the truck door and turned to face Amelia. “Thank you.”

"Thank you, Chogan." Amelia reached into her bag and pulled out two small boxes. "Could you give these to the girls for me?" she asked.

"What are they?" Chogan asked.

Amelia smiled. "Just something from the crafts that I think the girls will like."

"Why don't you give them to the girls?" Chogan watched Amelia's face for a reaction.

Amelia looked up surprised. "When?"

Chogan smiled. "Do you like to ride horses?"

"As a matter of fact, I do." Amelia felt her pulse beating faster than normal.

"Tomorrow is Sunday. Would you and Patricia like to join us for church in the morning and then go horseback riding with us tomorrow afternoon?" Chogan asked.

Patricia and Geoff walked up to the truck as Chogan extended the invitation.

"Amelia, you have to say yes!" Patricia prompted. "Geoff told me about their church and it sounds great."

Amelia smiled. "I'm assuming you have directions?"

Patricia laughed. "Don't need them; Geoff is picking us up at the condo."

Chapter Six

Amelia and Patricia arrived at the church with Geoff just as Chogan, Topanga, and Lovella were entering the doors.

Lovella spotted Amelia over her daddy's shoulder. "Mia, I want Mia, daddy!"

Chogan turned and gently sat Lovella down, watching her run to Amelia's arms.

Patricia laughed as Amelia scooped Lovella up and hugged her gently.

"Good morning, Lovella." Amelia smiled at the little girl. "You certainly look pretty today."

Lovella smoothed the material of her dress with her hands. "I am daddy's pretty girl," she said.

Topanga giggled. "Daddy told her that this morning."

"I think both of Daddy's girls look pretty this morning." Amelia spoke with diplomacy, knowing it was the best way to handle siblings.

Chogan turned and led the way into the sanctuary.

The service began with praise and worship and then the children were dismissed to children's church.

The pastor took the pulpit and opened his Bible.

"Open your Bibles to the book of James chapter two and we will read verses fourteen through seventeen."

14 What doth it profit, my brethren, though a man say he hath faith,
and have not works? Can faith save him?

15 If a brother or sister be naked, and destitute of daily food,

16 And one of you say unto them, Depart in peace, be ye warmed
and filled; notwithstanding ye give them not those things which are
needful to the body; what doth it profit?

17 Even so faith, if it hath not works, is dead, being alone.

"I have chosen for my title this morning, Faith without works is dead. As Christians we are taught that we are saved by faith and not by works. However, this morning I'd like to challenge you that your faith cannot stand without works."

The pastor's message spoke to Amelia's heart. His challenge to go beyond believing with faith and putting faith into action rang in her ears. She sat beside Chogan through the service and felt totally at ease, although she had only met him the day before.

After church, Geoff drove Patricia and Amelia to Chogan's ranch.

The entrance to the ranch was a lovely white archway. The driveway was centered between two rolling green pastures with large cedar trees lining the fence. The end of the driveway met a large lawn with a swing set, picnic table, and a large single level ranch style home with a wide veranda porch that surrounded three sides.

Chogan parked his truck and released the girls from their car seats. "Topanga, take your sister into the house and change into some play clothes," he instructed.

"Can Mia come with us daddy?" Topanga looked shyly at Amelia.

Chogan looked at Amelia. "Do you mind?" he asked.

Amelia laughed. "Topanga, lead the way."

Topanga's room was in perfect order. Her dolls, games and books lined the shelves like a museum. The walls were painted in sky blue and the ceiling was painted with white fluffy clouds. A white desk stood in the corner with a white wooden chair.

Hanging from the curtain rod over the window was a beautiful dream catcher with long feathers and beads hanging from it. Amelia touched the soft white feather lovingly.

"That's my dream catcher," Topanga whispered.

"It's lovely," Amelia offered.

Topanga smiled. "All Native American's believe, that if you hang a dream catcher over the window, it will catch the bad dreams and only allow the good dreams to flow through."

Amelia sat on the edge of the bed. "So can you tell me about this beautiful quilt on your bed?" she asked.

Topanga stroked it lovingly. "My mama made that before I was born. She used the colors of the flowers that grow in the meadow and sewed it with love."

Amelia felt the tears in her eyes. "Your mama must have loved you very much to sew such a pretty quilt for you."

Lovella tugged at Amelia's hand. "Mia, come see my room."

Topanga laughed. "Let me change clothes and I'll help you find Lovella's clothes; her room is a mess."

Lovella stuck out her lower lip. "My room is not a mess, its fun."

Amelia followed Lovella to her room and laughed out loud at what she saw. The room was cluttered with clothes, toys, and the bed looked like it had been used for undercover maneuvers.

The room was painted yellow with wildflowers painted on the walls. The quilt on her bed matched the colors in the wildflowers and obviously hand stitched by her mama. Over the window hung a dream catcher; Amelia smiled at the sentiment.

Once the girls were changed, Amelia allowed them to lead her outside to the picnic table.

"Did you survive?" Chogan teased.

Amelia laughed. "I can't say a word; I was a little girl once."

Lunch was full of laughter and as they finished, Amelia felt a nudge in her lower back. She turned to see a beautiful golden collie sitting behind her waiting patiently.

"What a beautiful dog." Amelia reached out a hand and lovingly stroked the collie. "What's her name?"

Topanga spoke first. "That's Amber."

Amber eased forward and laid her head in Amelia's lap.

Chogan stood abruptly and left the table, carrying some of the dishes back to the house; as a look of pain crossed his face.

Topanga and Lovella ran to the swing set to play.

"Whew, that was tough." Geoff spoke softly.

Patricia was confused. "What are you talking about?"

Geoff ran his hands through his hair. "Samantha raised Amber from a puppy. Amber would lay her head in Samantha's lap just like she did you."

Amelia looked stricken. "Doesn't she do that with everyone?" she asked.

"No," Geoff lowered his voice so the girls wouldn't hear. "Amber has been anti-social since Samantha died. She stays in the barn instead of the house. You are the first person she has reacted to."

Chogan returned to the table. “If you ladies would like to change clothes, we’ll head out to the barn and saddle up the horses.”

Patricia and Amelia changed quickly and walked with the children to the barn.

Chogan saddled four horses. “Amelia, you’ll be riding Dusty.” Dusty was a palomino with a gentle nature.

Chogan helped Amelia into the saddle but wouldn’t make eye contact with her.

Geoff helped Patricia on a deep brown quarter horse. Geoff’s horse was also a quarter horse.

Chogan was riding an Appaloosa and sat Topanga in front of him on the saddle.

Lovella insisted on riding with Amelia.

They rode across the pasture and followed a stream to the base of the mountain. The return trip wound through a rolling field that was filled with wildflowers. The girls were sleepy by the time they returned to the barn.

Amelia carried a sleeping Lovella to her room and tucked her into bed for a nap. She kissed her forehead softly. “Sweet dreams honey.”

Topanga stood in the doorway and watched Amelia. “Will you tuck me in too?”

Amelia took Topanga’s hand and walked back into her room and helped her into the bed. Amelia sat down on the side of the bed and pulled out the boxes she had purchased at the bazaar.

“What’s that?” Topanga asked.

“I found something at the bazaar that I thought you and Lovella would like.”

Topanga’s face lit up with excitement. “Can I open it?” she asked.

Amelia handed the box to Topanga and watched as she lifted the lid exposing the tortoise shell combs with turquoise stones.

Topanga lovingly stroked the combs. “They look just like mama’s,” she whispered.

“They will look beautiful in your hair.” Amelia tucked Topanga in and kissed her forehead softly.

"Will you come see me again, before you go home?" Topanga asked.

"I'll try," Amelia promised.

Both girls were sound asleep as Amelia walked back out to the front lawn.

Patricia and Geoff had taken a walk and Chogan was sitting on the porch swing with Amber lying at his feet.

"You're welcome to join me," Chogan invited.

Amelia smiled and sat down on the swing beside Chogan.

Amber walked over to Amelia and laid down at her feet gently swishing her tail back and forth.

"It's amazing," Chogan whispered.

Amelia didn't understand. "What's amazing?"

"You're a total stranger, and yet my children and even the dog, have taken an instant liking to you." Chogan took a deep breath.

"I'm sorry, Chogan. I didn't mean to cause you any pain." Amelia felt the tears well up in her eyes.

Chogan turned on the swing and looked at her. "It's me that should apologize. I acted like a jerk. I appreciate that you sacrificed a day of your vacation to spend it with my family."

"It wasn't a sacrifice." Amelia looked away. "I came on this vacation to forget a bad situation. Today was wonderful."

Chogan watched her closely. "Can you tell me what happened?" he asked sympathetically.

Amelia leaned back in the swing. "I was engaged for five years to my high school sweetheart." Amelia stared off in the distance, unaware that her face revealed the pain of heartache. "We were to be married this month."

"Five years is a long engagement," Chogan commented.

Amelia sighed. "Liam wanted to wait. I had college and he had the military."

"So what happened?" Chogan asked.

"Liam came to the house a few weeks before the wedding to tell me he had another woman in his life and was marrying her." Amelia ignored the tears that were falling. "He had been with her for six months, while he was stationed in Texas. Liam said he didn't break it off with me because if the relationship with Courtney didn't work out, he would marry me."

Chogan reached over and wiped a tear from Amelia's cheek.

Amelia didn't notice, her focus was fixed in the distance and she continued. "He had the nerve to ask for his ring back and I threw it at him."

Chogan whispered. "You're angry, hurt, and you're still in love with him, right?"

Amelia looked at Chogan and realization set in. "I'm working through the anger. I'm not sure that I even know what love is. How could I be so stupid as to allow a man to string me along for five years?" she asked.

Chogan smiled. "They say love is blind."

"I think in my case, love must be pretty stupid too," Amelia laughed. "You told me that you married Samantha right out of high school. You both knew you were in love and you committed to one another."

Chogan looked off in the distance and sighed. "We had each other and that was enough."

"That's what love is supposed to be," Amelia smiled sadly. "I think I'm angrier at myself than I am at Liam."

"Why are you angry with yourself?" Chogan was confused. "Liam had a woman who committed five years of her life to him and he threw that aside; I hope the other woman was worth it."

Amelia laughed out loud. "Thank you, Chogan."

"Thank you? What did I do?" Chogan asked in surprise.

"Thank you for showing me what real love and commitment look like." Amelia leaned her head back and took a deep breath. "Today is the first day of the rest of my life and it's time I started living again."

Patricia and Geoff walked up on the porch.

"So how was your walk?" Amelia asked.

Geoff grinned. "I'd say it was very educational."

Patricia giggled and changed the subject. "Chogan, your ranch is beautiful."

"Thank you." Chogan looked across the lawn at the Rocky Mountains. "If you want a real view of Colorado, you need to visit Rocky Mountain National Park."

"I think that's where we are headed tomorrow." Patricia pulled out her notepad from her bag. "Yep, tomorrow is Rocky Mountain National Park."

Amelia smiled. "Tuesday is our road trip, right?"

Patricia flipped the page, "Yep, Tuesday is our road trip."

Geoff leaned over Patricia's shoulder and glanced at the notepad. "Road trip to where?" he asked.

Patricia grinned. "We are driving up to Mount Rushmore."

Chogan laughed. "Driving to South Dakota; now that's what I call a road trip."

Geoff looked stricken. "How long are you staying?"

Patricia touched his cheek with her hand. "We're driving up to Rapid City and spending the night. We should be back sometime Wednesday."

"I was hoping to see you again before you head back to Florida." Geoff watched Patricia for a reaction.

Amelia watched the chemistry between them. "Are you off any days this week, Geoff?" she asked.

"I'm off Thursday."

"Why don't the two of you spend the day together?" Amelia suggested.

"That's not fair to you, Amelia." Patricia wanted to accept but didn't want to abandon her friend.

Amelia waved off her concerns. "Don't be silly. I have several things I'd like to do and I'll be just fine."

"Then it's a date." Geoff spoke before Patricia could change her mind. "I'll pick you up at 7:00 a.m. and we'll make a day of it."

"It's a date." Patricia agreed. "Amelia, are you ready to head back to the condo?"

Amelia stood and stretched. "Thank you, Chogan, for a lovely afternoon."

Patricia and Geoff walked on ahead, while Amelia gathered up her belongings.

Chogan carried her duffle bag. "I hope you enjoy your time here in Colorado."

Amelia stopped and turned to face him. "I already have."

Amelia unpacked her duffle and was downloading her digital photos to the laptop when Patricia joined her at the table. "You have stars in your eyes my friend." Amelia teased.

Patricia opened her soda and poured it over the ice in her glass. "Amelia, I think I'm falling in love."

Amelia watched her friend closely. "Well, something is going on between you two."

Patricia took a sip of her soda and smiled. "Geoff is from a large family and he's lived here all his life. He has never been married and he has been a firefighter since he graduated from high school."

"He's a nice looking young man. I'm surprised that he hasn't married before now." Amelia didn't want to discourage Patricia; however, she didn't want her hurt either.

"I ask him how he stayed single for so long." Patricia admitted. "He was engaged to be married."

Amelia looked up in surprise. "What happened?"

"She ran off with another man on the eve of their wedding and he's been alone ever since." Patricia watched Amelia for a reaction. "I knew you would understand."

"I understand perfectly." Amelia walked to the kitchen and brought a soda to the table. "So how long ago was Geoff engaged?"

Patricia paused before answering. "Geoff was engaged five years ago; he hasn't dated since, until now."

Amelia was stunned. Five years of waiting for the right person seemed like an eternity, and she totally understood. "Wow, he must have been devastated."

Patricia touched Amelia's hand. "I hope you won't be angry with me. I told him about you and Liam."

"There is nothing to be angry about." Amelia twirled her soda can slowly, deep in thought. "So what are you plans?"

Patricia looked confused. “Geoff and I are spending the day together Thursday. Are you sure you don’t mind?”

Amelia winked at her friend. “I meant what are your plans after this week is over? If you are falling in love with Geoff, you need Thursday to get to know one another.”

“Amelia, do you think I’m crazy?” Patricia asked worriedly.

“Why would I think that?” Amelia asked.

Patricia sighed as she responded. “Because I just met Geoff and I’ve never been in a serious relationship before.”

“I think you’re finally making time for what’s important in your life.” Amelia wanted her friend to be happy. “Don’t you think it’s amazing that of all the places in this country you could have chosen for vacation, you chose Frisco, Colorado?”

Patricia’s expression was dreamy. “Do you think God ordains relationships?” she asked softly.

“I think you opened your heart for God’s direction and He’s allowing you to find your way.” Amelia closed her laptop. “Yes, Patricia, I believe God ordains relationships.”

Patricia stretched and yawned. “I hope you’re right. This vacation is proving to be pretty amazing. I can’t wait to see what happens next!”

Chapter Seven

Amelia and Patricia drove to Rocky Mountain National Park. When they stepped out of the convertible they shivered.

Amelia pulled her jacket over her t-shirt. "Wow, it's really chilly up here!"

Patricia pulled her hair out of her sweatshirt and giggled. "Sure doesn't feel like Florida up here, does it?"

They took photos of the mountains and the wild rams and buffalo that were roaming in the distance. Amelia put her zoom lens on the digital camera and shot three quick photos. "Got them," she spoke appreciatively.

Patricia looked confused. "What are you taking pictures of? All I see is the stone wall and some trees."

Amelia set the camera to review and turned the viewfinder for Patricia to see.

Patricia laughed out loud. "I can't believe you saw those tiny chipmunks this far away. That looks like Alvin, Theodore, and Simon!"

Amelia grinned. "Topanga and Lovella would love these."

"Those little girls have stolen your heart my friend." Patricia watched Amelia's reaction as she spoke.

A warm smile stole over Amelia's face. "I spend most of my time with children in the classroom and with my niece and nephews." Amelia paused as she reset her camera and swung it over her shoulder. "So why is it that two little girls, total strangers, have invaded my heart so quickly?" she asked thoughtfully.

"Amelia, you are oblivious to the fact that children are absolutely drawn to you," Patricia explained.

"I don't know about that Patricia. You're students love your spontaneity and your enthusiasm. I've seen them give each other high fives when they find out you are their teacher."

Patricia shook her head. "You have got to be the most amazing person I have ever known."

"Why?" Amelia had no idea what Patricia was talking about.

"You have a natural ability to mother children. They respond to you immediately because you genuinely love them. There's a soft spirit about you that draws children and makes them feel safe and protected."

Amelia's eyes filled with tears. "Patricia, you're going to make me cry. I can't believe you really see all that in me."

Patricia grabbed Amelia's arm and headed towards the gift shop. "I am your best friend; I'm supposed to know you better than anyone!"

They spent over an hour touring the gift shop and buying souvenirs for friends and family back home. By the time they drove back through the park and back to Frisco, it was after 7:00 p.m.

The message light on the phone was blinking and Patricia checked the message while Amelia put her purchases in her room.

"That was a message from Chogan." Patricia watched Amelia's face for a reaction. "He wants you to call him back."

"The girls must want to talk to me." Amelia reasoned.

"Did you ever think that maybe Chogan wants to see you?" Patricia asked.

"I'm not ready for a relationship, Patricia." Amelia dialed the phone as she spoke. "I didn't do very well in my last attempt."

"Hello?" Chogan answered on the first ring.

"Hello, Chogan?" Amelia cleared her throat. "It's Amelia; you left a message for me to call?"

Chogan sat on the porch swing watching the girls playing on the swings in the lawn. "I called to see if you would like to spend the day with me Thursday?"

Amelia was stunned. "What did you have in mind?"

Chogan ran his hand through his hair. "I thought you might like to visit the Royal Gorge Bridge."

"I've seen that on the Internet, I'd love to see it." Amelia walked to the double doors as she talked. "Are the girls going with us?"

Chogan spoke softly. "No, my mom is coming to visit and the girls are spending the day with her."

Amelia was speechless.

Chogan waited for her to respond, after a lengthy silence he spoke softly. "I'm sorry Amelia; I didn't mean to put you on the spot." Chogan leaned back in the swing disappointed.

"There's no need to apologize," Amelia explained. "I was surprised at the invitation. I'd love to spend the day with you." She wondered at her reaction, didn't she just tell Patricia she was not interested in a relationship?

Chogan smiled. "I'll pick you up at 7:30 a.m. It will take us a little over two hours to get there."

"That sounds wonderful. I'll see you Thursday." Amelia couldn't stop smiling.

"Be careful on your trip to South Dakota," Chogan cautioned. "I'll see you Thursday. Goodbye, Amelia."

"Goodbye, Chogan." Amelia disconnected the call and turned to see Patricia grinning from ear-to-ear.

"You go girl!" Patricia cheered.

Amelia laughed out loud. "I can't believe I just did that. I haven't been on a date in almost a year." Amelia felt the panic start to set in. "What did I just do?"

Patricia wasn't about to let Amelia back out now. "You did exactly what any red-blooded woman would do. You accepted a date with a handsome man!"

The phone rang in Amelia's hand and she jumped. "Hello?"

"Is Patricia there?" Geoff's voice was familiar to Amelia.

"Hello, Geoff, Patricia is right here." Amelia handed Patricia the phone and walked into her bedroom to give her friend some privacy.

Patricia popped her head into Amelia's room a few moments later. "Would you mind if I met Geoff for dinner tonight?"

Amelia laughed. "Go and have fun. I'm going to sit in the hot tub and read my book."

Geoff picked Patricia up and drove downtown to the Silverheels At The Ore House restaurant.

Geoff ordered garden salads, followed by steak and shrimp. He grinned at Patricia as the waitress walked away. "I think you'll like the food here."

"I am sure I'll love the food." Patricia smiled as Geoff took her hand across the table. "I like the company I'm with even better," she admitted.

"I can't believe we just met." Geoff stroked the back of Patricia's hand with his thumb. "I feel like I've known you my entire life."

Patricia squeezed his hand. "I feel the same way."

"What do you want to do Thursday?" Geoff asked.

"This is your state, Geoff; I'm leaving the planning up to you," Patricia offered.

Geoff watched the candle flicker across Patricia's expressions. "I want to show you Red Rocks Park and Amphitheater."

"That sounds wonderful." Patricia felt her heart beating faster in her chest.

Geoff and Patricia finished their dinners and left the restaurant. Geoff took Patricia's hand and walked slowly down the sidewalk under the street lamps. They walked to the entrance to the main street and Geoff leaned against the rock wall and pulled Patricia closer.

"Will you be offended if I kiss you?" Geoff asked watching her expression closely.

Patricia smiled. "I'll be offended if you don't."

Geoff pulled her gently to him and kissed her softly. He leaned back and looked into her eyes. "Patricia, I've wanted to do that since the first day I saw you."

Patricia slipped her hands to the lapels of Geoff's jacket and kissed him slowly, enjoying the feel of his heart beating beneath her hands. She leaned back and smiled. "I've wanted you to kiss me since the first time I saw you."

Geoff pulled her closer and kissed her again, lingering as he slipped his arms around her and hugged her to him.

Patricia slipped her arms around his neck and enjoyed the feel of Geoff in her arms.

Geoff was breathing heavily as he pulled back. "I've got to get you back to your condo."

Patricia was having difficulty breathing normally too. "Yes, Amelia and I are leaving early for South Dakota."

Geoff stroked her cheek with his finger. "I want you to be careful."

"We will," she promised.

Geoff pulled Patricia close to him and walked back to his car with her in the circle of his arm. He drove to the condo and turned off the ignition.

"Can I kiss you one more time before you go in?" Geoff asked.

Patricia didn't answer. She placed her hand on Geoff's neck and pulled him close as she leaned forward.

Geoff kissed her slowly. "Be careful, I'll see you Thursday."

Patricia grinned and stroked his cheek with her hand. "I'll see you Thursday."

Chapter Eight

Amelia and Patricia left for South Dakota at 6:00 a.m. Tuesday morning. Patricia was driving when the exit for Rapid City appeared.

"Patricia, I think you just missed our turn for Rapid City, you're going east." Amelia teased.

"I'm taking a slight detour," Patricia grinned at Amelia. "I want to visit Wall, South Dakota first."

"Did you say Wall?" Amelia was puzzled.

Patricia laughed out loud. "Yes, Wall, is exactly what I said. Wall is nestled in Badlands National Park and is famous for Wall Drug Store. When the pioneers were traveling west; Wall, South Dakota was the first stop that offered real ice."

Amelia was intrigued. "So is this like an old west town?"

"Yep, when I found it on the Internet, I knew you'd love it."

Patricia and Amelia spent several hours touring Wall. They had lunch at the drug store and bought souvenirs before taking photos in the old church and along the main street.

Amelia drove when they visited Badlands National Park and it was early evening before they headed back to Rapid City.

"Thank you, Patricia," Amelia spoke with a smile.

"Your welcome; what are you thanking me for?" Patricia asked.

Amelia laughed. "I'm thanking you for taking us to Wall, South Dakota. We would have totally missed the Badlands if it weren't for your detour."

Patricia sighed and leaned back in the seat. "Seeing those Badlands reminded me of all those westerns we watched growing up."

"Myron still watches those same westerns with dad," Amelia admitted.

The hotel in Rapid City allowed a full view of Mount Rushmore from the room that Patricia and Amelia rented. They ate dinner and swam in the pool before going to bed.

Mount Rushmore National Monument was beautiful in the early morning sun. The fifty state flags that lined the walkway to the monument added an air of history to the beauty of the faces behind them.

Amelia and Patricia took photos and visited the museum before driving to the Crazy Horse Monument. They ended their visit to Rapid City with a drive through Bear Country.

Amelia giggled at the baby bears as they played in the trees next to the visitor's center at Bear Country. She found three stuffed bears and t-shirts for her nephews and niece.

Patricia looked at Amelia's bags and laughed. "You are going to have to buy another suitcase to get all that stuff home."

Amelia smiled knowingly. "Nope, I found the UPS store at Frisco and they are going to ship this for me."

On the drive back to Frisco, Amelia looked over at Patricia. "So you haven't said a word about your date with Geoff."

Patricia smiled dreamily. "It was lovely. We had salad, steak and shrimp and then we took a walk downtown."

"And…" Amelia prompted.

"And, he kissed me." Patricia's smile spoke volumes. "It was amazing, Amelia. I feel like I've known him forever."

Amelia watched Patricia closely. "I've never seen you react like this."

Patricia's eyes filled with tears and she whispered. "I think I've fallen in love with Geoff."

"That doesn't surprise me." Amelia continued. "The chemistry between the two of you is obvious to anyone who sees you together."

"So what do I do now?" Patricia asked.

"What do you want to do?" Amelia knew that Patricia was struggling with this relationship and the implications of falling in love with a man so far away from her home.

Patricia looked at her friend. "I don't want to leave."

Amelia pondered that. "Do you think Geoff feels the same way?"

"I've never been in love before," Patricia reminded her. "I hope he feels the same way."

It was after 9:00 p.m. when Amelia turned into the condo driveway. Patricia took the phone to the bedroom and called Geoff while Amelia downloaded her pictures to her laptop.

Amelia went to bed around 10:30 p.m. while Patricia was still on the phone with Geoff.

Geoff arrived at 7:00 a.m. Thursday morning and knocked on the door to the condo.

Patricia opened the door, “Good morning.”

Geoff pulled her into his arms and kissed her. As Patricia’s arms slipped around his waist, Geoff deepened his kiss and kept one hand on the small of her back and the other in her hair.

When Geoff released her; Patricia was breathless and flushed.

“I missed you,” Geoff whispered.

Patricia smiled. “I missed you too!”

They said goodbye to Amelia and slipped into Geoff’s car. Geoff leaned across the console and pulled Patricia close, kissing her softly. “I need just one more kiss, and then we’ll head out.”

Amelia watched them leave and hurried to get dressed. She slipped into blue jeans and floral peasant blouse. Amelia pulled her hair up & back and clipped it in place.

Chogan arrived at 7:30 a.m. and smiled when Amelia opened the door. “Hello there.”

Amelia smiled as she spoke, “Hello to you too.”

“Are you ready?” Chogan asked.

“Yes,” Amelia picked up a jacket and her camera and followed Chogan to his truck.

Chogan left Frisco and headed south. “Would you be offended if I made a stop before we go to Royal Gorge?”

“I wouldn’t be offended at all. Where are we going?” Amelia asked.

Chogan glanced over at Amelia before speaking. “I thought I’d take you to Cripple Creek, where I grew up.”

Amelia smiled. “That sounds lovely. Can you tell me about the town?”

“Cripple Creek was an old west gold town. The history is colorful and filled with tourist attractions like horseback riding, bicycling, and train rides. It's at the base of Pike's Peak and I think you'll find it pretty and a great place to take photos."

"Did you like growing up there?" Amelia asked.

Chogan smiled at the memory. "It was challenging." He glanced at Amelia before continuing. "My father is a full-blooded Ute and married my mother against her parents' wishes."

"What is your mother's ancestry?" Amelia was curious.

"My mother is from German ancestry and has beautiful blonde hair and blue eyes."

Amelia laughed. "That explains why your eyes are so blue."

Chogan grinned. "Your green eyes caught my attention too."

Amelia blushed. "So tell me about growing up in Cripple Creek," she said quickly to change the subject.

"Nice segway," Chogan teased. "It was tough being a half-breed but my parents filled our lives with love and laughter."

"So you have siblings?" Amelia asked intrigued.

"I have twin sisters." Chogan made a turn to a smaller country road and then continued. "They are fraternal twins, Onawa, looks like my mother. Talise, looks like my father."

"Those names are beautiful, what do they mean?"

"Onawa, means wide awake and Talise, means beautiful water." Chogan explained.

Amelia grinned. "Let me guess, Onawa didn't sleep much and Talise cried a lot?"

Chogan laughed out loud, "Exactly."

Chogan parked the truck in Cripple Creek and walked with Amelia through town. "Would you rather tour a gold mine underground or take a horseback ride through the Rocky Mountains?"

Amelia didn't hesitate. "Horseback riding is my favorite."

Chogan placed his hand at the small of her back and turned her towards the stables. Just the touch of her made Chogan's heart beat faster.

Chogan and Amelia rode the trail through the forest and followed it to the rolling meadow at the base of Pikes Peak.

Amelia's breath caught in her throat as they entered the meadow. The sunlight reflected off the snowcapped Rocky Mountains and lit the wildflowers like a painting. Amelia slipped her camera from her shoulder and snapped a photo of the elk at the edge of the forest. His antlers were huge and he rubbed the tree repeatedly.

"What is he doing?" Amelia whispered.

Chogan was sitting close to Amelia and leaned over to whisper in her ear. "He's rubbing the fuzz off of his antlers and trying to attract a female."

Amelia felt the color rise to her cheeks. She lifted her camera and took several photos of the mountains and the meadow itself; zooming in on the wildflowers growing in abundance.

Chogan smiled at the effect of his comment. "Look over to your left at the edge of the forest," he whispered.

Amelia turned her head to where he pointed and quietly lifted her camera. A herd of wild mustangs were grazing in the meadow. Amelia snapped a couple of photos and quietly slipped the camera to her shoulder.

Amelia turned to speak to Chogan, not realizing how close in proximity he was, and came face-to-face with him.

Their eyes met and neither could move. Chogan slowly lifted his fingers to her face and ran them gently down her cheek. The softness of her skin was like a magnet drawing him closer.

Amelia couldn't move. She was mesmerized by the deep blue of Chogan's eyes and the touch of his finger on her skin sent a shiver down her spine.

Chogan slid his finger to her chin and gently eased her closer. He kissed her softly on the forehead, waiting for her reaction.

Amelia closed her eyes and stayed perfectly still; not wanting to destroy the moment.

Chogan placed a feather soft kiss on her eyes and her cheek and then slowly touched her lips with his.

Amelia felt as if she had been struck by lightning. She trembled and opened her eyes, to find Chogan watching her closely.

His eyes looked through her eyes and into her soul. Amelia couldn't stop herself; she leaned forward and kissed Chogan softly.

Chogan trembled and sat perfectly still.

Amelia leaned back in her saddle and smiled.

Chogan smiled at Amelia. Words weren't necessary. Something special had happened between them and neither of them could speak.

They turned their horses and slowly rode back on the trail towards town.

Chogan helped Amelia into the truck and drove on to Royal Gorge Bridge. He paid the park fee and drove slowly across the bridge to the visitor's center.

Amelia took her camera and started out across the bridge with Chogan. She took photos of the gorge and the white water rafters in the water below.

Another couple was taking photos of one another and Amelia offered to take their photo for them.

"Can we take your picture for you?" they asked Amelia.

Amelia looked at Chogan for approval. She smiled when he handed her camera to the couple and took her hand leading her to the side of the bridge. Chogan wrapped his arm around Amelia and she wrapped her arm around his waist. The photo captured them smiling, holding one another close.

Amelia thanked the couple and waved as they walked away. "Thank you, Chogan. I wanted a photo of us together."

"Can you send me a copy of that photo?" Chogan asked.

"I'd be happy to." Amelia turned to walk back towards the truck and felt Chogan take her hand in his.

"Let's eat some lunch." Chogan suggested.

They ate at the visitor's center and watched children laughing and playing on the carousel in the park. While they ate, Amelia told Chogan about her family and her job.

The sun was starting to set as Chogan helped Amelia into the truck. He walked around to the driver's side and got in. Chogan didn't start the truck. He turned in the seat and faced Amelia with his arm across the back of the seat.

"I've enjoyed being with you today." Chogan spoke softly and watched the setting sun's rays play across Amelia's face.

"I enjoyed being with you too," Amelia admitted.

Chogan's expression turned serious. He unfastened Amelia's seat belt and pulled her gently to the middle of the seat.

Amelia slid willingly closer to Chogan. She watched his face as he slid his hand into her hair and released the clip, allowing her long blond hair to fall softly around her shoulders.

Chogan gently slid his hands on either side of Amelia's neck into her hair and pulled her to him. He kissed her tenderly and pulled back to watch her reaction. "Is this okay?" he asked softly.

Amelia's eyes were focused on Chogan's face and she smiled. Amelia slid her arms around Chogan and slowly leaned towards him.

Chogan needed no other encouragement. He pulled Amelia into his arms and kissed her slowly and lingering. When he pulled back, they were both trembling.

Chogan pulled Amelia into his arms and hugged her. Chogan buried his face in her hair and reveled in the scent of her cologne. She was soft and warm and the stone wall he had built around his heart, after his wife's death, began to crack.

Amelia felt the strength of Chogan's arms and buried her face in his shoulder. He was warm and strong and she felt safe and wanted.

Amelia shivered when Chogan released her, missing the warmth of his arms.

Chogan ran his finger down her cheek. "You are so beautiful."

Amelia blushed, "You make me feel beautiful."

"Please don't be angry with me for kissing you," Chogan whispered.

"I wanted you to kiss me," Amelia admitted. "Anger is the last thing that I'm feeling."

Chogan laughed softly and reached around Amelia to snap her seatbelt in place. "I'd like you to sit close on the drive home. Is that ok?" he asked.

Amelia didn't hesitate. "I can't think of anywhere I'd rather be."

Chogan drove back to Frisco with his arm around Amelia's shoulder.

Amelia allowed her head to rest on Chogan's shoulder and loved the feeling of protection she felt in his arms.

Chogan parked in front of Amelia's condo and turned off the truck. "It doesn't look like Patricia is back yet."

Amelia grinned. "I suspect they won't be back until later."

Chogan looked at his watch. "Why don't we get some dinner?"

"That sounds good to me." Amelia agreed.

Chogan started the truck and drove to the Arapahoe Café.

Amelia and Chogan ate Angus bacon burgers and fries with Coca-Cola to drink. Over dinner, Chogan listened to Amelia's stories from her classroom. They laughed and talked and became better acquainted. After dinner, they headed back to the condo.

Chogan walked Amelia to the door and waited in the dining area while she retrieved her laptop.

Amelia sat down beside Chogan and downloaded her photos from the day to her Vacation directory.

"You're very good with a camera," Chogan commented.

"It's not hard when you've got a really great camera." Amelia lifted the camera lovingly. "My brother and sister-in-law gave me this camera right before I left on vacation."

"How often do you take vacation?" he asked.

Amelia sat the camera down before she answered. "This is the first vacation I've ever taken without my family."

Chogan turned her to face him. "I don't want to lose touch with you after this week."

Amelia took Chogan's hand in hers. "As crazy as it sounds, I don't want to lose touch with you either."

Chogan leaned in and kissed Amelia. "What are your plans for tomorrow?" he asked.

Amelia's expression was sad. "Tomorrow is our last day in Frisco, we fly home Saturday."

Chogan drew in a deep breath. "I've got to work tomorrow, but I'd like to see you tomorrow night."

Amelia smiled. "I'd like that too. Topanga asked if I would come see her before I left."

Chogan smiled sadly. "I couldn't understand how my daughters could attach themselves to you so quickly." Chogan paused before he continued. "After today, I know exactly why."

"So will you call me when you get off work tomorrow?" Amelia asked.

"I could pick you up and we could take pizza to the house and eat with the girls." Chogan suggested.

"That sounds perfect!" Amelia agreed.

Chogan stood to leave and pulled Amelia into his arms. "I'll see you tomorrow, Amelia."

Amelia smiled up into Chogan's eyes. "I look forward to seeing you tomorrow, be careful driving home."

Chogan kissed her softly and left.

Chapter Nine

"Amelia, are you awake?" Patricia shook her friend gently. "Amelia?"

"What time is it?" Amelia was disoriented.

"It's 1:00 a.m." Patricia stood and paced the floor.

Amelia sat up in the bed and turned the table lamp on. "So why are you waking me up at 1:00 a.m.?" she asked.

Patricia sat down on the edge of the bed. "I'm sorry, Amelia, I don't know what to do."

"I've never seen you this distraught." Amelia knew it involved Geoff. "Did something happen?"

Patricia's eyes filled with tears. "I realized today that I am in love with Geoff."

Amelia smiled. "That's nothing to cry about, Patricia. How does Geoff feel about you?"

"He's in love with me too." Patricia looked at Amelia. "I don't want to go home, I want to stay here."

Amelia stood and grabbed her housecoat. "Come on, let's go to the kitchen."

Patricia looked confused. "Why are we going to the kitchen?"

Amelia rolled her eyes, "Wow, you are in love. Why else would you forget that any time we have had a crisis in our lives, we solved it with a pan of brownies."

Patricia grinned. "Where are we going to get brownies at 1:00 a.m.?"

"I brought brownie mix with me, just in case." Amelia snapped on the lights in the kitchen and pulled out the items needed to make the brownies. "You laughed when I bought the eggs and cooking oil."

Patricia sat on a bar stool facing the kitchen. "I had no idea that coming to Frisco, Colorado would change my life," she admitted.

Amelia set the temperature on the oven and started mixing the batter. "Tell me what happened today."

Patricia stared off into the distance. "Geoff picked me up and we stopped at Butterhorn to get some breakfast. We drove out to Red

Rocks Park and Amphitheater." Patricia smiled at the memory. "Geoff sat with me on the stage at the amphitheater and told me that he had fallen in love with me."

Amelia spread the batter into the baking pan and waited for Patricia to continue.

"I told Geoff that I had fallen in love with him too." Patricia sighed deeply. "We talked about spending our lives together. We even talked about marriage."

Amelia placed the brownies in the oven and set the timer. "So what you're telling me is that you have met the man you want to spend the rest of your life with."

"That's exactly what I'm saying." Patricia's eyes filled with tears. "How do I leave my family and my job in Florida and move to Colorado for a man that I've known less than a week?"

Amelia pulled out the stool next to her friend. "That's a tough question. Can you walk away from Geoff and never see him again?"

Patricia gasp audibly, "How can you ask me that? I'm in love with him."

"You've lived in Florida your entire life. Your family is in Florida. You have a job that you love. Can you walk away from all of that to make a life with Geoff?" Amelia watched Patricia for her answer.

"I don't know." Patricia drummed her fingers on the countertop. "I'm so confused."

"How do you feel about snow?" Amelia changed tactics. "Can you handle being snowed in for days on end?"

Patricia grinned. "That depends who I am snowed in with."

Amelia laughed. "Can I make a suggestion?"

"Please make a suggestion!" Patricia was desperate.

"Geoff has to work today, right?" Amelia asked.

Patricia was confused. "Yes, he's working all day and we're going out tonight."

"So that gives us all day to look into your options." Amelia stood as the timer sounded. She removed the brownies and put them on a pad to cool. "The first thing we'll do is pray."

"Pray?" Patricia looked at Amelia and grinned. "Pray for my sanity?"

"We will pray for God's direction in your life," Amelia laughed, "And then we'll pray for your sanity."

"And after we've prayed?" Patricia prompted.

"Then we'll go investigate the job market in Frisco. If you're seriously considering moving to Frisco, Colorado; you'll need to find a job." Amelia wanted to help her friend.

Patricia stretched and yawned. "That's why God made you my best friend; you always know what's best for me."

"So do we eat these brownies?" Amelia pointed to the pan on the counter.

Patricia stood and pushed her chair back to the counter. "I'm too tired for brownies and I think I'll pass and go to bed."

Amelia turned off the kitchen light. "That's the best idea you've had all day!"

Patricia and Amelia were up at 8:00 a.m. and showered and walking out the door when the phone rang.

"I'll get it," Amelia tossed the car keys to Patricia and picked up the receiver. "Hello?"

"Good Morning," Chogan's voice sounded wonderful to Amelia. "Did I wake you?"

Amelia laughed. "No, we were just walking out the door when the phone rang."

"I'm sorry, I won't keep you." Chogan started to hang up.

"Wait," Amelia amended. "What time are you coming by tonight?" she asked.

Chogan smiled. "I get off at 4:00 p.m. tonight and I'll pick up the pizza and swing by and pick you up."

"That sounds great," Amelia was grinning. "I'll see you tonight; have a good day."

"You too," Chogan hung up the phone grinning.

Amelia joined Patricia in the car. "I forgot to tell you last night that Chogan is picking me up to spend the evening with the girls."

Patricia turned in the seat and faced Amelia. "Fess up Amelia, you like this guy."

Amelia smiled. "I won't lie to you, my friend. I felt something with Chogan that I haven't felt in a long time."

"What about Liam?" Patricia didn't want Amelia to confuse rebounding from Liam's deception with real feelings for another man.

"Believe it or not, I'm over Liam." Amelia smiled. "I've spent five years of my life waiting for Liam to make a commitment; only to discover that he was committed to someone else."

Patricia knew this conversation was important. "So how does what you felt for Liam compare to what you're feeling for Chogan?"

"There's no comparison." Amelia felt as if a weight had lifted from her heart. "Chogan's love for his wife was pure and committed. That's the kind of love I want to find in my life. I'm grateful for the friendship that Chogan and I have found."

Patricia turned and started the car. "This vacation has been life-changing."

Amelia agreed.

Patricia filled out an application for a teacher's position with Frisco City Schools and for the county school system.

"So how did that feel?" Amelia asked.

"Scary! I applied for any openings from third grade through fifth grade since that's where my experience is." Patricia chewed her bottom lip. "Funny thing is, it was kind of exciting too."

"Patricia, this is a side of you I have never seen." Amelia watched her friend closely. "You've always been meticulous and organized and knew in advance just what direction your life was going to take."

Patricia laughed. "In other words, I've been boring."

"Not boring, consistent is what I meant." Amelia paused for a moment. "Do you remember the message that Pastor Greene preached before we left on vacation?"

Patricia nodded. "Actually, I remember it very well. He preached on Now Faith, and if memory serves, putting faith into action now."

Amelia smiled. "Sounds to me like you are allowing God to lead you with that now faith."

"There's only one thing that scares me about my relationship with Geoff," Patricia whispered.

"What one thing?" Amelia asked confused.

Patricia looked Amelia with tear filled eyes, "I won't have my best friend close by."

Amelia felt the tears and smiled in spite of them. "No matter how far apart we are, we will always be the best of friends."

Amelia and Patricia spent the remainder of the afternoon shopping for last minute souvenirs and gifts. They visited the UPS store and shipped their purchases home to Florida before heading back to the condo to get ready for their evening.

Amelia was wrapping the brownies to take with her to Chogan's as Patricia stood waiting for Geoff. "Where is Geoff taking you tonight?" she asked.

"I don't know," Patricia grinned. "He said tonight had to be special and that it was a surprise."

Patricia threw open the front door before Geoff could ring the bell. "Hi there," Patricia couldn't say anything else before Geoff pulled her into his arms and kissed her soundly.

Amelia giggled softly and slipped out of the room to give them privacy.

Geoff tucked the hair behind Patricia's ear with his hand. "Are you ready?" he asked anxiously.

"I suppose so," Patricia turned to pick up her jacket. "You didn't tell me where we are going so I didn't know how to dress?" Patricia had chosen a broomstick skirt in turquoise, yellow and brown with a matching yellow top that accentuated her tan. She had pulled her hair back into a French braid.

Geoff smiled, "You look perfect." He took her hand and led her to his car.

Patricia sat back in the car and watched as Geoff maneuvered the car into traffic and drove out of Frisco to the main highway. "Where are we going?"

Geoff reached over and took her hand. "It's a surprise."

Amelia looked at her reflection one last time. She had chosen a pair of soft stone-washed blue jeans and a pale pink polo shirt. She tied her hair back into a long pony tail with a pink ribbon.

The doorbell rang and Amelia grabbed her tote bag and the brownies and headed for the door.

"You look lovely." Chogan smiled as he spoke.

"Thank you kind sir," Amelia blushed. "You look very handsome."

Chogan laughed. "It's been a very long time since anyone has told me that."

Chogan took Amelia's hand and walked her to the driver's side of the truck and helped her up into the cab.

Amelia sat her items in the floor and stayed in the middle of the truck seat.

Chogan crawled into the cab of the truck and smiled as he placed his arm around her shoulders and drove to his ranch.

Topanga and Lovella were waiting on the porch with a couple that had to be Chogan's parents.

Chogan parked the truck and helped Amelia down. He handed the pizza to Topanga and led Amelia to the porch.

"Mom, Dad, this is Amelia." Chogan watched his parents for a reaction.

"Hello Amelia, I'm Uda, Chogan's mother," Uda held out her hand to Amelia and smiled warmly.

"It's very nice to meet you," Amelia saw the beautiful blue of Chogan's eyes reflected in his mother's eyes.

Chogan's father smiled and extended his hand, "Amelia, I'm Dakota, Chogan's father."

"I'm glad to meet you, sir." Amelia was stunned at the resemblance between father and son.

Lovella squeezed between her grandparents and extended her arms up to Amelia. "Mia, I want to hold you."

Amelia laughed and scooped the little girl into her arms. "I've missed you Lovella."

Chapter Ten

Geoff held Patricia's hand while he drove. "I know you and Amelia visited Rocky Mountain National Park, but I have a special place that I want to take you."

Patricia squeezed his hand. Tonight was their last night together and she wanted the memory to last forever.

Geoff drove through the park to an area that Patricia had not seen. He parked the car and removed a picnic basket and a blanket from the trunk. "Do you feel like walking?" Geoff asked as he reached for Patricia's hand.

Patricia smiled and took Geoff's hand. They walked about a quarter of a mile up the trail and through a clump of trees. When Patricia walked into the clearing she gasped in sheer delight. The Rocky Mountains stood tall and majestic in the background while the lake in front of her shone crystal clear in the afternoon sun.

Patricia tipped her head back and breathed in the cool mountain air. "Geoff, this is absolutely beautiful."

Geoff spread the blanket on the grass beneath a tree and sat the picnic basket to the side. He sat down on the blanket and extended his hand for Patricia to join him.

Patricia kicked off her shoes and sat down on the blanket tucking her feet under her skirt.

Geoff's expression was serious as he took Patricia's hands in his. "I know that you just met me six days ago." Geoff took a deep breath. "I am in love with you and I don't want to lose you when you leave for Florida tomorrow."

Patricia's eyes filled with tears. "Geoff, I'm in love with you too, but I don't know what to do."

Geoff smiled and wiped the tear from Patricia's cheek. "I brought you to this spot today because this is where I come to pray." Geoff watched Patricia's face as he spoke. "I asked God to help me find someone to love that would love me for who I am. I believe God brought you here this week to answer that prayer."

Geoff pulled a box from his pocket and opened it. "Will you marry me?"

Patricia couldn't stop the tears from falling. She stared at the solitaire diamond in the gold band. "I don't know what to say."

Geoff spoke softly, "Say yes and make me the happiest man in Colorado."

Patricia looked directly into Geoff's eyes, "You don't even know me. What if I say yes and you find out that I'm not what you wanted after all?"

"I know that you are a woman of faith; you love children; and you love me." Geoff smiled. "I want you in my life for now and forever. It doesn't matter how long we've known one another, if God has ordained our relationship, time will only make it stronger."

Patricia closed her eyes and took a deep breath. She prayed silently for the direction she needed to take.

Geoff sat back on the blanket and closed the box softly. "I'm sorry, Patricia, I've rushed you and you're not ready."

Patricia opened her eyes and shifted to her knees. She shifted her position until she was face to face with Geoff. Without saying a word, she leaned in and kissed him softly.

Geoff watched her expression and sat very still. "Patricia?" he questioned.

Patricia smiled and placed her hands on Geoff's face; she spoke from her heart. "I have been so lonely for so long that I asked God to send me someone to love." Patricia kissed Geoff softly and continued. "When I met you six days ago, I knew my life would never be the same. I am in love with you and I can't imagine my life without you in it."

Geoff kissed her questioningly, afraid to speak for fear of breaking the mood.

Patricia laughed softly. "I don't know how we're going to do this, but my answer is yes."

Geoff sat perfectly still. "Say it again."

Patricia felt the peace of her decision and started to giggle. "Yes, Geoff, I'll marry you."

Geoff pulled her into his lap and kissed her slowly. "I thought you were going to say no." He kissed her again and again holding her tightly in his arms.

Patricia slid her arms around him and held him close to her heart. "I can't say no, I don't think I can live without you in my life."

Geoff pulled back from Patricia and lifted her left hand. He slid the diamond onto her ring finger and lifted her hand to his lips. "I love you so much."

Patricia gazed at the diamond on her finger. "Geoff, we have to figure out how we're going to do this."

Geoff laughed and pulled her into the circle of his arms, holding her gently. "We'll take it one day at a time and before you know it, we'll be husband and wife."

Patricia leaned against his chest, loving the feel of this man holding her gently in his arms. "Promise me, you won't stop loving me before I can get back here to marry you."

Geoff kissed the top of her head. "I promise, I won't stop loving you. Promise me, you will come back to Colorado and become my wife."

Patricia cuddled closer in his arms. "I promise, I will come back to Colorado and become Mrs. Geoff Sandidge."

Uda and Dakota spent the evening with Chogan, Amelia and their granddaughters.

"Daddy, we want Mia to tuck us in." Topanga whispered.

Amelia said goodnight to Chogan's parents and took both girls by the hand and walked to their rooms.

"Chogan, she's lovely," Uda kissed her son's cheek in approval.

"Thanks mom. I wish she lived in Colorado." Chogan heard the girls giggling with Amelia as she readied them for bed. "The girls love her already."

Dakota watched his son carefully. "What about you son, do you love her?"

Chogan smiled. "I've only known her for a few days."

"Love knows no time or distance my son," Uda spoke from the heart. "If God means for Amelia to become a part of your home and family; He will work it out."

Chogan watched his parents leave, wondering if his mother was right.

Chogan stood in the doorway as Amelia tucked Topanga in bed. The moonlight shone through the window and bathed the room in a soft light.

"Goodnight sweet Topanga," Amelia whispered.

Topanga reached up and touched Amelia's face. "Mia, I love you. Please come back to me."

Amelia felt her eyes fill with tears. "I love you too, honey. If God allows me to come back, I will." Amelia hugged Topanga and kissed her forehead before moving to Lovella's room.

Lovella was sitting in the bed waiting. "Mia you have to tell me a story before you leave."

Amelia smiled. "Ok, slide down under the blankets and put your head on the pillow and I'll tell you a quick story."

Lovella did as she was told and watched Amelia in the moonlight.

"Once upon a time, there were two beautiful little girls, who lived on a lovely ranch in the mountains. Their daddy was a handsome prince who loved them very much and made them happy every day. They had horses, and toys and a beautiful puppy dog to play with." Amelia smiled in the moonlight as Lovella yawned and closed her eyes.

"One day the two beautiful little girls got separated from their daddy. A lonely princess found them and kept them safe until she could return them to the handsome prince. The handsome prince was so grateful that he learned to love the lonely princess and they lived happily ever after." Amelia smiled in the moonlight as she finished her story.

Lovella's soft snores revealed she had drifted off to sleep.

Amelia kissed her softly and whispered, "Goodnight Lovella, I love you."

Amelia slipped quietly from the room and found Chogan on the porch swing in the moonlight.

Chogan watched Amelia as she walked to the swing and sat down beside him. His arm was across the back of the swing and he wrapped it around her shoulder and pulled her closer to his side.

Amelia sighed and rested her head on his shoulder as the swing moved gently back and forth.

Chogan breathed in the scent of Amelia's hair and her cologne and felt the softness of her hair against his face. He kissed the top of her head softly never saying a word.

Amelia sat up slowly and allowed the moonlight to flow over her spirit. She felt at peace in this place. Chogan's arm around her offered security and comfort and she reveled in the feel of his strength.

Chogan turned her gently to face him and rained kisses from her forehead to her cheek. He tipped her chin and watched her expression in the moonlight as he moved to kiss her lips. He leaned back in the swing and untied the ribbon holding her hair in the pony tail.

The moonlight cast a glow on Amelia's hair and Chogan ran his hands through the silky strands loving the feel against his skin. "You are so lovely." Chogan whispered. "I haven't felt this way since, Samantha." He sighed deeply.

Amelia shivered. She looked into Chogan's eyes, searching for answers. "I didn't think I'd ever feel this way again."

Chogan touched her face. "How do you feel?" he asked softly.

Amelia smiled, "I can't explain it. When I feel your arms around me it's as if my heart has found a safe place to be."

"I will miss you when you leave tomorrow," Chogan whispered.

Amelia's eyes filled with tears. "I will miss you too."

Chogan pulled Amelia into his arms and held her against his chest. He rested his chin in her hair and gently rocked them in the swing.

"Can I call you and stay in touch?" Chogan asked.

Amelia smiled as she felt his heart beat beneath her cheek. "I would really like that."

A car came down the driveway and Amelia sat up slowly missing the warmth of Chogan's arms.

"It's my housekeeper, Alice. She stays with the girls when I work nights," Chogan explained.

Amelia gathered her things and walked slowly to the truck with Chogan. The ride back to the condo was quiet as Amelia sat in the circle of Chogan's arm.

Patricia and Geoff were still out when Amelia arrived back at the condo.

Chogan walked her to the door and came inside to say goodbye.

Amelia handed Chogan a folded piece of paper. "Here are my address, phone number, and email address."

Chogan tucked them in his pocket and pulled Amelia into his arms. "Thank you, Amelia, for spending this last day with me."

Amelia smiled. "I enjoyed being with you and the girls. Please keep me posted on them. I want to know how they are and what they are up to."

"I can't say goodbye to you, Amelia." Chogan leaned her back to look into her eyes. "I'll say goodnight and trust that I will see you again."

Amelia placed the palm of her hand on his face. "I hope I see you again too, Chogan. Thank you for sharing your family with me."

Chogan pulled her gently to him and felt her arms slip around his neck. He kissed her slowly, lingering to capture her in his memory.

Amelia didn't want the kiss to end. In all the time she had spent with Liam, his kisses had never affected her, the way Chogan's did.

Amelia felt her heart open and the warmth of love begin to flow as she watched Chogan return to his truck and drive away.

"Lord, thank you for allowing me to find Chogan. If you mean for us to have a life together, show me the path I must take." Amelia whispered the prayer as Chogan's truck disappeared out of sight.

Chapter Eleven

"Patricia, I've got everything in the car, are you ready?" Amelia stood outside the master bedroom door.

"I'll be right there; can you drive to the airport?" Patricia asked from inside the room.

Amelia laughed. "Yes ma'am, I'll wait for you in the car."

Patricia locked the condo door and ran to the car. "We have to stop and get some caffeine or I won't have the energy to walk on the plane!"

"I think a stop at Butterhorn Bakery is in order," Amelia teased.

Thirty minutes, two large cokes, and a bag of cinnamon rolls later; Amelia and Patricia were on their way to the airport.

The sunlight filtered through the windshield and reflected off the diamond on Patricia's hand and Amelia gasped when she saw it. "What is this?"

Patricia gazed at her hand lovingly, watching the sunlight create rainbows of color across the interior of the car. "Geoff and I are engaged."

Amelia smiled. "Have you set the date?"

"Not yet," Patricia sipped her coke before continuing. "I'm going to wait for a call from the school system in Frisco. In the meantime, Geoff and I will be in touch by phone, and email."

"I'm happy for you." Amelia smiled at her friend. "What can I do to help?"

"You can pray that I won't go crazy trying to plan this long distance wedding."

Amelia laughed out loud. "I will help you plan the wedding; after all I've had five years of experience."

Patricia was stunned. "Amelia, that's the first time I've heard you tease about your engagement to Liam."

"Don't you think it's about time that I lightened up?" Amelia asked.

Patricia giggled. "I think its past time!"

The flight from Denver to Orlando was smooth and arrived on time at 11:30 p.m.

Reggie and Cecilia were waiting just beyond the security check point. "There they are," Reggie pointed through the crowd and waved.

Amelia dropped her bag and hugged her father. "Hi daddy; thanks for picking us up."

Cecilia hugged both girls. "We couldn't wait to see you! Did you have fun?" she asked.

Patricia was glowing. "You won't believe how much fun I had."

Amelia took her daddy's arm and started to the baggage claim area. "Wait till you see the pictures that we took."

Cecilia grinned at her daughter. "Colorado must be amazing; you found your smile honey."

Amelia kissed her mom's cheek. "You're right, mom. I found my smile and I'm not going to let it go again."

Reggie pulled out of the airport and onto the interstate. He smiled in the darkness at the joy he saw on Amelia's face.

Amelia carried her luggage to her room and helped Patricia load her luggage into the trunk of her car. "You've got to tell my mom and dad about Geoff," Amelia whispered.

Patricia grinned, "I'm going to. I've already told my mom and dad by phone."

Cecilia had iced tea and snacks on the counter in the kitchen. "Girls, do you want a snack before you go to bed?"

Amelia winked at Patricia like a conspirator. "Mom, that sounds great, is daddy joining us?"

Reggie spoke from the sink. "I'm already here."

Cecilia and Reggie sat on one side of the counter, while Amelia and Patricia sat opposite.

Amelia nudged Patricia. "Tell them!"

"Tell us what?" Cecilia asked.

"This!" Patricia held her left hand across the counter, exposing the engagement ring.

Reggie let out a whistle, "Well look at that." He looked at the glow on Patricia's face. "So who is the lucky young man?"

Patricia's expression turned dreamy. "His name is Geoff Sandidge. He's a fireman and we met the first day we arrived in Frisco."

Cecilia was stunned. "You met a week ago and you're engaged to be married?"

Patricia's smile was dazzling. "We fell in love, and when he proposed, I accepted."

"So when are you moving to Colorado?" Reggie asked.

"As soon as a job opens up at the Frisco school system," Patricia spoke with confidence, "I'll be moving to my new home."

Amelia watched her parents' expressions change from surprise to concern. "I know you all would love Geoff. He's a very nice young man." Amelia wrapped her arm around Patricia's shoulder, "I wouldn't let my best friend move so far away if I wasn't convinced that this young man was the right one."

Cecilia came around the counter and hugged Patricia. "Congratulations honey; we wish you all the happiness you deserve."

Three days after Patricia returned from Colorado, she received a call on her cell phone. She came out of her bedroom and hugged her mother tightly. "Mom that was the school board in Frisco," Patricia spoke with excitement. "They've offered me a full time teaching position starting in September."

Nancy McAfee hugged her daughter. "I'm so proud of you."

Patricia hugged her mom close. "Mom, do you think I'm crazy for marrying a man I barely know, and moving to Colorado?"

Nancy laughed and looked at her daughter closely. "Your daddy and I knew each other exactly two weeks when we got married and we've been together over thirty years."

Patricia gasped. "That's right! I forgot all about that." Patricia stood perfectly still the color draining out of her face. "Mom?" she gasped.

"Honey, what's wrong? You look like you've seen a ghost," Nancy asked.

Patricia whispered. "I've got to plan a wedding and get moved to Colorado in the next six weeks!"

Nancy laughed out loud. "We can do this. Your daddy and I will help and I'm sure Amelia will help too.

Patricia hugged her mom and kissed her cheek. "Thanks mom, I love you so much!" Patricia grabbed her cell phone and hit the speed dial. "I've got to talk to Amelia."

Amelia hung up the phone and sat down on the edge of her bed. Patricia was moving to Colorado. Amelia was excited for her friend. The thought of her best friend living across the country was hard to fathom.

Amelia picked up her purse and keys and headed out to Ritz Camera to pick up her vacation photos. The warmth of the Florida sun seemed hotter after a week in Colorado.

Amelia paid for her photos and drove home. With a glass of lemonade, new photo albums and her photos; Amelia was ready to document her vacation. Amelia cataloged her trip in chronological order. She had just finished South Dakota, when she picked up the photo from the meadow at Cripple Creek. Amelia stared at the photo of the mustangs and her mind wandered back to the horseback ride with Chogan and his first kiss. A soft smile stole across her features.

Amelia placed the photos from Cripple Creek in the album and picked up the photo of Chogan with his arms around her at Royal Gorge Bridge. Amelia's heart started to beat faster and her eyes filled with tears. She stood with her arm around Chogan and wore an expression of pure joy. They made a handsome couple. Anyone looking at the photos would think they were in love.

Amelia caught her breath. She looked at the photo closely. Chogan was holding her close, as if nothing could come between them. Amelia smiled and placed the photo in the album.

Amelia had finished placing all the photos in her albums when her cell phone rang.

"Hello?" Amelia didn't recognize the number.

"Amelia?" Chogan's voice sounded deeper and Amelia clutched the phone.

"Chogan, it is so good to hear your voice." Amelia was smiling as she carried her albums to the bedroom.

"How are you?" Chogan asked.

"I'm fine, how are you?" she asked quickly.

Chogan let out a sigh, "I'm better now that I hear your voice."

Amelia sat down on the bed. "You must have been reading my mind."

"Why do you say that?"

Amelia smiled. "I was putting my vacation photos in albums and found the one of you and me, at Royal Gorge Bridge."

Chogan leaned back in the porch swing, smiling. "How do we look?"

"Happy," Amelia answered without thinking. "You look very handsome," she quickly amended.

"I liked your first answer better." Chogan was teasing her. "Do we both, look happy; or just me?"

Amelia laughed softly. "We both look pretty happy," she admitted.

"Are you happy now?" Chogan asked. He needed to know if Amelia felt what he felt.

Amelia sighed audibly. "I am trying to be."

"I miss you," Chogan whispered.

"I miss you too!" Amelia felt her eyes fill with tears and she dashed them away with the back of her hand. "I'll be seeing you very soon."

Chogan sat up in the swing. "When?"

Amelia smiled at the excitement she heard in Chogan's voice. "As soon as Geoff and Patricia plan the wedding; I'll be traveling back to Frisco for the ceremony."

"How long will you be here?" Chogan wanted more time with Amelia.

"Probably a week," Amelia glanced at her calendar. "Maybe two weeks, since I have to help Patricia get situated for her new job."

"Geoff is very excited." Chogan grinned at the thought. "He has been a real pain to work with since he found out that Patricia is coming back so soon."

Amelia laughed. "They are wonderful together; I'm very happy for them." Amelia meant that. "I'll miss Patricia very much; but I'm grateful that she's found someone to love."

Chogan smiled sadly. “I’m glad for them too. I just wish…” his voice trailed off without finishing his sentence.

Amelia pressed the phone closer to her ear, “What do you wish, Chogan?” she whispered.

“It’s not important,” Chogan cleared his throat and changed the subject. “Topanga and Lovella miss you.”

Amelia closed her eyes and smiled sadly. “I miss them too.”

“I miss you being here,” Chogan spoke so softly that Amelia barely heard what he said.

“I miss being there, Chogan,” Amelia admitted as the doorbell chimed. “That’s Patricia at the door. We’re making wedding plans today.”

Chogan smiled, “I’ll let you go. Let me know how the wedding plans are coming and when you’ll be here again; please?”

Amelia smiled as she headed for the door. “You’ll be the first to know,” she promised.

“Goodbye Amelia.”

“Goodbye Chogan.”

Chapter Twelve

Amelia and Patricia were driving to Colorado two weeks before the wedding. Patricia would need her car and Amelia agreed to drive with her and to fly home after the wedding. They had spent the five weeks after their vacation planning Patricia's wedding.

Amelia and Chogan had talked by phone and email at least three times every week over the summer. Their friendship had grown as they learned more about one another. Amelia couldn't believe how easily their conversations extended for hours. They never tired of sharing their day-to-day activities and laughed often at Topanga and Lovella's antics.

Amelia pulled into the hotel in St. Louis, Missouri and parked the car. "I am so glad we are here," she admitted tiredly.

Patricia stretched and yawned. "Flying to Colorado was much easier."

Amelia laughed. "I'll check us in to our room so you can call Geoff and let him know we made it."

Patricia smiled at her friend's understanding. "Thanks Amelia." She hit speed dial on her cell phone as Amelia walked through the doors of the hotel.

Amelia secured the room and requested a wake-up call for 6:00 a.m. She walked back to the car and found Patricia still on the phone.

"Geoff says hi," Patricia laughed.

"Tell Geoff, hello for me too." Amelia started the car and drove the parking place closest to their room.

Patricia giggled into the phone. "Geoff, we are at our room and I've got to get some sleep. Yes, I promise, we will be careful. I love you too!"

Amelia shook her head and laughed and she started removing their luggage for the night.

The hotel had given the girls a suite with queen beds and a large bathroom and mini kitchen area. Amelia threw herself across the bed and sighed contentedly. "This feels amazing!"

"I think you were right," Patricia stretched in pain. "Driving fifteen hours in a car is way too much for one day!"

Amelia rolled over and grinned. "And just whose idea was it to drive this trip in two days instead of three?"

Patricia paused for effect, "Hmmm, yours?" She ducked to avoid the pillow that Amelia threw at her in response.

"I'm thinking it was this crazy bride that I call my best friend; she had to see her fiancé and she couldn't wait one extra day!" Amelia laughed at the expression on Patricia's face.

"I'm sorry, Amelia, I know it's a lot to ask."

Amelia laughed out loud. "I'm teasing, Patricia. If I were in your shoes; you would have driven with me fifteen hours too."

Patricia sat down on the bed and tucked her feet beneath her. "I wish you were coming with me to stay." Patricia's eyes filled with tears.

"Hey what's with the tears? You love Geoff, don't you?" Amelia asked.

Patricia dashed the tears away and smiled. "Of course I love Geoff. I am just realizing how far away you're going to be. We've never been this far apart, our entire lives!"

Amelia stood and walked across the room. "I've thought about that too." She took a deep breath and spun around to cheer up her best friend. "I think this is the craziest thing we've ever done in our friendship and it's the most exciting event ever."

Patricia laughed. "I can't believe I'm going to be married in two weeks."

"I can't believe you found someone silly enough to marry you!" Amelia ducked as Patricia threw the pillow at her. "I'm just kidding."

They unpacked their suitcases and went for a swim in the indoor pool. While Patricia showered, Amelia ordered room service.

The food arrived just as Amelia finished her shower.

Patricia lifted the lid off the tray and grinned. "Steak, baked potato, tossed salad and rolls; this is exactly what I need!"

Amelia flipped on the TV while Patricia grabbed two cokes from the cooler.

The following morning, Patricia finished packing the trunk of her car while Amelia checked them out at 7:00 a.m.

The drive from St. Louis to Frisco, Colorado took over fourteen hours. Amelia was asleep when Patricia pulled into the registration lot at the condo.

Patricia eased out of the car and checked them into the same unit they had stayed in on vacation. Her mom and dad had rented the unit for two weeks as a wedding present. Patricia started the car and drove to their unit and parked.

"Hey sleepyhead, we're here." Patricia nudged Amelia's arm gently.

Amelia stretched and looked out the front window of the car. "Is this the same unit we had on vacation?" she asked.

"Yep, the manager said when my mom told him I was getting married that he had to put me in the same unit." Patricia smiled as she continued. "He gave my mom the two weeks for the price of one week to welcome me to Frisco."

Amelia grinned. "Now that's a friendly welcome. Come on let's get unpacked."

It was after 8:00 p.m. mountain time when Patricia dialed Geoff. "Hi honey, I'm here."

Amelia had unpacked the cooler into the fridge and took a shower to relax her tired muscles. She pulled on her sweats and a t-shirt and headed for the kitchen to get a soft drink when the doorbell rang. "I'll get it!"

Amelia opened the door knowing it would be Geoff and gasped.

"Hello Amelia." Chogan handed her a basket of pastries from the Butterhorn Bakery. "I thought I'd bring you a welcome basket."

Amelia took the basket and stepped back to allow Chogan to enter. "I thought you were Geoff."

Chogan laughed softly. "Geoff's on his way. He called me and told me you were here."

Amelia smiled and carried the basket to the kitchen. “Can I get you a soft drink?”

“Chogan!” Patricia ran into the kitchen and hugged Chogan before he could react. “Where is Geoff, isn’t he with you?” she asked excitedly.

Chogan laughed. “He stopped for a pizza and he’ll be right here.” No sooner had the words left his mouth when the doorbell rang.

Patricia ran for the door and threw it open. “Hi,” was all she could say as she stared at Geoff.

Geoff handed the pizza to Amelia and turned to take Patricia in his arms without uttering a word. He pulled Patricia close and kissed her again and again until she was breathless.

Amelia took the pizza to the kitchen and led Chogan to the patio so Patricia and Geoff could have some privacy.

Chogan slid the patio door closed behind them and moved to stand behind Amelia.

“The sky is beautiful tonight,” Amelia stared at the stars not daring to look at Chogan. She felt his hands on her shoulders and she trembled.

“You’re cold,” Chogan whispered in her ear.

Amelia smiled and closed her eyes feeling Chogan standing directly behind her.

Chogan stepped closer and pulled Amelia against his chest wrapping his arms around her waist from behind.

Amelia leaned into his strength and warmth. “Now this is nice,” she admitted contentedly.

“I’ve missed you,” Chogan whispered.

Amelia felt his breath at her temple and sighed. “I’ve missed you too.”

Chogan turned her slowly to face him and tipped her chin up. He ran his hands through her hair and traced the contours of her face with his fingers.

Amelia couldn’t move. Chogan’s touch mesmerized her. She stared up into his eyes longing for him to kiss her.

Chogan slowly lowered his head and kissed Amelia softly.

The world began to spin and Amelia clung to Chogan's jacket.

Chogan deepened his kiss and wrapped his arms around Amelia, pulling her close.

Amelia kissed him back. The five weeks of separation had haunted her memory. She had dreamed of Chogan and had mentally replayed every kiss in her mind. Her arms slipped around him and she ran her fingers in his hair, holding him close.

Chogan ended their embrace with feather like kisses. His breathing was labored as he leaned his forehead against Amelia's forehead. "I've wanted to hold you in my arms and kiss you since the day you left," he whispered.

Amelia touched his lips with her finger and her eyes misted over. "I looked at the pictures from Cripple Creek and all I could remember was how you kissed me that first time." Amelia took a deep breath and smiled. "When I opened the door and saw you tonight; all I could think of was being held in your arms."

Chogan pulled her close and hugged her against his body. He rested his head in her hair and breathed in her scent. "I'm so glad you're here."

Patricia leaned her head out the patio doors, "If you two would like to join us, Geoff brought pizza." She turned back to the living room and winked at Geoff. "I think you are right my love," she whispered.

Chogan and Geoff stayed until after midnight and both girls were yawning from their long drive.

Patricia walked Geoff to his car to say goodnight.

Chogan stood at the door and smiled down at Amelia. "You are exhausted, get some sleep."

"Will I see you tomorrow?" Amelia asked.

Chogan ran his finger down her cheek and kissed her softly. "Tomorrow is Sunday, I'll pick you up for church if you'd like."

Amelia stood on her tip toes and held onto Chogan's jacket for leverage. She kissed him gently, teasing his lips with hers. "That sounds wonderful; I'll see you in the morning," she promised.

Chogan left the condo whistling.

Amelia fell asleep as soon as her head hit the pillow. She didn't hear Patricia come upstairs and check on her. She was dreaming of Chogan.

Patricia smiled, "Sleep on my friend. You may just move here yet," she whispered.

Chapter Thirteen

Chogan rang the doorbell at the condo, Sunday morning.

Patricia opened the door and waved at Topanga and Lovella waiting in Chogan's truck. "Amelia will be right down."

Chogan grinned. "Are you coming with Geoff this morning?" he asked.

"Yes, Geoff will be here any minute." Patricia saw Geoff's car pulling in and ran to finish getting ready.

Amelia picked up her purse and walked with Chogan to the truck.

"Mia, I missed you!" Lovella was squirming in her car seat. "I want to hold you!"

Amelia turned to talk to the girls while Chogan drove to church. "I missed you girls too! Lovella, I'll hold you as soon as we get to church, ok?"

Lovella grinned. "Ok Mia, I can wait."

Topanga rolled her eyes. "Mia, look at my hair." She turned her head sideways and Amelia saw the turquoise combs she had bought.

"Topanga, you look beautiful in those." Amelia continued to talk to the girls as Chogan drove.

Chogan smiled as his girls chattered on and on, telling Amelia every detail she had missed for the past five weeks. He parked the truck and opened the back door, releasing Lovella from her car seat.

As soon as Amelia opened the back door for Topanga she was wrapped in a hug.

"I missed you so much, Mia." Topanga whispered.

"I missed you too," Amelia assured her.

Lovella was tugging at Amelia's hand, "I want to hold you!"

Chogan walked beside Amelia as she carried Lovella in her left arm and held Topanga's hand with her right hand. He smiled at the bond his daughters had forged with Amelia.

Immediately following the service, Geoff and Patricia met with the pastor to plan the ceremony.

Amelia and Chogan took the girls back to the ranch for lunch. Amelia helped the girls change out of their dresses, while Chogan started the grill.

Amelia carried the potato salad, deviled eggs, fruit, buns and tea to the table, while Chogan grilled the meat.

Patricia and Geoff arrived with dessert just as Chogan finished grilling.

"Girls, come and eat." Chogan called.

Topanga helped Lovella from the swing and they ran to the picnic table laughing.

"Daddy, I want to pray grace." Topanga had memorized the blessing. "Hold hands," she instructed.

They all joined hands around the table and Topanga took a deep breath. "Bow your heads." After she was sure everyone's eyes were closed she began, "God is great, God is good, let us thank Him for this food; by His hands we all are fed, thank You Lord for our daily bread. Amen."

"That was wonderful, Topanga." Amelia praised.

Lunch was full of little girl giggles and stories. Amelia felt a soft nudge at her back as they finished eating and she turned to see Amber waiting patiently behind her.

"Hello Amber, I've missed you." Amelia leaned down and stroked Amber's fur. The collie laid her head in Amelia's lap and looked up at her lovingly.

Topanga and Lovella were excused from the table and ran back to the swings to play.

"Geoff, we have to finish this order of service for the wedding." Patricia prompted.

Geoff rolled his eyes and sat the dishes back on the table. "Yes ma'am."

Chogan laughed out loud. "You two plan the wedding and Amelia and I can clean up this food."

Amelia carried the grill items into the house and started a sink full of dish water, while Chogan carried in the food.

Amelia was up to her elbows in dishwater when Chogan walked up behind her and wrapped his arms around her waist.

"This is nice." He whispered.

Amelia smiled. "What's nice, someone else doing the dishes?" she teased.

Chogan laughed. "Yes that's nice, but I was talking about having you here in my kitchen."

"Hmmm, so you think I'd made a good housekeeper?" she asked teasing.

Chogan slid her hair back and kissed her neck softly.

Amelia shivered. "Is that how you greet all your housekeepers?"

Chogan rained kisses up her neck and across her cheek, "Only the ones I want to keep."

Amelia giggled. "And how many have you kept with this method."

Chogan whispered. "Only one; but I think it's time that I found another one to keep."

Amelia couldn't move. The underlying message in Chogan's teasing sent a chill up her spine. She wanted to believe what her heart was telling her.

Topanga ran into the kitchen, interrupting the moment. "Daddy, Lovella fell off the swing and she's crying."

Chogan followed his daughter to the yard and carried Lovella into the house. He carefully washed his daughter's knee and bandaged it for her.

Lovella wrapped her arms around Chogan's neck and kissed him. "Thank you daddy, my boo-boo is all better now."

"You're welcome sweetheart." Chogan stood and put the medicine kit away.

Topanga and Lovella returned to the swings to play.

Chogan walked into the kitchen and found all the dishes put away, the sink cleaned and Amelia was gone. He walked out to the yard and found Amelia at the table with Geoff and Patricia.

It was after 8:00 p.m. when Geoff and Patricia left. They were meeting with the caterer to discuss the food for the reception.

Topanga and Lovella were exhausted. They had missed their naps and the fresh air had them yawning at the table.

"Girls, it's time for you to get your baths and go to bed." Chogan spoke with gentle authority.

"Daddy, can Mia help us?" Topanga was sitting in Amelia's lap and could barely keep her eyes open.

Amelia hugged her. "I think that's a great idea. Come on, girls; let's get you ready for bed."

Chogan heard the giggles and the splashing of water in the bathroom as he straightened up the living room.

Amelia tucked Lovella into bed first and sang her a lullaby. Lovella was asleep before Amelia finished the chorus.

Chogan watched Amelia kiss Lovella softly and tuck the blanket gently around her little body. He was standing at the edge of the den where he could view both girls' rooms.

Amelia entered Topanga's room and brushed the little girl's hair until it shown. She braided Topanga's hair into a loose braid and tied a soft ribbon at the bottom. They whispered and giggled and Topanga hugged Amelia tight before lying down in the bed.

"I love you, Mia." Topanga watched Amelia's face closely. "I'm glad you came back to me."

Amelia's heart turned over. "I love you too, Topanga. I'm very glad to be back here and be able to see you again."

"Do you have to leave again?" Topanga asked.

Amelia smiled sadly. "I have to go back to Florida. I have a job there and my family is there."

Topanga's eyes filled with unshed tears. "So I won't see you again?"

Amelia gently stroked Topanga's cheek. "Oh honey, I'll be back to visit. Patricia is moving here to marry Geoff and I'll come to visit as often as I can."

Topanga took a deep breath to try and stop the tears that were falling down her cheeks. "I wish you were moving here. I miss you so much when you're not here."

"I miss you, when I'm not here." Amelia spoke from the heart. "I'll have to find a way to see you more often ok?"

Topanga yawned and smiled. "Ok, goodnight Mia."

Amelia kissed her forehead and tucked the blankets around her. "Goodnight my love."

Chogan walked out to the porch and sat down on the swing.

Amelia turned off Topanga's light and walked out onto the porch.

"Want to join me?" Chogan asked softly.

Amelia walked slowly to the swing and sat down beside Chogan. The gentle motion of the swing soothed her troubled mind.

Chogan slipped his arm around her shoulders and slid her against his side. "Something wrong?" he asked.

Amelia smiled. "I'm afraid I made Topanga cry tonight." There were tears in Amelia's voice.

Chogan hugged her close. "I think my daughters love you very much."

Amelia felt the tears slide. "I love them too."

Chogan sat quietly, rocking the swing back and forth gently. "I came back to the kitchen to finish our conversation this afternoon, but you were gone."

Amelia was confused. "What conversation?"

Chogan grinned. "I was telling you about my need for a housekeeper."

Amelia smiled in the moonlight. "Ahh yes, I remember that conversation. I think you were showing me how you keep a housekeeper."

Chogan laughed softly. "That's not quite how the conversation went."

Amelia played along. "Really? Maybe you should refresh my memory," she prompted.

Chogan lifted her chin and kissed her forehead and then softly placed kisses down her cheek stopping just before her lips. "I was telling you that I've only had one permanent housekeeper that enjoyed this and that I thought it was time for another."

Amelia was distracted by the feel of Chogan's lips across her skin. "I can see how that would be a good idea."

Chogan smiled and continued to rain kisses across Amelia's cheeks, never kissing her lips. "So you agree, I need to find someone?"

Amelia closed her eyes, enjoying the teasing. "Oh yes, I think it's time for you to find someone."

"Are you available?" Chogan whispered.

Amelia was stunned. She opened her eyes and stared into Chogan's eyes. "What?"

Chogan touched her cheek with his finger. "I'm asking if you are available to be in a full time position." Chogan watched her expression.

"As your housekeeper?" Amelia asked.

"I'm asking you to become a permanent part of my home." Chogan spoke softly. "My daughters love you and I know you love them. They need someone permanent."

Alice's car came into the yard, interrupting their conversation.

Amelia stood and walked across the porch. Her heart was shattered. Chogan wanted her for a surrogate mother to his daughters. Amelia wanted more; she wanted love.

Chogan helped Amelia into the truck and drove her back to the condo. He parked the truck and turned off the ignition. "Are you ok? You're awfully quiet."

Amelia smiled in the darkness. "I'm fine; I'm very tired."

Chogan kissed her softly. "Can I call you tomorrow?"

"Sure," Amelia answered quietly. "Patricia and I will be in and out all day making wedding arrangements."

Amelia slid across the seat and got out the passenger door. "Thank you for a lovely day, Chogan."

"Goodnight Amelia." Chogan watched her walk to the condo.

Amelia let herself in and went directly to her bedroom. She threw herself across the bed and cried herself to sleep.

Chogan drove home slowly and sat out on the porch swing long after Alice left for home. He couldn't understand what happened. Amelia enjoyed his company, she was responding to his kisses and then she went cold. Chogan thought carefully about the conversation and then sat up in the swing. "You idiot," he scolded himself. "You ask her to be your housekeeper." Chogan sat back in the swing and ran his hands through his hair. No wonder Amelia was quiet; she was offended and hurt. He was teasing and trying to ask her to become a permanent part of his life, as his wife. He had to fix this. Chogan called the condo and couldn't get an answer.

"God please, don't let me ruin this relationship." Chogan paced the porch. "I'm in love with her, Lord. Please help me to make her love me too."

Chapter Fourteen

Amelia and Patricia were up at 7:00 a.m. and on their way to Denver by 8:00 a.m. Patricia had ordered her wedding dress from a shop in Denver and today was her fitting.

Amelia was standing up with Patricia and Chogan was standing up with Geoff. Amelia was having her final fitting today also.

Patricia had asked Henry, Harmon, and Hilary to be in the wedding. Henry would serve as a junior usher, Harmon would serve as ring bearer and Hilary would serve as flower girl.

Amelia drove to Denver while Patricia made a list of the items that still needed to be finished.

"You're awfully quiet this morning. How was your evening with Chogan?"

Amelia forced a smile. "It was very nice. I helped the girls with their baths and then tucked them in."

Patricia shoved her notepad and pen in her purse and turned sideways in the seat. "Okay, fess up, Amelia. You have lost your smile again and it's obvious to me that you've been crying."

Amelia felt her eyes fill with tears. "I'm an idiot, Patricia."

Patricia was stunned. "What are you talking about? You are the most intelligent person I now."

Amelia laughed bitterly. "I waited five years for Liam; and he dumped me. I rushed into a sort-of relationship with Chogan, and he offers me a position as his housekeeper."

"His housekeeper? Am I missing something?" Patricia asked confused.

"Yesterday at lunch, Chogan and I were teasing one another in the kitchen about his needing a housekeeper full time to take care of him and the girls." Amelia smiled at the memory of Chogan holding her from behind and teasing her with kisses.

Patricia watched Amelia closely. "That doesn't sound bad, so what happened?"

"Lovella fell from the swings and Chogan had to bandage her knee. After I tucked the girls in, we were sitting on the swing and the teasing picked up where we left off in the kitchen," Amelia spoke sadly.

Patricia couldn't figure out what went wrong. "Ok, so where did it go wrong?"

"Chogan asked me if I was interested in a full time position. I asked him if he was asking me to be his housekeeper." A tear fell down Amelia's cheek and she brushed it away. "He told me that his girls loved me and they needed someone to care for them full time."

Patricia was shocked. "Please tell me he amended that."

Amelia shook her head sadly. "No, Alice pulled in the driveway and Chogan drove me back to the condo."

Patricia touched Amelia's arm. "I am so sorry, Amelia. I can't imagine what Chogan was thinking. I honestly thought that he was falling in love with you."

"I thought so too," Amelia whispered. "That's why I'm an idiot; I fell in love with him," she admitted.

"You're not an idiot, Amelia." Patricia needed to help her best friend. "You are a warm, caring, compassionate woman; Chogan acted like he truly cared for you."

Amelia took a deep breath as she reached the city limits. "I'm going to be just fine. I'm going to help my best friend marry the love of her life. Then I'm going to return to Florida and figure out what to do with the rest of my life."

Patricia put on her wedding dress and came out of the dressing room to stand before the mirrors; while the attendants pinned & tucked the final fitting.

Amelia snapped photos of the entire process. "You are beautiful, Patricia."

Patricia smiled as she turned to face Amelia. "Do you think Geoff will like it?"

Amelia laughed. "He won't be able to take his eyes off of you, that dress is perfect!"

Patricia had chosen a winter white gown of shimmering satin. It was gathered in layers that accentuated her slim figure. The top was strapless and gathered at the bodice with rhinestones. The bolo style jacket had tiny rhinestones that lined the edge of the collar and the entire edge of the jacket; the jacket fell just to the top of Patricia's waist.

"How are you going to fix your hair?" Amelia asked as she took more photos.

Patricia pulled her hair up and back. "I'm going to pull it up and back and have loose cascading curls falling down my back."

"Are you wearing a veil?"

Patricia smiled. "I chose this instead."

The attendant grinned and brought a beautiful tiara that sparkled like real diamonds.

Amelia gasped. "It is beautiful! You are going to look like a princess."

Patricia's eyes filled with tears. I thought that a modern dress needed something different than a veil. What do you think?"

Amelia's eyes were filled with happy tears. "I think you are the most beautiful bride I have ever seen."

Amelia was fitted for her dress next. She wore a yellow satin gown that was gathered at the bodice with rhinestones that sparkled and reflected off the satin. The dress had tiny spaghetti straps and a bolo jacket styled like the bridal gown.

One of the bridal shop attendants took photos of Amelia and Patricia in front of the mirrors.

Amelia and Patricia drove back to Frisco and ate lunch at Butterhorn Bakery. They left the bakery and met with the florist to order the altar arrangements and the wedding flowers. It was after 5:00 p.m. when they drove back to the condo.

Patricia took a shower while Amelia downloaded the photos to her laptop. She was just finishing when the doorbell rang.

Amelia opened the door and grinned at Geoff. "Ah the bridegroom," she teased.

Geoff kissed her cheek. "Is my bride ready?"

Amelia laughed. "She'll be down in just a minute. Are you ready for the wedding?"

"More than you know." Geoff pulled out a stool at the bar. "Can I ask you something?"

"If you want to know Patricia's deep, dark secrets, you'll have to figure them out for yourself." Amelia laughed at the expression on Geoff's face.

"Actually, I wanted to ask you what happened between you and Chogan." Geoff saw the look of pain cross Amelia's face. "Chogan was like a grizzly bear today and that's not like him."

Amelia smiled softly. "I'm sorry he was ill with you, maybe he was having a bad day."

Patricia overheard the conversation and walked quietly into the room. "Hi Geoff, are you ready to go?"

Geoff slipped his arm around Patricia's waist and kissed her softly. "Amelia, do you want to join us for dinner?"

"No Geoff, but thank you for inviting me. You two lovebirds go and have a wonderful time." Amelia watched them leave.

Geoff backed the car out of the parking place and headed for town. "What happened last night?"

Patricia squeezed his hand. "Your friend Chogan offered Amelia a permanent position as his housekeeper."

"He offered her a position?" Geoff was confused. "You're kidding right? He proposed and it was too soon?"

Patricia sighed. "I wish I was kidding. He hurt her, Geoff; she didn't deserve that."

"Amelia is in love with Chogan, isn't she?" Geoff asked.

"Yes," Patricia confirmed. "She opened up to Chogan after being humiliated by Liam and now she feels like it was all a mistake."

"I really thought that Chogan was in love with her too." Geoff turned into the parking lot of the restaurant and parked the car. He turned to face Patricia as he spoke. "I was there when Samantha died; Chogan was heartbroken. I didn't think he'd ever open his heart to a woman again. Then he met Amelia. He's talked about her non-stop since you all left for home."

Patricia squeezed Geoff's hand. "If he loves her, why did he offer her a housekeeper's position?"

Geoff pulled Patricia into his arms. “I don’t know, but I promise you, I’m going to find out.”

Chogan sat in his truck at the fire station and dialed the condo number. After the fifth ring, Chogan left a message and disconnected the call. He started the truck, determined to drive over to the condo and find Amelia so he could straighten out this misunderstanding.

Amelia gathered her camera as soon as Patricia and Geoff left for dinner. She chose the walking trail that ran from the condo through the city park and all the way to the town of Frisco. The fresh air and the beautiful wild flowers were a balm to Amelia’s wounded spirit.

As Chogan started out of the fire station parking lot, the alarm sounded. He backed up, parked the truck and ran inside. Within five minutes, Chogan was in full gear and headed out with the trucks to a forest fire.

Amelia heard the fire trucks as she neared the edge of town; she caught sight of Chogan in the first vehicle as it rushed by, sirens blaring.

Geoff hung up his cell phone and returned to the table.

“Do you need to go?” Patricia respected Geoff’s job as a fireman.

“No. The captain said that I wasn’t needed on this one. It’s a small forest fire at the base of Rocky Mountain National Park.” Geoff took Patricia’s hand in his. “I never asked you how you felt about marrying a fireman. I can be called out any time, day or night.”

Patricia smiled softly. “Geoff, your position as a fireman is just one of the many reasons that I love you.”

Geoff looked relieved. “I can’t imagine doing anything else.”

“You are serving the community as a fireman, and I’m proud of you.” Patricia stroked the back of Geoff’s hand with her thumb. “How do you feel about me being an elementary school teacher?”

Geoff grinned. “If I had teachers that looked like you, when I was in school; my grades would have been much better.”

Patricia laughed out loud.

“I figure anyone that can handle an entire classroom full of small children, will be a great mother to mine.” Geoff watched her for a reaction.

Patricia smiled dreamily, "Our children, I like the sound of that."

Geoff's expression turned serious. "I love children, Patricia. I told you I'm from a large family and you're going to meet them at the wedding. I have three sisters and two brothers."

Patricia took a deep breath. "Are you sure they didn't want to be in the wedding?" she asked.

Geoff grinned. "They are so happy to see me take the plunge they want to sit back and watch," he teased.

"Tell me about them," Patricia prompted.

"Isabella is the youngest at twenty-one. She's a junior in college. Kaitlyn is next and she's twenty-three. She has a bachelor's degree in chemistry and is now a first year grad student working on her pharmacology degree," Geoff spoke proudly. "Adriana is twenty-seven, just two years older than me, and is married and living in North Dakota with her husband who serves in the military. Justin is twenty-nine and is married and living in Texas. And last but not least is George; he's the oldest at thirty-one. He's married and lives in Washington DC."

"Wow," Patricia spoke in awe. "Your family is spread out everywhere. Where do your parents live?" she asked.

"They live in Wyoming and are both retired and waiting for grandchildren," Geoff grinned.

"Do you think they'll like me?" Patricia asked worrying.

Geoff leaned across the table and kissed her. "They are going to love you as much as I do," he promised.

Amelia picked up a sandwich and headed back to the condo along the trail. The message light was blinking on the answering machine. Amelia pressed the button and heard Chogan's voice. "Amelia, it's Chogan, I need to talk to you, please. If you get this message, can you call me back?"

Amelia deleted the message. She grabbed a soda from the fridge and headed for the patio with her sandwich. Amelia offered the blessing over her dinner as her cell phone rang. She placed her food on the table. "Hello?"

"Hello Amelia, you're a hard woman to find."

"Liam?" Amelia was stunned. "Why are you calling me?"

Liam stared out the window of his car. "I need a friend Amelia."

"You should talk to your wife." Amelia was angry.

"Amelia, don't be that way. I know that I don't have a right to ask you for anything after the way I treated you, but you've always been my friend," Liam spoke with charm trying to ease back into Amelia's life.

"Liam, our relationship is over. I don't want to talk to you." Amelia felt betrayed.

"I'm sorry, Amelia." Liam's voice sounded strained. "My marriage to Courtney was a mistake."

Amelia stood and paced the patio. "That is your problem, you chose Courtney over me."

Liam changed tactics. "I heard you were in Colorado for Patricia's wedding."

"Yes, Patricia is marrying a wonderful guy," Amelia spoke firmly.

"You're not seeing anyone, are you?" Liam didn't want Amelia to be with anyone else. If his relationship with Courtney failed, he was sure he could win Amelia back.

"That's none of your business Liam." Amelia felt her heart grow cold. "Don't call me again. Goodbye." Amelia disconnected the phone before Liam could respond.

Amelia tossed her sandwich in the trash. She had lost her appetite and needed to work off the stress she was feeling. Amelia headed to her room, changed into her swimsuit and headed for the indoor pool.

The pool was deserted and Amelia swam lap after lap until she was exhausted. The physical exertion helped ease the stress of betrayal Amelia felt. When she couldn't swim another lap, Amelia crawled out of the pool and put on her robe. The sound of sirens greeted her as she exited the pool house and headed back to the condo.

Geoff ran past Amelia, never seeing her, in his rush to leave.

"Patricia?" Amelia walked into the condo and saw Patricia pacing the living room. "Is something wrong?"

Patricia turned towards Amelia, with tears streaming down her face. "Where have you been?" she asked.

Amelia shivered in fear. “I’m sorry; I went to the pool to swim. What’s happened?”

Patricia walked over to her friend. “Amelia, there’s a forest fire at Rocky Mountain National Park.”

“I saw the fire trucks earlier,” Amelia paused as she thought of Chogan in the first truck. “It’s Chogan isn’t it?”

Patricia’s eyes filled with tears. “The fire shifted and trapped Chogan and another fireman behind the fire.”

Amelia’s knees buckled and she fell to the couch. “Oh God no, please God, don’t let him die,” she prayed in desperation.

Patricia knelt in front of Amelia. “Listen to me,” she tipped Amelia’s chin up and made eye contact with her. “Amelia, we need to pray, right here and right now.”

Amelia fell to her knees beside her best friend and they joined hands and prayed for the safe return of the firefighters.

Chapter Fifteen

The news was full of reports on the raging fire for three days. Patricia and Amelia paced the condo, worrying about the men that were fighting the fire and trying to rescue their friends.

The phone rang early Friday morning and Patricia answered it, anxious for news. "Hello?"

"Hi honey," Geoff's voice sounded exhausted.

Patricia went weak in the knees and grasped the phone closer to her ear. "Geoff, it is so good to hear your voice. Is the fire out? Did you find Chogan and the other fire fighter?" she asked hurriedly.

Geoff cleared his throat and spoke slowly; his voice was raspy from the smoke he had inhaled. "We found them. They are alive and on their way to the hospital in Denver."

"How badly are they injured?" Patricia asked as her heart constricted in fear.

"Ben was hit by a falling tree and broke his leg. Chogan pulled him to safety and protected him until we could get through the wall of fire," Geoff explained.

"Are you ok?" Patricia wanted to be with Geoff.

"I'm fine, just exhausted and the smoke has done a number on my voice." Geoff coughed trying to clear his lungs before he continued. "They are giving all of us a breathing treatment and we've been ordered to rest."

Patricia felt the tears of relief, "Geoff, is Chogan going to be ok?"

Geoff spoke quietly. "I hope and pray he's going to be ok. Those girls have already lost one parent."

"Get some sleep, sweetheart." Patricia hung the phone up and turned to see Amelia standing in the doorway, tears streaming down her face.

"Are they alive?" Amelia whispered.

"Yes." Patricia replaced the receiver. "Chogan saved Ben's life and protected him until the firemen could rescue both of them."

Amelia fell to the floor and sobbed.

Patricia rushed to Amelia's side and wrapped her arms around her. "He's in the hospital, but Geoff says they think he will be ok."

Amelia stood. "I have to be there."

Patricia nodded in agreement. "Come on, let's shower and head to Denver."

The hospital waiting room was full of firemen. Amelia walked slowly into the room and was met with a tiny cry.

"Mia!" Topanga ran into Amelia's waiting arms sobbing on her shoulder.

Amelia lifted her gently and rocked her back and forth."Shhhh, Topanga its ok, honey. Don't cry, please don't cry."

Topanga clung to Amelia's neck and sobbed into her shoulder.

Uda held a sleeping Lovella in her arms and smiled at Amelia from across the waiting room.

Dakota walked over and gently hugged Amelia. "Thank you for coming, Amelia."

Amelia smiled, the tears falling slowly down her cheeks. "Have you seen him?"

Dakota shook his head slowly. "Ben was taken to surgery for his injuries and Chogan is still being examined."

Geoff walked through the hospital doors and straight into Patricia's arms. "I knew you'd come," he whispered in her ear.

Patricia kissed him and stroked his face. "You are exhausted, you need some sleep."

"I promise, I'll get some rest once I know Chogan is ok." Geoff walked over and shook Dakota's hand.

"Dakota, this is my fiancée, Patricia. Patricia, this is Chogan's dad, Dakota." Geoff made the introductions with a tired voice.

Patricia extended her hand. "It's so nice to meet you."

"My son has told me about the beautiful woman who stole Geoff's heart," Dakota spoke softly.

Patricia blushed. "I believe it was Geoff who stole my heart the first time I saw him."

Amelia smiled and walked slowly to the couch to sit beside Uda. Topanga had cried herself to sleep in Amelia's arms.

"My granddaughters love you very much, Amelia," Uda commented.

"I love them too." Amelia stroked Topanga's back loving the feel of this little girl in her arms.

"And how do you feel about my son?" Uda spoke softly and watched Amelia's face for her answer. "Is there love in your heart for him?" she asked.

Amelia's eyes filled with tears. "I fell in love with Chogan before I left Colorado the first time," she admitted honestly.

"My son's heart was lost after Samantha died," Uda confided. "I have prayed often that God would send a woman of compassion who would love my son and my granddaughters."

Amelia cried softly, unable to speak or explain the conflicting emotions she felt.

Uda placed her hand over Amelia's. "My dear Amelia, if God has ordained a love between you and my son, He will make a way for you to be together."

The doctor walked in to the waiting room and spoke with the firemen and then with Dakota.

Dakota walked over to Uda. "Chogan is in intensive care. They will allow us to visit with him, but the girls are not permitted in that unit."

"I'll stay with the girls," Amelia offered.

Uda placed Lovella on the couch beside Amelia and covered her with a blanket.

Geoff had fallen asleep with his head on Patricia's shoulder.

"Patricia, why don't you drive Geoff home so he can get some rest and I'll bring your car back to the condo?" Amelia offered.

"Amelia, you haven't slept in three days. Are you sure you'll be ok to drive?" Patricia asked.

"I will be fine. You take care of Geoff." Amelia smiled as Patricia gently woke Geoff and persuaded him to leave.

Uda walked back into the waiting room after seeing her son and smiled. Amelia had turned sideways against the corner of the couch and fallen asleep with Topanga asleep across her chest and Lovella curled up beside her, with her head in Amelia's lap.

Dakota stood beside Uda. "I never thought Chogan would find someone to replace Samantha."

Uda spoke softly. "I think the Lord has sent this woman for our son, and for our granddaughters."

"We need to take the girls home." Dakota gently lifted Topanga from Amelia's arms without waking her.

Amelia opened her eyes as Topanga was lifted from her arms. "I'm sorry, I must have fallen asleep."

Uda kissed her forehead. "My sweet Amelia, you look exhausted."

Amelia smiled. "I'm fine. Do you need me to take the girls home?"

"We will take the girls home and get them to bed." Dakota waited while Uda removed Lovella without waking her. "You can go and visit with Chogan."

Amelia watched them leave and stretched. She took the elevator to the intensive care unit and was directed to Chogan's room.

Chogan was hooked to oxygen and his hands were bandaged. His left hand was bandaged from fingertip to elbow. His right hand was bandaged from the palm to the shoulder.

Amelia touched the fingers of Chogan's right hand and stroked them softly. Tears fell softly down her cheeks as she listened to his labored breathing.

The nurse came in to check Chogan's vitals. "You can talk to him. He's heavily sedated but he can hear you."

Amelia wiped her eyes. "Is he going to be ok?" she asked.

"He's got second and third degree burns on his arms and chest. He has smoke inhalation that will cause him some breathing difficulties; however, he should recover." The nurse adjusted the IV and returned to the nurses' station.

Amelia walked closer to the bed and kissed Chogan's forehead softly. She pulled a chair up next to Chogan's bed and gently held his fingers in her hand. "Lord, please heal Chogan's body. Strengthen him and give him breath." Amelia sat for hours before she fell asleep at Chogan's bedside.

Chogan struggled to wake from the sedative. He opened his eyes slowly and looked around the room. Chogan lifted his left hand and looked at the bandages. He looked over at his right hand and saw Amelia sleeping in the chair with her hand holding his fingers.

Amelia stirred and opened her eyes. She stood and stroked Chogan's fingers with her hand. "You're awake." Tears fell slowly down Amelia's cheeks and she smiled. "Are you in pain?" she asked.

Chogan tried to speak but started to cough with the effort.

The nurse rushed in and raised the bed to give Chogan a breathing treatment. She gave Chogan a shot of sedative and spoke softly to him. "You have to try not to speak. Your voice will come back with time, but you've got to give your throat time to heal."

Chogan watched the nurse until she left and he searched the room for Amelia.

Amelia moved to the bedside, and took Chogan's fingers in her hand when he reached for her. "You need to rest." Amelia started to leave and Chogan clung to her hand with his fingers. "Do you need the nurse?" she asked, her voice filled with concern.

Chogan shook his head slowly back and forth, struggling against the effects of the sedative. He needed to talk to Amelia but he couldn't speak.

Amelia brushed the hair from his forehead and kissed him softly. "Sleep Chogan, I won't leave you," she promised.

Chogan's eyes filled with tears and he clung to Amelia's hand.

Amelia wiped the tears from Chogan's face and gently stroked his face until he relaxed and allowed the sedative to take effect. She returned to the chair at his bedside and sat quietly watching him sleep.

Geoff and Patricia came to visit at lunchtime. "How is he?" Geoff asked softly.

"He's heavily sedated," Amelia spoke softly. "He can't talk because the smoke damaged his throat and lungs."

Geoff walked over and touched Chogan's hand. "I hate seeing him like this."

Patricia wrapped her arms around Geoff and hugged him. "He saved Ben's life, Geoff. God honors that kind of sacrifice."

Geoff hugged Patricia to him. “He has to get better, he’s my best man.”

Geoff and Patricia stayed for just a few minutes and left to go and visit Ben.

Dakota arrived in the afternoon and found Amelia sitting quietly at Chogan’s side holding his hand. “How is he doing?”

Amelia stood and moved so Dakota could visit with his son. “He’s sedated. He tried to talk and they had to give him a breathing treatment and sedative to make him rest.”

Dakota stroked his son’s hair. “He won’t be able to talk until his throat heals. The girls won’t like that.”

Amelia smiled. “If Topanga and Lovella are anything like I was as a child; they’ll talk enough for him.”

Dakota laughed. “They can certainly fill a room with conversation.”

Amelia yawned revealing the exhaustion she felt.

“Why don’t you go and get some rest. You’ve been here all night.”

Amelia smiled. “I should I guess.” Amelia wrote the number to the condo on a pad of paper next to the bed. “Call me and let me know how he is, please?”

Dakota hugged her gently. “We will call and give you an update. Get some rest.”

Amelia turned to leave the room.

“Amelia,” Dakota called her name softly. “Thank you for caring for my son, and my granddaughters.”

Amelia turned with sad eyes. “He’s a very special man. It was my pleasure.”

Chapter Sixteen

Chogan was in ICU for two days and then moved to a step-down unit. He was frustrated with the inability to speak. Chogan couldn't write with the burns on his hands.

Dakota and Uda took turns at the hospital so that one of them could stay with the girls.

Amelia and Patricia drove to Denver on Monday to meet their families who had flown in for the wedding.

Geoff was working extra shifts at the fire station to make up for Ben and Chogan's absence. An alternate fire fighter would arrive from the Breckenridge fire station the following week while Geoff and Patricia went on a honeymoon.

Nancy and Gerald McAfee were the first passengers off the plane. Nancy hugged her daughter close. "Patricia, this is the most exciting thing you have ever done."

Gerald laughed. "Our daughter meets a man in Colorado, decides to marry him and move away; and you think it's exciting."

Patricia looked hurt. "Daddy, do you think I'm making a mistake?"

Gerald hugged her close. "Honey, I'm proud of you. You're my daughter and it will be my pleasure to walk you down the aisle."

Amelia heard Hilary before she saw her. "Mia!"

Amelia knelt down and scooped up her niece and hugged her tight. "Hi sweetie, did you like riding on that big plane?"

Hilary pushed her hair out of her eyes and gestured with her arms. "It was wild. We went way up in the sky and I saw clouds and mountains."

Harmon and Henry ran to Amelia and waited patiently for their hug.

Amelia grinned as Henry whispered in her ear. "Is there gonna be anything for us to do while we're here?"

"There's an indoor pool at the condo, and I think I can find something fun to do while you're here." Amelia saw the sparkle in his eye as he hugged her tight.

Reggie hugged Amelia and walked with her while the children walked with Myron and Anne. "So how is your friend Chogan?"

Amelia smiled. "He's being released from the hospital tomorrow. He won't be able to talk for several weeks and he can't write since both hands are burned."

"Ouch!" Reggie hugged Amelia close. "So does Chogan have someone to help him when he gets home?"

"His mom and dad are taking care of the girls and will stay until he can take care of them again." Amelia had a far-away look in her eyes.

"Will we get to meet this young man?" Reggie wanted to meet the man that had stolen his daughter's heart.

Amelia laughed. "Yes daddy, you'll meet him at the wedding, he's Geoff's best man."

Myron gathered their luggage while Anne picked up their minivan from the rental counter.

Nancy and Gerald rode with Patricia back to Frisco; while Amelia drove her family in the minivan.

Amelia had rented the three bedroom condo next door for her family. She took Henry, Harmon, and Hilary swimming while the adults unpacked and settled in.

Patricia and Geoff walked into the pool house with Topanga and Lovella.

"Mia!" Topanga ran for the pool and Amelia captured her in her arms.

"Who is that, Mia?" Hilary asked from the water.

Amelia smiled as she helped Topanga remove her robe. "This is Topanga and she's come to swim with you."

"Don't forget me, Mia!" Lovella had removed her robe over her swimsuit and was trying to put her water wings on her arms.

Amelia helped the little girl. "Hilary this is Topanga's little sister, Lovella."

Within minutes the five children were swimming and splashing in the pool.

Myron and Anne joined them, dressed to swim. "Hey sis, I'll take over lifeguarding."

Amelia grinned. "Big brother, you have five to watch now. Are you sure you can handle it?"

"He's got me to help," Anne slipped off her robe and dived into the water.

Amelia was watching the children and didn't notice the door to the pool house open and close.

Chogan walked slowly towards the pool and touched Amelia's shoulder with his unbandaged fingers.

Amelia spun around and slowly stood to come face to face with the man she loved. "Hey, you should be home resting," she gently scolded.

Chogan touched her cheek with his fingers and smiled.

Geoff grinned. "He would not allow us to take him home. When he found out that Uda was bringing the girls to swim with you, he insisted we bring him here."

Amelia looked confused. "How did you insist?" She looked at his bandaged hands and knew he couldn't talk yet.

Patricia grinned and held up her palm pilot and pen. "Where there's a will, there's a way."

Chogan touched Amelia's hand with his fingers and nodded towards the door.

"I can't leave the children." Amelia turned to look towards the pool.

"Little sister, Anne and I can handle these kids. Go and talk to your friend." Myron took one look at Amelia's face and knew his instincts had been right.

Patricia pressed her palm pilot and pen into Amelia's hand and shoved her towards the door.

Chogan walked slowly with his fingers touching Amelia's hand. He led her down the park walkway until he came to a bench where they could sit. Chogan eased himself to the bench and his face contorted in pain.

"Chogan, you need to go home and get some rest. You're not well yet." The concern in Amelia's voice was evident.

Chogan shook his head slowly and touched Amelia's face with his fingertips. He pointed to the palm pilot and took the pen and tapped out a message. "Can I kiss you?"

Amelia's eyes filled with tears as she nodded her head in agreement.

Chogan leaned gently towards Amelia and kissed her lips softly. He leaned back and looked at her closely.

Amelia couldn't stand it. She reached up and gently stroked his face with her hand. "I thought I'd never see you again." The tears flowed unstoppable down her cheeks. Amelia leaned forward and kissed Chogan.

Chogan wrapped his right arm around Amelia and drew her into his arms. He groaned softly as he ignored the pain to feel her close to his heart. He kissed her again and again, longing to tell her what his heart needed to say.

A soft smile stole across Amelia's face. "You may be injured, but you haven't lost your ability to kiss," she teased.

Chogan grinned and then flinched in pain.

Amelia was immediately concerned. "We've got to get you home so you can rest."

Chogan shook his head no vehemently. He took the pen in his fingers and tapped out a message. "I tried to call you, before the fire."

Amelia's expression turned sad. "It's ok, I understand."

Chogan lifted her chin with his unbandaged fingers to look her in the eyes and shook his head no. "I need to talk to you," A fit of coughing caused Chogan to drop the pen and clutch his chest. He tried to get the inhaler from his pocket but couldn't with his bandaged hands.

Amelia shook the inhaler and held it to his lips, gently giving him puffs to open his throat.

Chogan gasped for breath and beads of sweat appeared on his forehead as he struggled to get control.

Amelia waited until he was breathing normally. "I'm not going to take no for an answer." She helped Chogan to stand and wrapped her arm around his waist. She walked slowly with him feeling his body flinch in pain.

Geoff was waiting outside the pool house watching for their return. "You overdid it, Chogan. No arguments, I'm taking you home."

Chogan turned to Amelia, the frustration evident on his face.

"I'll see you before I leave," Amelia promised. "Get some rest, please."

Chogan leaned heavily on Geoff as he walked to the car. He longed to tell Amelia how he felt and prayed he'd have a chance before she left Frisco for good.

The phone in Amelia and Patricia's condo rang at 8:00 a.m. on Tuesday morning. Amelia answered it on the first ring.

"Amelia?" Uda's voice was as soft on the phone as it was in person.

"Hello, Uda, how is Chogan today?" Amelia asked.

Uda laughed softly. "He's being very difficult at the moment. Would you consider bringing your family to the ranch today?"

Amelia laughed. "Uda, there are eight of us."

"The more the merrier my dear; Dakota thought the children would enjoy riding the horses around the coral."

Amelia grinned. "Hang on and I'll ask them."

"Hey guys, would you like to visit a working ranch today?"

Henry answered first. "Can we ride a horse?"

"Yes you can." Amelia covered the receiver to smother the shouts from the children.

"Uda, as you probably heard, that was a yes," Amelia responded laughing.

"Wonderful, we'll be ready when you get here." Uda paused for a moment. "Amelia,"

"Yes ma'am?"

"Don't worry about bringing anything except your smile and your family," Uda instructed.

Amelia loved the warmth of Chogan's mother. "I'll do that, Uda. We'll see you soon," she promised.

Patricia walked into the condo as Amelia hung up the phone. "So what time are you taking your family to Chogan's?" Patricia asked.

Amelia was startled. "How did you know we were going?"

Patricia grinned. “Because, we are all going; Myron I hope you can still ride a horse.”

The children ran and played and spent hours with the horses and with Dakota. Topanga and Lovella had bonded with Myron’s children and were playing like siblings.

Myron, Anne, Geoff, Patricia, Reggie and Gerald took the children and went for a long ride on the horses. Cecilia and Nancy stayed in the house visiting with Uda.

Chogan was alone on the porch swing and he motioned for Amelia to join him.

Amelia walked to the swing remembering the last night she had sat in his arms and how that evening had ended.

The memory brought a look of sadness to Amelia’s face that Chogan recognized immediately. He tapped Amelia’s pocket for the palm pilot and took the pen as she sat down beside him. “I need to tell you something before we are interrupted again.” Chogan tapped the pen on the palm pilot and nudged Amelia to read what he typed.

“You don’t have to explain.” Amelia didn’t want Chogan to feel obligated.

Chogan shook his head and touched her arm with a look of pleading in his eyes. “Please, Amelia, give me a chance to explain,” he typed.

Amelia nodded slowly.

“I was teasing you that night about the housekeeper.” Chogan watched Amelia’s expression.

“I misunderstood, Chogan.” Amelia tried to smile. “I just wasn’t expecting a job offer.”

Chogan tried to speak and stopped himself before he started coughing. He tapped out what he couldn’t say. “I wasn’t offering you a job; I was trying to ask you to be a permanent part of my home and my life.”

Amelia read the words slowly, looking up at Chogan for confirmation.

Chogan tapped the pen trying to get his feelings out. “I love you, Amelia.”

Amelia turned in the swing and looked Chogan directly in the eye. She whispered, “I love you too. I’ve loved you since I left Colorado the first time.”

Chogan took his fingers and pulled Amelia close kissing her deeply. He placed his left arm across the back of the swing and hugged Amelia close, ignoring the pain. He pressed his face into her hair and sighed. Chogan held Amelia in his arms and rocked the swing slowly back and forth.

Amelia sat up slowly; Chogan was asleep against the cushion of the swing. She smiled at the expression he wore. He looked content and happy.

Chapter Seventeen

The wedding rehearsal took several hours and the children were restless by the time it was over. The entire wedding party headed to Butterhorn Bakery for the rehearsal dinner.

Geoff stood and raised his glass of coke in a toast. "To my beautiful bride-to-be; it is fitting that we have our rehearsal dinner where we first met. I will forever be grateful that you walked into this café and into my heart. I love you Patricia."

The entire room erupted in applause. Patricia stood and raised her glass. "To my husband-to-be; I will forever be grateful that you walked through those doors and into my heart. I love you now and forever, Geoff."

Geoff's parents, Allison and Edwin had arrived from Wyoming for the wedding. Edwin stood and lifted his glass in a toast. "To my son and future daughter-in-law, I wish you love, laughter, and many years of happiness. I also pray that you are blessed with many children so that your mother and I can spoil them rotten."

The room erupted in laughter.

Allison took the floor and lifted her glass. "Geoff you have found a beautiful young lady to share your life with. Patricia, welcome to our family."

Geoff leaned over and whispered to Patricia, "Tomorrow you meet the rest of my family."

Patricia kissed him softly. "Geoff, I'm an only child; being part of your family is going to be wonderful."

The toasts and good wishes continued until 11:00 p.m. The party broke up and everyone headed for their cars.

Chogan stopped Amelia with his finger and motioned for her to stay. He tapped out a message on the palm pilot and turned it where she could read it. "When do you fly home?"

Amelia spoke softly. "Sunday morning."

Chogan turned the palm pilot and tapped out another message. "I don't want you to leave."

"I know, it's hard for me to leave too." Amelia sighed. "I have to go back to work Monday."

Chogan frowned. "I wish I could talk to you instead of tapping out my words," he wrote.

Amelia smiled sadly. "I miss your voice too; but you'll be talking in no time. You can call me so we can talk," she offered hopefully.

"Will you come back?" Chogan had to know. He watched Amelia read this message hoping for a positive answer.

"Yes Chogan, I'll be back to visit. Will you keep in touch with me?" she asked.

Chogan nodded his head yes. Chogan stood and waited for Amelia to slip her shawl around her shoulders. He kissed her softly as she joined Myron's family in the minivan.

Chogan walked over to Geoff's car and waited until Patricia and Geoff said goodnight.

The morning of the wedding was warm and sunny. The church was full by 1:00 p.m. and Patricia paced slowly across the room anxious for the ceremony to start.

Amelia giggled as she watched Patricia. "You're as nervous as a cat on a hot tin roof."

Patricia sighed. "I'm ready to get married." She turned to face Amelia. "Just wait until you and Chogan get married. You'll know exactly how I feel."

"What makes you think we are getting married?" Amelia asked.

Patricia laughed. "You're kidding right? You two are so in love that it's amazing you haven't already gotten engaged."

Amelia was solemn. "He hasn't asked me."

"What would your answer be?" Patricia wanted her friend close by, but she wanted Amelia to be happy most of all.

"If I could find a job as quickly as you did, I'd probably say yes!" Amelia admitted.

Patricia hugged Amelia. "I'm going to miss you."

"Hey, none of that," Amelia touched Patricia's cheek. "I'm very happy for you, Patricia. I know that you and Geoff are going to be very happy."

The wedding music started and Hilary started down the aisle dropping her rose petals as she walked. Harmon walked solemnly behind her carrying the ring pillow like a soldier.

Amelia started down the aisle and she couldn't take her eyes off of Chogan. His burned arms were covered by the black tuxedo he wore and his eyes were fixed on Amelia. The smile he wore; warmed her heart.

Chogan sucked in his breath when Amelia appeared at the back of the church. She was breathtakingly beautiful in the yellow satin dress. Her hair was curled in long tendrils that cascaded down her back. Chogan longed to ask her to become his wife. In less than twenty-four hours she would be leaving for Florida and his heart was breaking at the thought.

The bride's music started and everyone stood. Geoff stared in wonder as Patricia walked slowly down the aisle on her daddy's arm. Geoff accepted her hand from her father and slowly walked up the steps to the pastor. It seemed like only minutes passed until they were pronounced husband and wife.

Patricia met Geoff's brothers and sisters and the spouses at the reception. They shared stories of Geoff's childhood that made her laugh and made Geoff roll his eyes.

The reception was held in the fellowship hall; the toasts were made, the cake was cut, the bouquet and garter were thrown. Geoff and Patricia drove away from the reception under a shower of bird seed and headed off to their honeymoon.

Patricia sat cuddled up close to Geoff in the car with her head on his shoulder and her arm around his waist as he drove. "Mr. Sandidge, can you tell me where we are headed for our honeymoon?"

Geoff stroked Patricia's arm with his fingers as he drove. "We are catching a flight in Denver and flying to Los Angeles."

"I've never been to California." Patricia smiled. "Have you been to Los Angeles before?" she asked.

Geoff squeezed her shoulder. "Nope, and we aren't staying in Los Angeles."

Patricia sat up confused. "Where are we going?"

Geoff pulled the tickets from his tuxedo and handed them to Patricia.

"A cruise? We're going on a cruise?" Patricia was thrilled.

Geoff grinned at her reaction. "I thought a nice cruise to Mexico would give us time to relax and really get to know each other."

Patricia giggled and snuggled close to Geoff. "My dear husband, I hope we know each other very well, before this week is over."

Amelia was the last person to leave the reception. She walked slowly down the steps of the fellowship hall and saw Chogan waiting for her.

"Hello stranger, are you waiting for me?" Amelia teased.

Chogan nodded yes and wrapped his arm around her waist as they walked. He helped her into his truck and got in behind the wheel.

Amelia was surprised. "Can you drive?"

Chogan grinned and turned the key with his fingers. His left hand bandages had been changed and his fingers were exposed.

Amelia sat quietly while Chogan drove. She didn't say anything when Chogan drove away from Frisco.

It was two hours later that Chogan drove across the Royal Gorge Bridge. He smiled at Amelia as he parked the truck.

Amelia was still in her yellow satin dress from the wedding, and Chogan was still in his tuxedo.

Visitors at the bridge smiled and whispered as they passed. Chogan took Amelia's hand with his fingers and led her to the spot on the bridge where they had their photo made. He pulled the photo of the two of them from his pocket and handed it to Amelia.

"Do you carry this with you?" Amelia gently unfolded the picture.

Chogan nodded his head yes. He pulled Amelia into his arms and hugged her close.

Amelia hugged Chogan and held on tight knowing that this was their last night together.

"I love you." Chogan whispered in her ear his voice raspy from the damage of the fire.

Amelia looked up into Chogan's face. "You're not supposed to talk! Your voice needs to heal," she scolded gently.

Chogan placed his finger on Amelia's lips stilling her words. "I love you. The day we stood here and had our photo made, I knew I was in love with you." Chogan looked down in her eyes. "When we sat together on my porch swing and I asked you if you were available," Chogan took a deep breath as his voice began to fade. "I was trying to propose."

Amelia gasped.

Chogan took Amelia's hands in his fingers and stared into her eyes. He whispered, "I love you, Amelia, marry me!"

Amelia was stunned. "Chogan, I don't have a job here, and I have responsibilities in Florida." Amelia turned and stood watching the sun set. Her heart said yes, but her mind was troubled.

Chogan wrapped his arms around her from behind and gently rained kissed across her neck and up her cheek. He was reminding her of how their misunderstanding got started.

Amelia closed her eyes; she trembled as Chogan's kisses opened her heart and mind to the true desire in her heart. She wanted a family, she wanted a husband to love and cherish. Amelia's prayer from the night on Chogan's porch rang through her mind and she smiled. She had prayed for Chogan to propose.

Chogan held her close and whispered, "I love you. I had to tell you before you leave tomorrow."

Amelia turned and placed her hands on the lapel of Chogan's tuxedo. She smiled as she looked up into Chogan's face. "I love you too." Amelia pulled Chogan to her and kissed him tenderly. "Yes."

Chogan stood perfectly still, if he heard Amelia right, she said yes. "Marry me?" Chogan whispered.

Amelia smiled and looked directly into Chogan's eyes. "Yes Chogan, I'll marry you," she confirmed.

Chogan didn't need to hear anything else. He kissed her, wrapping her in his arms and holding her close. He didn't know how or when, but it didn't matter, Amelia was going to be his wife.

Chapter Eighteen

Amelia exited the plane in Orlando with mixed emotions. She had a hard time saying goodbye to Chogan the night before when he dropped her off at the condo. She could still feel his kiss and hear his voice whisper, "I'll be waiting for you."

Myron, Anne and the children said their goodbyes at the airport and headed for home.

Amelia placed her luggage with her parents' luggage before crawling into the back seat for the ride home.

Reggie watched Amelia through the rearview mirror. "Amelia, are you ok? You're awfully quiet."

Amelia smiled at her daddy's reflection. "I'm just sorting out some things in my mind, daddy."

Reggie smiled. "So when are we heading back to Colorado?"

"What are you talking about?" Amelia asked in surprise.

Cecilia took her cue from the squeeze of Reggie's hand. "We were just wondering if you and Chogan had set the date for your wedding."

"You know about his proposal?" Amelia was stunned. "He just asked me last night."

Reggie laughed. "That's funny; he asked me and your mother for your hand at the ranch that first day we visited."

A smile crept across Amelia's face. "I said yes."

Cecilia reached across the seat and squeezed Amelia's hand. "I'll miss you but I have no doubt that you are going to be happy with that young man."

Amelia squeezed her mother's hand. "We just have to work out the details. I'll miss my family very much; but I feel like I belong in Colorado."

Amelia unpacked her things and opened her laptop to check her email. The first email was from Patricia and Geoff.

"Greetings from the Pacific Ocean…We boarded the cruise ship in Los Angeles, California and we are on our way to Mexico. Marriage is WONDERFUL, Amelia! I love you and miss you bunches! Patricia and Geoff."

Amelia read through all of her emails expecting to see one from Chogan, but there were none. She typed out an email to him and the girls, telling him how much she loved and missed him and that she couldn't wait to return to Colorado.

The first week of a new school year kept Amelia busy from morning till late evening. She went home every night hoping for an email from Chogan. She didn't want to call, knowing that his voice still needed time to heal.

Amelia slept in her first Saturday after returning from Colorado. She ate breakfast and then opened her email. Patricia had emailed her from the night before.

"Hello Amelia. Life is wonderful! Geoff and I have loved every minute of the cruise and I feel like a new woman, well at least a married one, hee hee. I can't wait to show you all the pictures we took and to talk to you. We are headed back to Colorado tomorrow. Hope your first week back at school was great. Love, Patricia."

Amelia grinned and opened her next email. Her smile turned instantly to a frown and before she finished reading the email she was trembling.

"Hello Amelia. I understand that you have found a married man with two rugrats in Colorado. If you think you're going to be happy living in squalor with someone's leftovers, you're crazy. I was the best thing that ever happened to you and you won't be happy until we are back together. I'm not giving up. Liam."

Amelia trembled. The email from Liam reminded her of the phone call in Colorado. Something had changed Liam from the man she fell in love with in high school to the stalker he now appeared to be.

Amelia started to delete the email and changed her mind. She forwarded the email to her brother Myron with a note. "Myron, I received this email tonight. Liam also called my cell phone while I was in Colorado. I'm concerned, what should I do? Love, Amelia."

Amelia went through the remainder of her email surprised that she still hadn't received one from Chogan. She closed her laptop and went to bed, troubled by the email from Liam.

Amelia had a migraine headache the following morning. She vetoed going to church and took her prescription medicine with a glass of juice and went back to bed.

Reggie and Cecilia checked on her before they left for morning worship.

The prescription medicine on an empty stomach combined with the lack of sleep the night before had Amelia completely oblivious to her surroundings. She didn't hear the door open, nor did she know that someone came and left her room. She slept soundly until her parents returned home three hours later.

Amelia woke to the tapping on her bedroom door. "Honey, its mom; are you feeling any better?"

Amelia struggled to sit up. "Come on in, mom. I'm lightheaded but the migraine has gone."

Cecilia sat down beside her daughter. "I've got some fruit and sandwiches if you think you can eat something."

Amelia hugged her mom and placed her head on Cecilia's shoulder. "Thanks mom, that should help me feel better."

They walked into the kitchen and Amelia ate a light dinner before retiring for the evening. She had to return to class the following morning; she wanted to be rested and ready.

Chogan opened his computer to see if Amelia had answered his email yet. There was a message in his inbox from her email address and he smiled as he opened it. Chogan's smile turned to anger as he viewed the photos that were attached and read the message that came with them. "Chogan, when I returned to Florida, Liam was waiting for me. We've reconciled and he's left his wife. I won't be returning to Colorado and I'm sure these pictures will convince you that I need to be with the man I have loved for years. Please don't contact me again. Amelia."

Chogan was sick at his stomach. The photos that were attached were of Amelia in the arms of another man in bed. She used him to make her ex-boyfriend jealous. She went back to a married man. Chogan deleted the email and closed the computer. His heart was broken.

Amelia checked her email one last time before she went to bed. Still nothing from Chogan and she was surprised. She had emailed him again the night before and really believed that he would have responded by now. Amelia checked her cell phone but there were no missed calls, no voice mails, and no messages. She went to bed troubled.

Amelia drove home on Friday evening after her second week of school. She was tired and very worried that she still hadn't heard from Chogan. She wanted to call his home but her pride wouldn't allow her to do that.

Amelia's cell phone rang as she drove and she touched the Bluetooth in her ear to answer it. "Hello?"

"Hey Amelia, it's Myron, we need to talk."

"Big brother you sound distraught, what's up?" Amelia teased.

"Can you come to my office?" Myron's voice was strained and Amelia knew her brother well enough to know that he wasn't easily disturbed."

"Sure, I'll be there in about ten minutes." Amelia switched lanes and drove to Myron's office. The receptionist cleared her to enter the offices and Amelia took the elevator to Myron's floor in the IT department."

Myron was pacing his office when she arrived. "I'm glad you came." He hugged her and held her tight.

"What's wrong?" Amelia had never seen her brother so upset. "Has something happened to Anne, to one of the children?"

"No, they're fine." Myron led Amelia to the chair opposite his desk and sat down facing her. "Do you remember that email from Liam that you sent me?"

Amelia shook her head yes. "Of course, that email disturbed me."

Myron took Amelia's hands in his. "Have you been with Liam?"

Amelia was shocked. "What? No, of course not, he's married and I want nothing to do with him. Why would you ask me such a question?"

Myron ran his hands through his hair. “I traced that email that Liam sent you and I put a tracer on his IP address. I intercepted these photos.” Myron turned the screen for Amelia to see.

Amelia gasped. “How did he get photos of us in my bed? I’ve never been to bed with him.”

Myron stared at his sister. “These are time stamped from this past Sunday. You weren’t in church Amelia, what did you do?”

Amelia’s eyes filled with tears. “Myron, I had a migraine and I took my prescription and went to bed. I didn’t wake up until mom and dad came home from church.”

Myron stood and paced the floor. “Amelia, does Liam still have a key to the house?”

Amelia thought for a moment and the color drained out of her face. She stared at the photos and started to tremble. “I never thought to ask for the key. Look at me in these pictures Myron; my eyes are closed and my hands are limp.”

Myron zoomed in on the photo and highlighted Amelia’s eyes and hands. “He must have staged these while you were sleeping under the migraine medicine.”

Amelia started to cry, she trembled in fear. “He called me while I was in Colorado, Myron. I told him I wanted nothing to do with him and to go back to his wife.”

Myron took the seat across from Amelia and forced her to look in his eyes. “Listen baby sister, I know you’re scared and you have every right to be. This isn’t a joke, it’s a real threat. I think you need to be under protection.”

Amelia shook her head. “I’m not afraid of Liam, I’m angry.”

Myron squeezed her hands. “I know how brave you are, Amelia, but something isn’t right about Liam and I’m not convinced that he isn’t a real threat to you. If he’s brazen enough to stalk you and crawl into bed with you; what else is he willing to try?”

Amelia agreed. “Ok, so what do I do now?”

Myron hugged her. “You leave that up to me. Go home and act like nothing is wrong. I’m going to start an investigation and I want you to be extremely careful. Try not to be out after dark and let us know when you leave home and school so we can watch out for you."

Amelia hugged Myron tightly. "I'm so glad you work for the police department Myron. You will never hear me tease you about being a geek again."

Amelia left Myron's office and drove home.

Reggie and Cecilia were waiting when she walked through the door. "Honey, are you ok?" Reggie wrapped her in his arms and held her close.

"I'm fine daddy. Did Myron call you?" Amelia asked.

Cecilia spoke softly. "Yes, and we are going to make sure that Liam never gets back into this house. We've had the locks changed, here's your new key."

Amelia felt violated and scared. She opened her email that night and couldn't believe that she still had not heard from Chogan. She needed to hear his voice so she dialed his cell phone and he answered on the second ring.

"Hello?" Chogan didn't check the caller id before he answered.

"Chogan, it's me Amelia, it's so good to hear your voice," she spoke in relief.

Chogan felt the anger rise in his chest. He walked to the porch so the girls wouldn't hear what he had to say. "What do you want Amelia?" he asked brusquely.

Amelia was shocked by his tone. "I just needed to hear your voice; it's been a very rough week."

"Is that so?" Chogan felt betrayed. "It's been a pretty rough week here too, but I guess that doesn't matter to you."

Amelia was trembling. "Chogan, are you angry with me?" Amelia asked as she felt the tears well up in her eyes.

"I don't think angry is the right word to describe how I feel about you, Amelia. I'm going to make this easy for you. I got your message loud and clear and I'd appreciate it if you never call here again."

Amelia was speechless, hurt and confused. She disconnected the call without saying a word and cried herself to sleep.

Chogan paced the porch after his conversation with Amelia. He felt raw inside. He honestly loved Amelia and thought she was in love with him too. Tears of anger and frustration filled his eyes.

"Son, what's wrong?" Dakota had followed Chogan to the porch. "Was that Amelia on the phone?"

Chogan turned his troubled eyes to his dad. "It's over, dad."

"What's over?" Dakota asked.

"My so-called relationship, with Amelia, is over," Chogan spat out.

Dakota walked over to the porch swing and sat down. "Son, I don't understand. I thought she agreed to marry you."

Chogan's laugh was filled with bitterness. "Yes, she agreed to marry me and then went back home to her ex fiancé, who is now married, and went to bed with him."

Dakota's voice was calm. "Son, I don't believe that."

"I wouldn't have believed it either; it I hadn't seen it with my own eyes." Chogan threw himself into the swing next to his father. "How could I have been so wrong about her?"

Dakota turned in the swing to face his son. "Tell me what happened, from the beginning."

Chogan ran his hands through his hair. "I sent Amelia an email right after she left for Florida. I hadn't heard from her in over a week. I assumed that she was busy with starting the new school year and working late. I sent two or three more emails but still heard nothing from her. Then this past Sunday, I got an email from her."

Dakota watched Chogan closely. "Son, tell me what the email said."

Chogan's eyes filled with angry tears. "She told me that she reunited with her ex and that he had left his wife. She included photos of the two of them in bed, and she asked me not to contact her again."

Dakota was shocked. "Can I see the email?"

"I deleted it." Chogan stood and walked over to the rail of the porch leaning heavily against the support beam. "I feel like my heart has been ripped out of my chest. I promised myself after Samantha died that I would never care for another woman; too bad I didn't keep my promise."

Dakota stood and put his hand on Chogan's shoulder. "Son, I know you're angry and you have every right to be. I have to wonder why Amelia would call you tonight if she truly never wanted to hear from you again. What did she say on the phone?"

Chogan turned to look at his father. "She said it was good to hear my voice and that she'd had a very rough week and needed me."

Dakota was troubled. "That sounds like the Amelia that I met. The Amelia in your email doesn't sound like her at all."

Chogan stood very still. "She asked me if I was angry with her and I told her that anger didn't begin to say how I felt. I also told her that I never wanted to hear from her again."

Dakota spoke very softly. "Son, I think you just made a huge mistake."

"Mistake, you think I made a mistake?" Chogan was stunned. "Dad, she ripped my heart out with that email and then has the nerve to call and act like it never happened. What am I supposed to do?" he asked angrily.

"I'd like to see the email," Dakota responded.

"Dad, I deleted it." Chogan couldn't understand his dad's persistence.

"Did you empty your trash?" Dakota asked.

Chogan was confused. "What does my trash have to do with my email from Amelia?"

Dakota laughed softly. "Son, let's go get your laptop." They walked into the house and while Uda gave the girls their baths, Chogan opened his email.

"Dad, I told you I deleted it," Chogan said in disgust.

"Son, if you didn't empty your trash in email, Amelia's email is still here." Dakota turned the laptop towards him and opened the email trash file. "Is this it?"

Chogan nodded his head yes.

"May I open it?" Dakota asked.

Chogan stood and walked away. "Be my guest; it will turn your stomach."

Dakota opened the email and read the message before viewing the photos. "Chogan did you look at these pictures?"

Chogan kept his back to the screen. "Once was enough to burn them into my memory."

"Son, come here." Dakota waited until Chogan joined him. "Look at Amelia's face. Her eyes are closed."

Chogan felt the pain of betrayal. "What's your point, dad?"

Dakota chose his words carefully. "Son, look at the picture, really look at it. She's asleep. Look at her body language; these photos look staged."

Chogan forced himself to look at the photos. "You may be right, but what difference does it make? The message was loud and clear."

Dakota sat back from the computer for a moment. "Son, forward this email to me."

"Why? What possible reason could you want to have this email?" Chogan was frustrated and wanted to put the email out of his mind.

"Trust me, Chogan." Dakota waited while Chogan hit the forward button. Dakota took a breath and stopped Chogan from hitting send. "Look," he pointed at the message header.

"What am I looking at?" Chogan asked confused and frustrated.

Dakota pointed to the copied header from the original email. "Do you see Amelia's email address?"

Chogan looked closely. "Of course I do its right there."

"Look how her email address is in brackets and the text preceding it is not." Dakota pointed as he explained.

"Dad, I know your job in security has you working on computers, but I'm lost. I don't understand what you're trying to tell me," Chogan said.

"Son, I'm telling you Amelia didn't send this email. This email has been packaged by someone else to make it look like it was from her," Dakota confirmed.

Chogan sat very still. "What about the other emails that I sent her, why didn't she respond to those?"

Dakota typed a test message into the computer and attached a read receipt. "I'm going to send a test message and let's just see what happens."

After Dakota's message was confirmed, he waited until a new message appeared. Dakota smiled knowingly and turned the screen towards Chogan. "Look at this."

The read receipt message had arrived. When Chogan opened it, Amelia's email address was again in brackets. "Dad, I still don't understand."

"Someone has intercepted Amelia's email and is channeling which messages she can receive and I suspect the messages she can send."

Chogan stood and walked away from the computer. "I don't know what to believe anymore, dad."

Dakota forwarded the test message to his email account at work and closed the laptop. "Son, I think it's time you trusted your heart."

"I fell in love with Amelia and my heart is broken. Sorry Dad, I don't have a lot of faith in anything right now." Chogan voice was tinged with bitterness and hurt.

Dakota hugged his son. "I watched that young lady sit at the hospital all night, caring for your daughters. She sat with you for over twenty-four hours and wouldn't leave until we insisted that she get some rest."

Uda had heard Chogan's remark about his lack of faith and joined the conversation. "Son, you are wrong about Amelia. She loves you very much. I don't know what's happened but I'll tell you what I told her, if God means for you to be together; He will work it out. You must rely on your faith."

Chapter Nineteen

Amelia turned her cell phone off for the weekend and didn't open her laptop. She asked her mom and dad to intercept any calls for her on the home phone.

Amelia sat listening to the message on Sunday morning and tried to concentrate on the pastor's words. She rode home with her parents and changed out of her church clothes into her swimsuit to sit beside the pool.

Cecilia brought Amelia a glass of lemonade. "Penny for your thoughts, Amelia," she prompted.

Amelia took the glass and smiled sadly. "I remember the message that pastor preached the first weekend after Liam dumped me. Do you remember, mom?"

Cecilia took a seat in the lawn chair. "Honestly, no I don't remember, tell me."

Amelia smiled. "He preached on now faith. He talked about putting our faith into action and trusting God now for the needs in our lives."

"Did you do that?" Cecilia prompted.

Tears welled up in Amelia's eyes. "I found my faith in Frisco, mom."

"So why have you lost that faith now?" Cecilia asked quietly.

"I gave my heart to Liam and he tossed it aside for Courtney. I walked in faith when I met Chogan and I gave my heart to him. He told me he never wants to hear from me again." Amelia was crying openly now. All the hurt and anguish came tumbling out.

Cecilia took the glass from Amelia's hand and held her daughter in her arms. "Honey, I don't know what drove this wedge between you and Chogan. I do know that he loves you very much. If God led you to be together, then your faith has to be strong enough to allow God to work it out."

Amelia hugged her mother close. "Thanks mom, for listening. Would you pray for me that God will show me what I need to do?"

Cecilia wiped her daughter's eyes with a soft tissue. "Yes Amelia, that's what moms are for."

Amelia drove to work on Monday in a thunderstorm. The children were distracted by the lightning and thunder. Amelia was grateful to hear the bell announcing the end of the school day. She carefully tucked her papers to grade in her satchel and pulled her raincoat on before running across the wet pavement to her car.

Traffic was snarled from the heavy rain and Amelia drove slowly trying to avoid an accident. Myron had left her a message to come to his office and Amelia took the exit that would take her away from the downtown congestion and around the bypass to Myron's office.

Amelia was just a couple of miles away from Myron's office, when another vehicle struck her car from behind. Amelia glanced into her rearview mirror and could only see the grill of a large commercial truck pushing her. She felt the car accelerate and she switched lanes to get away from the maniac behind her. She tapped the brakes and felt no response. Amelia pumped the brakes to avoid hydroplaning and screamed as the truck hit her again and drove her off the road and into the guardrail and darkness.

The phone rang and Reggie answered it on the first ring. "Hello?"

"Hi Reggie, its Patricia, is Amelia home?"

Reggie grinned. "Hello sweetheart, how is married life?"

Patricia grinned. "I love it. Geoff and I are so happy."

"Amelia isn't home yet, but it's stormed here all day so she may be late. Do you want me to have her call you?" Reggie asked.

"Yes, please have her call. I'll be home all night." Patricia talked to Reggie a few more minutes and then hung up the phone to start dinner.

Geoff walked through the door as Patricia slipped a dish of chicken pot pie into the oven. He wrapped his arms around Patricia and nuzzled her neck. "Mmmm, pretty wife, I love coming home to you."

Patricia giggled. "Geoff, did you get a chance to talk to Chogan today?"

Geoff pulled out the chair at the table and pulled Patricia into his lap. "Yes, I finally got him to tell me what's going on."

Patricia sat very still.

"Chogan got an email from Amelia two weeks after she left Colorado," Geoff explained.

Patricia frowned. "That's odd. I would have thought that Amelia would email him right away."

Geoff chose his words carefully, torn between his love for his wife and his loyalty to his oldest friend. "Amelia told him in the email that she was reunited with Liam and that he had left his wife. She told Chogan that she never wanted to hear from him again."

Patricia jumped up and spun around in anger. "I don't believe it. Amelia would never take Liam back. She told me that she was in love with Chogan and that her heart belonged to him."

Geoff struggled to find the words. "I'm sorry honey, I couldn't believe it either. Unfortunately, there were photos."

"Photos of what?" Patricia asked.

Geoff took a deep breath. "Photos of Amelia in bed with Liam," he spoke cautiously.

Patricia laughed sarcastically. "Ok this has to be a joke. I have known Amelia since we were small children. Amelia and I took the promise pledge as teenagers and neither of us broke it."

"Amelia called Chogan this past Friday," Geoff quietly continued.

Patricia took a calming breath. "So what did she say? She had to have an explanation."

Geoff was troubled. "This is the part I don't understand. Chogan said that Amelia told him she needed to hear his voice and that she had a bad week."

Patricia smiled. "That sounds like Amelia. Did Chogan talk to her?" she asked hopefully.

Geoff didn't want to answer that question. "Chogan was angry over the email and he told Amelia that she had made her point perfectly clear. He told her he never wanted to hear from her again."

Patricia burst into tears.

Geoff stood and wrapped her in his arms trying to comfort her. Patricia's sobs tore at his heart. "Honey, I'm sorry."

Patricia wrapped her arms around Geoff and tried to stop the flow of tears. "Geoff, you don't know Amelia like I do. She's tough as nails when she's hurting. There is no way she would deliberately send an email to hurt the man she loves. Something is wrong."

Myron paced his office. Amelia was thirty minutes late. He looked out the window and watched the lightning. The weather was pretty nasty, that had to be what was keeping her.

"Myron, there's a call for you from the squad room."

Myron thanked his administrative assistant and picked up the call. "This is Myron Cantrell, how can I help you?" he asked.

"This is Mahoney from traffic. There's been an accident on the bypass and I believe your sister Amelia was involved."

Myron's blood ran cold. He took down the details confirming that Amelia was on her way to the hospital and called his parents. Myron left instructions that Amelia's car was to be impounded directly to the police yard for further investigation. He called Anne on his way to the hospital.

"Hi honey, what time are you coming home?" Anne kept an eye on the children while she stirred the sauce on the stove.

"Anne, I'm headed to the hospital. Amelia has been involved in an accident and I'm not sure how badly she's injured."

"Drive safely, Myron. I'll call the prayer chain. I love you." Anne disconnected the phone and called the first person on the prayer chain. Within minutes prayers were going up for Amelia's health and safety.

Reggie and Cecilia arrived at the hospital just as Myron finished talking to the traffic cop that handled the accident scene.

"Son, what happened to your sister? Is she alright?" Reggie's voice was shaking.

"Amelia was struck from behind by a large commercial truck. He ran her off the road and then left the scene. There is an APB out for him now." Myron leaned against the counter for support. "Amelia is in the trauma unit and I don't have the details yet, they wouldn't allow me to go back until they finished examining her."

Reggie, Cecilia, and Myron had to wait for over an hour before they were permitted to see Amelia. Her face was stitched from the corner of her eye to the middle of her jaw and the bruising had already started turning her face purple.

Cecilia leaned across the rail and kissed Amelia's forehead. "My baby girl, are you alright?"

Amelia started to cry. "Mom, I totaled my car," she whimpered.

Cecilia laughed softly. "Honey, we can replace your car; we can't replace you."

Reggie picked up Amelia's hand from the opposite side of the bed and kissed it softly. "Do you remember what happened?" he asked.

Amelia motioned for Myron to come and stand by her dad. "Myron, my accident was deliberate. Someone ran me off the road." The look of fear and terror in Amelia's eyes were Myron's undoing.

"I know sis, there was an eyewitness and the police are searching for the truck and driver now." Myron tried to reassure her.

Amelia closed her eyes and grimaced in pain. "I've got to contact the school. I think I'm going to need to take a sick day tomorrow.

Myron laughed. "Amelia, you're going to need several sick days."

Amelia was admitted to the hospital with a concussion and a fractured collar bone. She was bruised from head to foot and was feeling the pain of the stitches in her face.

Cecilia stayed at her daughter's bedside throughout the night.

Patricia's cell phone rang at 10:00 p.m. mountain time and she grabbed it from the night stand. "Hello? Reggie? What's wrong?"

Geoff turned on the lamp beside the bed and saw the tears streaming down Patricia's face.

"Thanks for calling me Reggie. Give Amelia my love and please keep me posted. You can call my cell phone anytime day or night." Patricia closed her cell phone and burst into tears.

Geoff sat up and wrapped her in his arms. "What's wrong?"

Patricia was crying so hard she couldn't speak.

"Patricia? Please honey, tell me what's happened." Geoff brushed the hair back from her face and tried to calm the sobbing.

Patricia pulled back from Geoff and grabbed her tissue from the night stand. "It's Amelia," she managed between sobs. "She's been in an accident."

Geoff had a bad feeling in his gut. "How bad is it?"

Patricia looked up with tears still streaming down her face. "She's got a broken collar bone and a concussion and she has stitches from her eye to her jaw." Patricia blew her nose and stood pacing the bedroom. "Someone ran her off the road, Geoff. Someone tried to kill my best friend!"

Geoff went white with fear. "Do they know who or why?"

Patricia spun around the anger replacing her tears. "They've got a pretty good idea. Liam."

"Why would he do that?" Geoff started piecing the story together in his head. "This has something to do with the email and the phone call between Amelia and Chogan, doesn't it?"

Patricia pulled out several Kleenex and blew her nose. "Amelia got a call from Liam while she was here for our wedding. She told him in no uncertain terms to go back to his wife that she was not interested in him." Patricia stood and started pacing again, trying to control her temper. "Liam had a house key to Amelia's house from when they were engaged. He came into her room while she was asleep, from prescription migraine medicine, and took those photos that Chogan told you about." Patricia threw the Kleenex away and grabbed another handful. "Liam sent Amelia a threatening email and Amelia sent it to her brother Myron."

"Doesn't Myron work IT for the police?" Geoff asked trying to keep the story straight in his head.

Patricia laughed bitterly. "He doesn't just work IT; he's the head of their information technology department. The guy is amazing at forensic technology."

Geoff was impressed. "So what did Myron find out?"

Patricia stopped pacing and faced Geoff. "Myron found out that Liam had intercepted Amelia's email account and was deleting messages he didn't want her to receive and deleting messages he didn't want her to send. None of Chogan's emails were delivered and none of Amelia's arrived. He also packaged her email to send it to others like it was being sent from her."

Geoff stood and faced Patricia. "Then the email that Chogan received from Amelia was actually from Liam."

"Yes!" Patricia was angry. "If Chogan truly loved Amelia, he would have given her a chance to explain by asking her about the email. He doesn't deserve my best friend. She's lying in a hospital bed bruised and broken and he's walking around like he's the victim."

Geoff wrapped Patricia in his arms. "Remind me to never make you angry at me."

Patricia hugged Geoff close. "I warned you when we got married that there was a side of me you probably wouldn't like."

Geoff leaned back and kissed Patricia slowly. He continued to kiss her until the tension in her body relaxed and she kissed him back. "I love this side of you." Geoff whispered against her lips. "Your love and compassion for Amelia is just proof that you are the most amazing woman I have ever known."

Chapter Twenty

Geoff walked into the fire station Tuesday morning and waited for Chogan to arrive.

Chogan walked to his locker and hung up his jacket. He closed the door and turned to see Geoff waiting.

"We need to talk." Geoff spoke with firmness that was unusual.

Chogan laughed. "Not now, I'm not in the mood to talk to anyone."

"Well that's too bad," Geoff persisted. "I need to talk, and you need to listen. Captain gave me twenty minutes to talk to you and you are going to hear me out."

Chogan was shocked. Geoff had never raised his voice in all the years that Chogan had known him. He followed Geoff to the office and sat down while Geoff closed the door.

"Do you have any idea how very stupid you are?" Geoff asked.

"What are you talking about?" Chogan responded, stunned by Geoff's vehemence.

"You always think the worst of people. You couldn't give Amelia the benefit of the doubt when you got that stupid email. You couldn't ask her why it was sent; you just assumed that she was out to hurt you." Geoff was angry. "I've got news for you Chogan, that young lady loved you deeply and you just ruined the gift that God sent you."

Chogan stood to leave. "Geoff, what's gotten in to you? You don't know anything about my relationship with Amelia and frankly, it's none of your business."

Geoff closed the space between them his eyes flashing in anger. "I'm making it my business. Amelia is my wife's best friend; she's also my friend. When something happens, that breaks Patricia's heart; it makes me angry; so sit down and hear me out."

Chogan sat down without responding. He had never seen Geoff this angry.

"Amelia didn't send you that email. She called you because she was in trouble. Did you give her a chance to ask you for help or just to listen to her problem?" Chogan tried to speak but Geoff continued without giving him a chance. "Amelia didn't go back to Liam; Liam was stalking her. He called her the week of our wedding and when she got back to Florida, he threatened her via email."

Chogan felt the blood drain from his face. His hands went cold and he remembered his dad's words about the email and about giving Amelia a chance.

"Amelia turned to her brother Myron for help. Myron discovered that Liam had hacked into Amelia's account and was intercepting her incoming and outgoing emails. Liam snuck into Amelia's house while she was under prescription medication for a migraine and staged those photos you claim were so bad." Geoff drew in a deep breath trying to find a way to tell Chogan about the accident.

Chogan kept hearing his dad's words, "These photos look staged." What had he done?

Geoff walked to the door and then walked back and sat on the edge of the desk. "Late last night Patricia received a phone call from Amelia's dad." Geoff stood and walked to the door leaning against it. "Amelia was in a car accident last night. Someone deliberately ran her off the road and totaled her car in a heavy storm. They were trying to kill her."

Chogan began to shake. He lost Samantha and because he didn't trust his heart, he had lost Amelia. "Oh God no," Chogan groaned and dropped his head into his hands not wanting to hear any more.

Geoff softened his voice. "Amelia survived the accident Chogan. She's got a concussion, a broken collar bone and her face was cut from her eye to her jaw."

Chogan lifted his eyes to Geoff. "Is she going to be ok?" She had to be ok. If Amelia never forgave him or never spoke to him again; he couldn't blame her but she had to be ok.

Geoff sat down next to Chogan, the anger in him spent. "Reggie said, the doctors think she will be ok, but she's in a lot of pain and she'll be in the hospital for a few days."

"Why would someone run her off the road or want to kill her?" Chogan asked in desperation.

Geoff spoke softly. "Liam wants her and if he can't have her, no one will."

The alarm sounded and Geoff and Chogan ran for their stations.

Amelia's shoulder throbbed, her body shook with spasms of pain, and her face felt like it was on fire. She cried softly in agony, trying not to disturb Cecilia who was sleeping in the chair next to her hospital bed.

"Honey, what's wrong? Are you in pain?" Cecilia rang for the nurse.

"I'm sorry mom; I didn't mean to wake you," Amelia apologized.

Cecilia smoothed Amelia's hair back, "Amelia, I'm here to take care of you. You don't need to worry about me."

The nurse arrived and took one look at Amelia and smiled. "I'd say you're ready for some pain medication. We couldn't give you anything until the twenty-four hours had passed after your concussion. But it's time now." She left the room and returned within minutes with a shot that she injected into Amelia's IV. "You should feel the effects of this shot very soon," she whispered with a smile.

Amelia felt the warmth up her arm and into her shoulder before the sweet darkness took over. She dreamed of riding horses in a beautiful meadow at the base of the Rocky Mountains.

The nurse monitored Amelia's vitals until she was sure Amelia was asleep. "Mrs. Cantrell, please press the call button for me if she has any more pain. We don't want her trying to suffer through this. Her body is badly bruised and the best thing for her is rest."

Cecilia smiled. "Thank you so much for taking care of my daughter. She's very special to me."

The nurse smiled. "Would you like a snack or something to drink? You've been here all night and we don't want you getting sick."

"Thanks for offering, but her daddy is bringing me something in just a bit." Cecilia watched the nurse check the IV and quietly make a notation in Amelia's chart before heading down the hall to another patient.

Reggie walked softly into the room carrying a bag and a tray with beverages. "How is she this afternoon?"

Cecilia's eyes filled with tears. "She's in a lot of pain. They gave her some pain medicine and said to not allow her to try and suffer through the pain. They want her to rest so her body will start to heal."

Reggie handed Cecilia a large sweet tea and a sub sandwich with chips. "You need to eat; we've got to help Amelia through this."

Cecilia leaned back in the chair and nibbled her sandwich. "Have they found out anything about the accident?"

Reggie glanced at his watch. "Myron said he was coming by after work to tell us the latest on the investigation."

Myron arrived at 6:00 p.m. and walked over to the bed. He leaned over and kissed Amelia's forehead softly. "Wow she is going to have some serious bruises."

Reggie grimaced. "She's feeling those bruises now."

"Ok you guys; don't talk about me like I'm not in the room," Amelia whispered.

Myron leaned over the bed and gently hugged his sister. "Amelia, I'm glad you're awake. Do you feel up to talking about the accident?"

Amelia shifted in the bed and her face went white with pain. "Can they shift my bed to let me sit up a little? I think it would take the pressure off my shoulder."

The nurse came in and helped shift Amelia up into a reclining position. "Honey, your pain medication has worn off and I think it's time to get you something else."

Amelia touched her hand with tears in her eyes. "Could I wait until my brother tells me about the accident? Please?"

The nurse smiled and squeezed Amelia's hand. "Tell you what I'll do; I'll get you a soda and a sandwich to eat while you're talking to your family. Then I'll bring your pain medication in and let you get some rest."

Amelia smiled. "Do you have coke?"

The nurse winked and headed down the hall.

Myron pulled out a chair. "We examined your car, Amelia."

"It's totaled, isn't it?" She asked.

Myron grinned. "Totaled doesn't begin to describe the damage to your car. However, we also discovered that your brake line had been cut."

Amelia turned pale. "Liam is determined to kill me."

Myron didn't want to frighten his family, but they needed to know the truth. "Yes, we are pretty sure Liam is the culprit. The only thing that saved your life in this accident is the fact that you hit those barrels that are placed at the exit ramp for the explicit purpose of accident prevention. They are filled with sand to allow the car to lose momentum and save lives."

Amelia shivered. "Did you catch him?"

Myron wore a frown. "Not yet, but we discovered that Courtney left him over a month ago. He beat her and sent her to the emergency room and she's in the process of a divorce and has a restraining order against him."

Amelia was shocked. "Poor Courtney, she didn't deserve that. What happened to Liam? He was never like this before."

Myron shook his head. "According to our investigation, Liam started drinking heavily while he was stationed in Texas. He started mixing prescription pain medication with his alcohol and he's turned into a very mean person."

Amelia shifted in pain and sipped at the coke that the nurse had brought. "Can you catch him before he hurts someone else?"

Myron grinned. "Our department is really good at their jobs. We've got proof that he was driving the truck that hit you. Liam will be caught and when he is, he'll be spending a very long time behind bars."

Amelia ate half of her sandwich and her face turned pale. Beads of sweat formed on her forehead as the spasms of pain twisted her body.

Cecilia rang for the nurse.

Within minutes the nurse had administered pain medication and Amelia was drifting off to sweet sleep where there was no pain.

Chapter Twenty-One

Amelia had spent almost a week in the hospital and she was moving home today. She was given a pain injection and wheeled out to her parents' car in a wheelchair. Amelia stood slowly trying to ignore the pain in her left shoulder. The brace for the broken collar bone was stiff and unyielding and it pressed against Amelia's soft skin and the bruises from the accident.

By the time Reggie pulled into the driveway, Amelia was groggy but able to get from the car to her room without as much pain.

Amelia stopped in the doorway of her room and stared at the new bed. "What is this?" she asked.

Cecilia smiled and eased Amelia into the room. "The doctor said you needed rest and your bed was flat and difficult to get in and out of. Your daddy and I bought you a bed that has therapeutic incline so you can get in and out of bed easier; and so you can recline without lying flat while you're resting."

"Thanks mom. You and dad have been amazing through all of this and I am so sorry to be such a burden," Amelia spoke gratefully.

"Honey, you are our daughter. No matter what age your children are, you never stop being a parent."

Amelia felt woozy from the injection and sat down gently on the edge of the bed. "Mom, can you help me out of these clothes and into some pajamas?"

Cecilia helped Amelia out of her pants and top. "Do you want to see the bruises?" Cecilia asked.

Amelia spoke softly. "Yes, I'd like to see how bad I look."

Cecilia carried a full length mirror into the room and stood it where Amelia could view her body. She expected tears.

Amelia took one look at her reflection and started to giggle. She laughed so hard that tears of mirth streamed down her face. "I look like a painted clown!"

Cecilia laughed too. "Amelia, I have always thought your sense of humor was odd, but today you have proved just how funny you are."

"Mom, did they take photos of me at the hospital?" Amelia asked.

Cecilia thought for a moment. "Myron said they did. He said they had to document your injuries for the trial."

Amelia looked closely at her face. "If you'll help me get my pajamas on, I'd like you to take some photos of my face so I can send them to Patricia."

Cecilia leaned the mirror against the wall and finished dressing Amelia in soft pajamas. She took Amelia's camera and snapped several photos of Amelia's face. "Amelia, lean back in the bed and I'll take one with your shoulder brace too."

Amelia eased into the bed and sighed in relief as she rested against the elevated head of the bed. "Mom, I appreciate you and dad getting this bed for me to recuperate in. It is amazing."

Cecilia took additional photos of Amelia with her brace and sat the camera on the bed next to Amelia. "Let me get your laptop, or do you want to rest for a bit?" she asked.

Amelia spoke immediately. "I'm ok now that the pain medication has kicked in; I'd like to download these photos and email them to Patricia."

Cecilia took the laptop from the dresser and the USB cable for the camera and helped Amelia get them connected. Cecilia left the room to prepare some lunch for Amelia.

Amelia opened her email and immediately noticed the security settings that Myron had put in place to protect her account from being hacked. She also found an email from Myron with her emergency room injury photos. She downloaded the pictures from the camera and from Myron's email to the laptop and stated her email to Patricia. It was difficult to type with only one hand but Amelia needed to assure her friend that she was on the mend.

"Patricia, I wanted to send you an update to tell you to stop worrying; I'm getting better every day. I'm sending you some photos that mom took for me today and some that the police took after the accident; but I wouldn't open them on an empty stomach. I miss you very much. Please give Geoff my love. Before I forget, or the pain medication kicks in, whichever comes first, I am home from the hospital now. I love you both, Amelia."

Amelia opened the folder where the photos were downloaded and viewed the photos of her car. Myron had taken her camera to the impound lot and taken pictures of the car from every angle. Amelia closed her eyes and whispered a prayer. “Thank you, Lord, for sparing my life, in this accident. I am grateful for the guardian angels that watched over me that day.”

Amelia attached images of the car, the photos from the hospital, and the photos her mom had taken that afternoon. She pressed send and waited to make sure the email was successful. Amelia closed the laptop and laid it beside her in the bed and leaned back into the soft pillows. She was asleep in just a few minutes and didn’t hear her mom come into the room to check on her.

Cecilia disconnected the camera and USB cable from the laptop and placed them safely on Amelia’s desk. She left the laptop on the bed where Amelia would be able to use it when she woke up. Cecilia then pulled Amelia’s favorite blanket up over her and closed the door gently so her daughter could rest.

Patricia arrived home from work and opened her laptop at the kitchen table. She wanted to check her email before she started dinner for Geoff. There was a message from Amelia and Patricia opened it quickly. She read the short message, smiling at the comment about the pain medication, and then opened the photos.

Geoff walked through the door and heard Patricia crying in the kitchen. He threw his jacket across the chair and entered the kitchen to find Patricia at the table sobbing in front of her laptop. “Patricia? What’s wrong?” Geoff asked.

Patricia wiped at the tears and held her hand out to Geoff. “I got an email from Amelia.” Patricia felt the tears well up and took a deep breath to control the tears before she continued. “Geoff, Amelia sent photos.”

Geoff pulled out a chair and placed it next to Patricia. “Ok Patricia, I’m ready. Let me see Amelia’s email.” Geoff read the email and smiled at Amelia’s humor. “Amelia has a sense of humor just like yours. It’s no wonder you two are best friends.” Geoff commented. “Can I see the photos?”

Patricia took a deep breath and opened the folder where she had downloaded Amelia's photos.

Geoff gasped audibly when the first photo showed Amelia's car crushed from the front fender to the passenger seat. The rear of the car had been crushed to the driver's seat. The convertible top was twisted in with the glass from the windows. He viewed the photos of the car from all angles. "My God, it's a miracle she wasn't killed," Geoff whispered with a sick feeling in his stomach. "Are there more?" he asked.

Patricia nodded her head and snatched a handful of Kleenex. "These next ones are of Amelia's injuries," Patricia explained.

The first photo was taken by the EMTs at the hospital ER. Amelia's face was covered in blood and the gaping wound from her eye to her jaw was obvious. The next photo showed her shoulder injury and the broken collar bone under the skin of her left shoulder. The third photo revealed the bruising across Amelia's back. The fourth photo showed Amelia's legs bruised and bloody from the shards of glass.

Geoff placed his hand across Patricia's and took a deep breath. "Patricia, I've worked on more accidents than I care to remember, but this is our friend. I need a minute." Geoff stood and poured himself a coke and gathered his emotions before he sat back down. "Ok, I'm ready," he spoke softly.

Patricia opened the next photo and it showed the stitches from Amelia's eye to her jaw. The bruising had just started and Amelia's cheek was stained with beta dine from the suchers. Her eyes were swollen and the pain was evident on her face. The following photo showed Amelia in her brace for the broken collar bone. Patricia opened the next photo and started to cry. Amelia was smiling into the camera and her face was purple, black, and green from the bruising of the airbag. Her eyes were open but the swelling was severe. The last photo showed Amelia in her room, reclining against an elevated bed, smiling into the camera. Patricia closed the folder and sat quietly waiting for Geoff's reaction.

Geoff stood and pulled Patricia into his arms. "Amelia's an amazing woman, Patricia. Even with all the pain of the accident, she's smiling into the camera."

Patricia clung to Geoff as she spoke. "She's trying to cheer me up so I won't worry about her, but it isn't working."

Geoff kissed Patricia and wiped her tears with his thumbs. "Amelia has a tender heart. She'd rather make you smile than to have you worrying about her. I'm glad she sent those photos. I know you needed to see her to know she was okay."

The doorbell rang and Geoff left the kitchen to answer it.

"Hello Chogan." Geoff stepped back and invited Chogan into the house.

"Honey, who was at the door?" Patricia asked as she walked into the living room. She stopped in her tracks when she saw Chogan.

"Hello Patricia." Chogan spoke softly watching Patricia's face for a reaction. "Am I welcome here?" he asked.

Patricia frowned. "What a stupid question, Chogan. You are Geoff's friend and Geoff's friends are welcome here.

"I thought you and I were friends too?" Chogan asked hopefully.

Patricia thought for a moment before she responded. She checked her temper. "We were friends, but I'm angry with you for mistreating Amelia. She's my best friend and I need time to get over it," Patricia spoke honestly.

Chogan smiled sadly. "That's more than I hoped for. Have you heard from Amelia?" he asked hopefully.

Patricia looked at Geoff and he held up his arms leaving the answer to that question in her control. "As a matter of fact, Geoff and I were just reading her email in the kitchen." Patricia wiped the tears from her eyes and tried to control her anger.

Chogan felt the pain of guilt deep in his chest. "Patricia, I don't have a right to ask this, and if you say no, I'll understand; can I see the email?"

Patricia motioned for Chogan to follow her and she pulled out a chair for Chogan to sit in front of the laptop. Patricia waited until he was seated and she opened the email.

Chogan read Amelia's words with a heavy heart. He felt guilty needing to know how she was after he brutally turned her away on the phone. "This email says she sent photos, can I see them?" Chogan asked. One look at Patricia's face made Chogan ask again, "Please Patricia, I know I have no right to ask, but I'm begging you."

Patricia heard the hurt in Chogan's voice. She took the mouse and opened the folder containing the photos. Patricia walked out of the kitchen and into the bedroom, closing the door behind her.

Chogan opened the photos of the car and felt like a knife had been stabbed into his heart. Amelia had called him scared, hurting, and in need of a friend. He had turned her away and the words he said to her made him ache with guilt and regret. When he opened the photo of Amelia in the ER with her face laid open and the blood covering her cheek and down into her beautiful blond hair; Chogan hung his head and cried, his body shook with shame and remorse.

Geoff walked over and squeezed Chogan's shoulder. "You need to see all the photos." He handed Chogan the box of Kleenex and leaned back against the counter waiting for Chogan to continue.

Chogan clicked to the next picture and saw the contorted collar bone beneath Amelia's skin. His stomach felt queasy and he tasted the bile of bitterness. Chogan willed his stomach to remain calm and opened the next photo of the stitches in Amelia's face. He traced the incision from her eye to her jaw with his finger touching the screen. Chogan longed to be with Amelia to try and beg her forgiveness. He carefully viewed the remaining photos of Amelia with the bruising and in the shoulder brace.

Chogan stood and walked across the kitchen with his back to Geoff. He spoke slowly, "Geoff, you were right; I am an idiot."

Geoff waited quietly for Chogan to continue.

Chogan turned facing his friend with tears streaming down his face. "I had the most beautiful caring woman in this world agree to marry me and I allowed my temper and ignorance to push her away. I don't deserve her and I don't think I ever did." Chogan walked from the room and out the door. He crawled into his truck and drove to the church in Frisco.

Pastor Taylor opened his office and allowed Chogan to precede him through the door. The pastor moved around the desk and took his seat watching the emotions on Chogan's face. Pastor spoke softly, "Chogan, I've known you a long time. You look deeply troubled tonight."

"Pastor, I've done a foolish and unforgiveable thing and I don't know what to do about it." Chogan leaned back against the chair. "Do you remember Patricia's friend, Amelia?"

Pastor smiled as he spoke. "Of course, Amelia is a fine young woman. I heard that the two of you were going to follow in Geoff and Patricia's direction and get married."

A look of pain passed over Chogan's face. "We were, until I destroyed our relationship."

"What did you do, Chogan?" Pastor asked.

Chogan spent the next half hour pouring out his heart to the pastor. He explained in detail how he had misinterpreted the email and how he had spoken harshly to Amelia; telling her he never wanted to hear from her again.

When he finished, Pastor sat with his hands folded under this chin. "Chogan, I wish I had an easy answer for you. I can only imagine the guilt you are feeling about Amelia's accident and injuries. What do you want to do?" he asked.

Chogan shook his head slowly. "I want to make this better. I had no intention of falling in love after Samantha died. My girls fell for Amelia and before I knew it, I was in love with her. She agreed to marry me Pastor. I want to beg her forgiveness but I don't have a right to be in her life, not after the way I've treated her."

"Have you tried to contact Amelia?" Pastor asked.

"No." Chogan was ashamed. "I'm afraid of causing her more pain."

"Are you afraid of causing her pain, or are you afraid she'll tell you to leave her alone and you'll lose her forever?" Pastor asked.

Chogan sighed. "Both, I'm afraid. I have to do something. Those pictures will haunt me the rest of my life. If Amelia will forgive me, that's more than I can hope for."

"Chogan, you love Amelia don't you?" Pastor asked.

"With all my heart," Chogan whispered. "I love her enough to let her go."

Pastor smiled as he spoke. "God is the author and finisher of our faith, Chogan. Let's pray for God's direction in this situation."

Chogan left the church and drove slowly home. He kissed the girls goodnight and waited on the porch swing while his mom tucked them in.

Uda joined her son on the swing. "Chogan? Are you ok?" she asked.

Chogan's eyes were filled with unshed tears. "Mom, do you remember when you told me that if God wanted Amelia and I together, He would work it out?"

Uda nodded her head. "Yes, I do." Uda placed her hand on Chogan's arm. "Son, that young lady loves you. This accident could have killed her, but it didn't. You need to follow your heart."

Chogan hugged Uda tightly. "Mom, I need a favor."

"What do you need?" Uda asked.

"I need you to stay with the girls this weekend, I'm going to go and see Amelia." Chogan spoke with determination.

"I think that's a grand idea." Uda smiled in the darkness and Chogan went in to make the arrangements. "Lord, please guide Chogan and Amelia and if it is Your will for them to be together, help them to see past their hurt and find forgiveness."

Chapter Twenty-Two

Chogan's flight from Denver to Orlando arrived at 3:00 p.m. on Friday afternoon. Chogan had talked to Reggie and Cecilia and made sure he would be welcome to visit Amelia.

Chogan pulled into the driveway and parked the rental car. He took a deep breath and tried to calm his nerves before he went inside. "Lord, please guide me as I talk to Amelia. Help her to find forgiveness in her heart for me."

Chogan picked up the bouquet of wildflowers he had purchased at the airport and headed for the door. He was sweating profusely and he hoped it was caused by the heat of Florida and not the fear that was gripping his heart.

Cecilia answered the door. "Hello Chogan." She spoke softly and smiled before she hugged him. "I'm glad you came."

Chogan spoke from his heart. "I'm very sorry for the hurt I've caused your daughter. Please forgive me."

"Honey, you're human. There was no way you could have known that Liam was behind that email and those photos." Cecilia's compassion was evident as she spoke.

"I should have trusted Amelia and given her the benefit of the doubt." Chogan spoke through the guilt he felt. "If she will forgive me, I'll be content with that."

"Amelia was getting claustrophobic and needed some air so I helped her out to the sunroom." Cecilia took Chogan's arm and led him to the sunroom through the kitchen. "Just follow your heart, Chogan." She gave him a gentle shove and watched him approach Amelia. Cecilia smiled as Chogan stood watching Amelia sleep in the chaise lounge. She turned back to the counter to finish dinner and give them privacy.

Chogan walked over to the lounge and stared at the damage to Amelia's face. The bruises and the stitches tore his heart with pain. She was propped up against pillows to alleviate the pain of the shoulder brace. Amelia's soft even breathing made Chogan smile. At least she had found some measure of rest and he was grateful for any relief she could find from the injuries.

Chogan placed the flowers on the table and knelt down quietly beside Amelia's chair. His eyes filled with tears as he leaned over and softly kissed her forehead.

Amelia opened her eyes at the touch of his lips. "Chogan?" She had to be dreaming. She couldn't be looking into Chogan's eyes and seeing the love that she had seen when he proposed. Amelia stared at him, hoping he was really there and not just a figment of her imagination. She reached up with her right hand and gently laid her palm against his cheek. "I can't believe you're here," she whispered as she began to cry.

"Please don't cry, Amelia." Chogan didn't know what to do. Her tears were like nails to his heart; he was causing her pain. "I'm sorry, I didn't mean to upset you, and I can leave if it makes you…"

Amelia placed her finger on his lips, stilling his words. "Please don't go," she whispered through the tears.

Chogan needed to kiss her. He moved forward slowly and placed a gentle kiss on Amelia's forehead.

Amelia closed her eyes and sighed with a sad smile on her face.

Chogan kissed her uninjured cheek softly so he wouldn't hurt her. "Amelia?" Chogan wanted to kiss her but he didn't want to take advantage of her weakened state.

Amelia opened her eyes and reached up to grasp Chogan's shirt with her right hand. She pulled him gently closer until his lips were close to hers.

Chogan kissed her lips gently. When Amelia responded he lingered kissing her tenderly; trying to show her how much he loved her. Hope began to grow in Chogan's heart. He felt the tears sliding down her face and pulled away slowly. Chogan sat down on the edge of the chaise lounge facing Amelia.

"I came to apologize," Chogan spoke with the conviction of his guilt. "I have no right to be here, Amelia; after the way I mistreated you. I am begging you to forgive me for being so rude and arrogant and turning you away when you called me for help." His heart was breaking at the tears flowing from Amelia's eyes.

Amelia's words came from hours of thinking. She spoke softly through the pain in her body and her heart. "Chogan, I am so sorry that I hurt you. I had no idea that Liam had hacked into my email. I've brought you nothing but pain and you deserve much more than that. You deserve to be loved."

Chogan was crushed. "Please don't apologize, Amelia. I let you down. You deserve someone who will always stand beside you and protect you. More importantly, you didn't fail me, I failed you. I should have trusted you." Chogan held her hand and stroked it with his finger. "I should have listened to my heart and had faith in you."

Amelia flinched and her face turned pale. "Chogan, can you get my mom, please."

Chogan stood and hurried into the kitchen. "Cecilia, Amelia's asking for you."

Cecilia wiped her hands quickly. "Chogan, take a glass from that cabinet and fill it with ice and coke, and bring it to us, please."

Chogan did as he was instructed and hurried back to the sun porch. He grimaced at the pain he saw in Amelia's face.

Cecilia helped Amelia to shift from the Chaise lounge to the porch swing. Cecilia stacked pillows under Amelia's left arm to take the weight off her bad shoulder. "Ok Chogan, we'll take that coke now."Cecilia spoke with gentle authority.

Chogan hurried over and watched as Cecilia took the pain medication from her apron pocket and held it for Amelia.

Amelia's hand trembled as she swallowed the pills and tried to hold the coke with her good hand.

Cecilia took the glass and handed it to Chogan. "She'll drink all of that if you'll help her with the glass. Amelia's hand is still a little weak."

Cecilia returned to the kitchen to finish dinner.

Amelia spoke quietly. "You can join me, I won't break."

Chogan eased himself onto the swing and turned to look at Amelia. "I've missed you so much."

Amelia touched Chogan's hand with hers. "I've missed you too. You'll never know how hard it was to fly home after Patricia's wedding. I sent you an email every day and when I didn't hear back from you, I had to call."

Chogan held her hand in his. "I sent you an email every day and I should have called when you didn't respond." Chogan was angry with himself. "I would give anything if I had married you after Patricia's wedding and kept you with me."

"That would have been a lot less painful than this." Amelia spoke solemnly but laughed at her own joke.

Chogan laughed at Amelia's ability to make light of her injuries. "I promise you it wouldn't have been painful at all," he spoke seriously.

"How are Patricia and Geoff?" Amelia asked.

"They are amazing. You would think those two had known one another all their lives." Chogan helped Amelia take a sip of her coke.

"I sent Patricia some photos from the accident." Amelia touched her cheek and gently scratched her healing incision. "I know Patricia well enough to know that she needed details before she would believe that I'm ok."

Chogan hung his head. "I saw the photos too. Geoff read me the riot act after your accident. He told me how stupid I was and he was right." Chogan stood and walked away from the swing and then back. "I couldn't find out any details about your accident and I was dying inside not knowing if you were okay. I went to see Patricia and Geoff and you had just emailed Patricia."

Amelia sat quietly, allowing Chogan to work through his feelings.

Chogan sat down gently, joining Amelia on the swing. "Patricia is still very angry with me and she has every right to be. I hurt her best friend." Chogan reached up and touched Amelia's hair allowing the soft tendrils to flow through his fingers. "Patricia opened the photos and then left me alone with Geoff to view them."

"Pretty aren't they?" Amelia teased.

Chogan looked directly into Amelia's eyes, his own eyes filled with tears. "Those photos broke my heart." Chogan couldn't stop the tears as he continued, "When I saw the photo of the damage to your face, I lost it." Chogan took a deep breath and ignored the tears as they fell from his eyes. "I blame myself for not protecting you. I went to see Pastor Taylor and asked him how I could make this better," he spoke honestly.

Amelia was surprised. "What did Pastor Taylor say?" she asked.

"He told me that God is the author and finisher of our faith and that I needed to trust in Him for the right direction." Chogan smiled sadly at Amelia. "I prayed for guidance, asked my mom to babysit the girls, and called your parents for permission to come and see you."

"You talked to my mom and dad?" Amelia asked in surprise.

"Yes." Chogan grinned. "First I apologized over and over for being an idiot. Then I asked if I could come and see you."

Amelia took Chogan's hand. "I'm glad you came. Your voice sounds like it's healed."

"My voice is fine; too bad it wasn't out of commission the night you called," Chogan chided himself.

Amelia laughed and then flinched in pain. "Now that's funny, Chogan. Unfortunately, it hurts when I laugh."

Chogan was immediately contrite. "I'm sorry, are you okay? Do you need anything?"

Amelia grinned at Chogan. "I will be fine, really. I haven't laughed much lately and although it hurt, it also felt wonderful."

"I love the sound of your laughter," Chogan whispered.

"I love the sound of your voice," Amelia said. "I still can't believe you're here." Amelia yawned as the pain medication began to take effect. "I'm sorry, that medicine makes me sleepy," she explained.

Chogan eased closer and allowed Amelia to rest her head on his shoulder.

"Chogan, I…" Amelia's words ended as she drifted off to sleep.

Chogan kissed the top of her head and whispered. "Sleep Amelia, I'm here." Chogan trembled at the thought of losing this woman in his arms. Her body flinched in pain even with the pain medication and it tore at his heart. Chogan could see the dark angry bruises on Amelia's left arm and her legs. He whispered a prayer as he held her close. "God, please heal Amelia, take away her pain and make her body whole again. Forgive me God for not protecting her and please allow her to forgive me too." Chogan felt the tears falling again and he didn't try to stop them. He just held Amelia tenderly as she slept; grateful that she was alive and close to his heart.

Cecilia slipped to the sunroom to check on Amelia and saw her sleeping with her head on Chogan's shoulder. She quietly moved back to the kitchen and whispered a prayer for their relationship and God's divine direction.

Amelia's shoulder sent a spasm of pain through her body and woke her an hour later. She eased herself back against the pillows. "You're really here," she whispered to Chogan.

Chogan smiled at Amelia. "Yes Amelia, I'm here."

Amelia searched his face with her eyes. "I thought I was dreaming," she admitted.

Chogan took her hand in his. "Do you think you can find it in your heart to forgive me? If you need time to think about it, I'll understand."

Amelia didn't need time to think about it. "Chogan, there is nothing to forgive. The night you were injured in the fire, your mom asked me if I was in love with you." Amelia smiled at the memory. "At that moment I was under the impression that you wanted me for a housekeeper. Your mom told me that if God meant for us to be together then He would find a way," she explained.

"My mother told me the same thing. I couldn't believe when I woke up in ICU that you were sitting at my bedside. I wanted to propose properly and I couldn't speak." Chogan's voice was filled with frustration.

"You found enough voice to propose on Royal Gorge Bridge," Amelia reminded him.

Chogan extended his hand to the table and pulled the wildflowers to Amelia. "I bought these for you at the airport. They reminded me of our ride through the meadow the first day you came to my ranch."

Amelia breathed in their scent. "They are lovely. I'll have mom put them in a vase."

Cecilia appeared in the doorway. "Chogan we will be having dinner in about ten minutes. Can you help Amelia to the dining room?"

Chogan handed the flowers to Cecilia. "I'd be happy to." He stood and gently wrapped his arm around Cecilia's waist lifting her gently to her feet.

Amelia stood slowly, trembling from the effects of the pain medication. Chogan's arm was still around her waist and Amelia leaned against him. Amelia slid her good arm around Chogan's waist and hugged him gently. "I've missed you." She whispered.

Chogan held her close, allowing Amelia to lean her weight against him. "I've longed to hold you like this." Chogan spoke into Amelia's ear. "I love you, Amelia. I know I don't deserve you, but I love you with all my heart."

Amelia leaned back slowly and looked into Chogan's eyes. "I love you, too."

Chogan helped Amelia to the table and enjoyed the company of her family.

After dinner, Cecilia helped an exhausted Amelia to her room and into her pajamas. She shifted the pillows and helped Amelia to get situated before bringing her medication. "Chogan would like to say goodnight."

Amelia hugged her mother. "Thanks mom."

"What did I do?" Cecilia asked.

"You welcomed the man I love to come and see me. That's the best medicine I've had since the accident." Amelia spoke with sincerity.

Cecilia kissed Amelia's forehead and winked. "Sleep tight honey."

Chogan walked into Amelia's room and smiled. The walls were filled with her awards, diploma, and her college degree. "I wanted to say goodnight." Chogan said.

Amelia patted the mattress beside her. "Come sit with me for a minute, please?" she asked.

Chogan sat down facing Amelia and eased his weight so he wouldn't hurt her.

Amelia covered her mouth and yawned, feeling the effects of the medication. "Chogan, how long are you staying?" she asked.

Chogan picked up her hand and laid her palm against his cheek. "I have a flight Sunday afternoon."

"Will I see you tomorrow?" Amelia asked.

"Yes." Chogan caressed her hand with his thumb.

Amelia's eyes were heavy. She leaned her head back against the pillows as she spoke. "I'm so glad you're here, I need you, Chogan." Amelia's eyes closed and she fell asleep.

Chogan sat holding her hand and watching her sleep. He stood and pulled the blanket up around her and kissed her lips. "I need you too, Amelia," Chogan whispered. "Sweet dreams my love. I'll see you tomorrow."

Chogan talked with Reggie before leaving and left Amelia's home with a feeling of joy in his heart. That night in his hotel, his sleep was peaceful and he dreamed of what could be.

Chapter Twenty-Three

Amelia woke early and eased herself out of bed. She walked slowly to the kitchen and smiled as she saw her flowers on the counter. Amelia breathed in their scent and turned them to see the variety of colors included in the bouquet.

"Good morning, Amelia." Reggie stood watching his daughter with a smile on his face. "From the smile on your face, I'd say your visit with Chogan went very well."

Amelia eased herself into a chair. "Daddy, I'm in love with Chogan. He came to apologize but he didn't need to. I can't say that I would have reacted any differently than he did if I had received an email telling me it was over and with incriminating photos."

Reggie brought Amelia a glass of iced tea with a straw and sat across from her at the table. "Are you going to marry him?"

Amelia thought about that question before she responded. "If he asks me again, my answer will be yes. I love him and I want to spend the rest of my life as his wife and as a mother to his children."

"I'll miss you." Reggie smiled as he spoke. "Your mother and I knew when we met Chogan that he was the one that you would marry. We were actually surprised that you came back with us after Patricia's wedding."

Amelia was stunned. "How did you know?"

Reggie laughed. "When you left on vacation, you were hurt, rejected and questioning your faith. When you returned from vacation, you had found your faith again; and your smile was the smile of a woman in love."

"So what do I do now?" Amelia asked.

Reggie was surprised by the question. "What do you mean?"

Amelia turned the glass with her good hand. "Should I plan for a move to Colorado or should I wait until Chogan proposes again?"

"Why don't you put a fleece before the Lord," Reggie said. "You remember how Joshua laid the fleece in the grass and put his situation before the Lord. Joshua asked the Lord to allow the fleece to be wet and the grass dry. The following morning, God proved faithful. Joshua wanted to be sure of his decision so he asked God to allow the fleece to be dry and the grass wet the following morning. Once again God proved faithful."

Amelia thought about the story. "Dad, I found my faith in Frisco, I need to trust God for the right direction; just like Joshua."

Reggie stood and kissed her forehead. "You can't go wrong if you keep your faith in God, Amelia."

Cecilia helped Amelia to shower, wash her hair and dress for the day. "You slept very well last night, Amelia."

Amelia smiled as Cecilia pulled her hair into a long French braid. "I dreamed I was riding a horse through a beautiful meadow full of wildflowers."

Cecilia grinned at Amelia through the reflection in the mirror. "And were you riding alone?" she teased.

Amelia laughed. "Of course not, Chogan was riding beside me."

Cecilia sat down on the bed. "Are we planning a wedding for Colorado or Florida?" Cecilia asked.

"If Chogan proposes again, my answer will be yes. However, I don't know what to do about where to get married." Amelia didn't want to hurt her family.

"Your daddy and I will be there, no matter where you choose to marry," Cecilia offered.

"I don't know what to do mom. I guess I should wait until I'm actually engaged," Amelia laughed as she responded. She was still laughing when Chogan arrived.

Cecilia helped Amelia to stand. "Follow your heart, Amelia," she whispered.

Amelia walked slowly and painfully to the sunroom and watched as Reggie walked with Chogan around the pool.

"My daughters love to swim," Chogan was saying. "When Patricia took them to swim with your grandchildren at the condo, they were ecstatic!"

"Amelia grew up in the water," Reggie spoke with pride. "She learned to swim before she could walk and she's been in or around a pool ever since."

Amelia joined the conversation. “I just hope my shoulder heals well enough that I can still swim.”

“The doctor said that swimming will strengthen your arm and shoulder, after you are released from rehab.” Reggie said.

“Daddy, you think of everything.” Amelia was grinning as she spoke.

“I’ve got to take your mother shopping. Do you need anything before we go, Amelia?”

“I’d love some strawberries,” she teased.

Reggie pulled his car keys from his pocket and kissed Amelia on the cheek. “Your daddy will bring you some strawberries.”

Amelia grinned at him.

Chogan watched her parents leave and he moved slowly to Amelia’s side. “Can I help you sit so you’ll be more comfortable?” he offered.

Amelia turned to face Chogan. “I’d be very comfortable if you would hold me for just a minute.”

Chogan slipped his arms around Amelia’s body and allowed her to lean her weight against him. He felt her arm wrap around his waist and her face press against his shoulder. Chogan breathed in the scent of her hair. “I can’t believe how good you feel in my arms.” Chogan spoke as he splayed his hand across her lower back, holding her gently against his strength.

Amelia sighed. “I’ve missed being in your arms. If my shoulder wasn’t injured, I’d give you a real hug.”

Chogan leaned back and tipped Amelia’s chin up. “I’ve really missed this,” he spoke softly as he moved closer and kissed Amelia, being careful not to hurt her.

Amelia clung to his waist and her heart began to race. She felt the bond between them being restored and didn’t want Chogan’s kiss to stop. Amelia felt loved.

Chogan pulled apart from their kiss and looked into Amelia’s eyes. “Let’s get you more comfortable,” he suggested.

“Help me to the chaise, please?” Amelia asked.

Chogan eased her down onto the lounge chair and quickly shifted pillows to ease the pain in her shoulder. "Can I fix you a coke?" he asked.

"You could fix us both one," Amelia offered.

"Coming right up," Chogan replied. He returned from the kitchen and sat the cokes on the table beside the chaise lounge. He stood staring down at Amelia, loving her.

"You can sit with me if you like," Amelia had shifted far enough to allow Chogan to sit facing her.

Chogan sat down facing her and ran his finger down her face. "I love you, Amelia."

Amelia's eyes filled with tears at the touch of Chogan's hand.

"What's wrong? Are you in pain?" Chogan asked.

"I'm sorry I'm so ugly," Amelia whispered as she lowered her head and felt the tears falling.

Chogan sucked in his breath and lifted Amelia's chin forcing her to look into his eyes. "Amelia, how can you think that? Your body is broken from the accident but you are still beautiful to me and always will be," Chogan assured her.

Amelia looked deep into his eyes, "Chogan, I'm going to have an ugly scar on my face that's never going to go away. I don't want you to be disappointed in me."

Chogan leaned in and kissed Amelia very softly. "My beautiful Amelia, you are a precious gift from God sent to fill the lonely void in my heart and in my life. I could never be disappointed in you. Your beauty is more than just how you look, it's who you are."

Chogan stood and tossed a cushion to the floor. He knelt down beside the chaise lounge and took Amelia's hand in his. "Amelia, I love you with every fiber of my being. I need you in my life, in my home, and in my arms. Marry me, Amelia. Give me a chance to make you happy and to always be there when you need me. You told me yes once, if you'll give me another chance, I won't let you down again," he pleaded.

Amelia smiled slowly before she spoke. "Chogan, I love you. I can't imagine my life without you. I need you in every aspect of my life; I want your home to be our home, and I long to be held in your arms." Amelia's eyes filled with tears. "If you can look beyond the damage to my body and love me anyway; yes, Chogan, I'll marry you."

Chogan pulled a box from his pocket and opened it. He held it for Amelia to remove the ring. "Will you accept this ring and seal our engagement?" he asked.

"It's beautiful," Amelia whispered solemnly. The ring Chogan had picked was a solitaire diamond in a princess cut set in a tri-color band of black hills rose, yellow, and white gold.

Chogan pulled out another box and opened it. "These are the wedding bands that go with the engagement ring." Chogan had selected the black hills gold set to honor his Native American heritage. The diamond engagement ring was traditional. The wedding band was also tri-color black hills gold. The groom's band matched Amelia's wedding band and held a diamond with two canary diamonds on either side of the center setting.

"Chogan, how did you find these, they are so unusual," Amelia asked.

"The solitary white diamond represents our hearts becoming one as Christ ordained in marriage. The two canary diamonds are for my daughters that you have taken into your heart." Chogan spoke with feeling.

Amelia's eyes filled with happy tears. "I know that I can never replace Samantha, but I promise to be a good mother to Topanga and Lovella."

Chogan closed the box with the wedding bands and tucked it into his pocket. He lifted the engagement ring from the box and gently lifted Amelia's left hand and slid it in place. Chogan pulled himself up to the chaise lounge and leaned across Amelia holding her face tenderly in his hands. He kissed her lips very gently to avoid hurting her.

Amelia slid her hand into Chogan's hair at the base of his neck. She pulled him closer and leaned her forehead against his, claiming the man she loved.

Chogan pulled back relieved, his eyes were filled with hope. "Please tell me this won't be a long engagement."

Amelia laughed, feeling the same urgency as Chogan. "I don't think a long engagement is a good idea. I want to be able to kiss you any time, any place." Amelia's honesty struck a common chord in Chogan's emotions.

Chogan kissed her softly, "When?" he asked.

Amelia was so caught up in her emotions that she had trouble comprehending what he was asking her. "When what?"

Chogan laughed. "When are we getting married?"

Amelia stared at this man that she loved. "I was thinking Christmas."

"That's three months away." Chogan looked disappointed.

Amelia squeezed his hand. "Chogan, I have to wear this shoulder brace for six more weeks."

Chogan stroked her hand with his. "I'm sorry my love, I didn't mean to pressure you. I'll marry you whenever and wherever you say, Amelia."

Amelia spoke shyly, "Can I make a suggestion for the honeymoon?"

Chogan's hand stilled and his eyes grew dark. "Anywhere you want to go, I'll take you," he promised.

Amelia smiled wistfully. "I was thinking if we were married in Colorado and then took a family honeymoon here in Florida, the girls could experience Disneyworld."

Chogan chose his words carefully. "I love my daughters, but I have other plans for our honeymoon and Mickey Mouse is not on the agenda."

Amelia laughed out loud. "I was talking about a delayed honeymoon, like in the spring when we can travel easier."

"It doesn't matter to me whether we are married here or in Colorado, I just don't want to lose you, again." Chogan's voice reflected the emotion he was feeling.

"And the honeymoon?" Amelia prompted. "I'd like to hear more about this honeymoon."

"You focus on getting well and planning the wedding; I'll take care of the honeymoon." Chogan spoke softly and with passion that appealed to Amelia.

"Knock, Knock, anybody home?" Myron shouted from the door so that he wouldn't scare Amelia if she were there alone.

Amelia shouted back from the sunroom. "Hey big brother, we're in here."

Myron grinned when he saw Chogan. "Hello Chogan, what brings you to Florida; as if I didn't know?" he asked teasing.

Chogan shook Myron's hand. "I had to make sure that your sister was still willing to marry me."

Myron looked from one to the other. "I'm surprised you're not already married!" he teased. Myron pulled a chair close to the chaise lounge and sat down. "We need to talk, sis."

Amelia spoke softly. "You've found Liam."

Myron nodded his head. "I wanted you to hear the news from me, before the press gets a hold of it."

Amelia was puzzled. "They've arrested him, right?" She trembled with fear.

Chogan took Amelia's hand in his. "Did he admit to trying to kill Amelia?" Chogan asked.

Myron chose his words carefully. "Yes. Liam knew that he was headed for a dishonorable discharge and prison when he was caught." Myron watched Amelia; he didn't want to upset her. "Amelia, Liam is dead."

Amelia's eyes filled with tears. No matter what Liam had done, the fact that he was dead shocked her. "What? How did he die?"

"Liam knew where he was headed and he turned himself in yesterday. He signed a full confession to attempted murder. He asked to speak with the chaplain last night." Myron drew in a deep breath and continued. "This morning Liam collapsed in his cell, he was rushed to the hospital but never responded. He was pronounced dead just before noon." Myron was angry. "I don't understand how a man like Liam could destroy his life. It makes me angry."

Amelia shook her head slowly. "I am so sorry for his family. I did not want to face Liam in court for the accident; but I would never have wished him dead. Do they know what happened?" she asked sadly.

Myron spoke softly. "They are performing an autopsy but the doctors are pretty sure it was a heart attack brought on by damage caused by drug usage." Myron looked at his watch and stood to leave. "I've got to go pick up the kids." Myron walked over and kissed Amelia's forehead. "I'll bring them by tomorrow after church to swim if you think you're up to it."

Amelia smiled up at Myron as she spoke. "Please bring them by; I miss them terribly."

Chogan sat quietly after Myron left. He looked over at Amelia and spoke what was on his heart. "You loved Liam. I'm so sorry for your loss."

Amelia shuddered. "I love Liam all through high school. I planned to marry him for five years. During that time we were growing apart and I was so wrapped up in the dream of being married that I didn't even see what was happening." Tears fell slowly down Amelia's cheeks as she continued. "When Liam called off our wedding, I was angry. The trip to Colorado made me realize that my faith was in a dream and not in reality. I was in love with a fantasy that I had created in my mind. God protected me from making the worse mistake of my life."

Chogan held Amelia's hand and chose his words carefully. "I knew you were emotionally hurt when I met you. What amazed me was your ability to put your personal feelings aside and be so kind and compassionate to Lovella and Topanga." Chogan smiled at the memory of Amelia's visit to his ranch. "You even found a special bond with a very lonely dog."

"Can we have Amber in the house after we are married?" Amelia asked.

"She has already returned to the house. She keeps watching the door and I know she's waiting for you to come home. Do you think you'll be happy living so far away from your family?" Chogan asked.

Amelia pulled Chogan closer with her good arm and kissed him. She whispered for effect, "When we are married, you, Lovella, Topanga, and even Amber will be my family. I will be happy and I'll do my best to make you and the girls happy, too."

"We can visit your folks and they can visit us, often." Chogan spoke with conviction.

"Chogan, can you help me up and over to the swing? I'm getting stiff." Amelia's voice was strained with pain.

"Do you need something for pain?" Chogan ask with concern.

Amelia shook her head slowly. "No, I've got to move around a bit more to alleviate this stiffness and then I won't be so uncomfortable. Besides, the pain pills make me sleep and I need to be with you."

Chogan wrapped his arm around Amelia's waist and lifted her to her feet. "I need to be with you too, Amelia." He walked with her to the swing and helped her get situated. Chogan moved the side table close to the swing and brought their cokes.

Amelia sighed as she shifted the weight of the brace to the pillows.

"When will you give your notice at the elementary school?" Chogan asked.

Amelia thought for a moment. "I need to give it to them now. Chogan, I'm not sure how quickly I'll find a job teaching in Frisco."

"Does it matter?" Chogan asked.

"I like teaching, Chogan. I'll feel like I'm helping our household if I'm working." Amelia waited for his reaction.

"Whatever makes you happy; is fine with me." Chogan touched Amelia's face with his finger. "I want you to be happy, Amelia." His voice dropped to a whisper. "I never want to lose you again."

Chapter Twenty-Four

Chogan had dinner with Amelia and her family. He returned to the hotel knowing he would only have a couple of hours with Amelia the following morning; before he returned to Colorado.

Reggie and Cecilia left for church, while Amelia waited for Chogan.

The doorbell rang and Amelia moved slowly to the door. "Good morning, Chogan."

Chogan stepped inside and closed the door behind him. He moved closer to Amelia and pulled her gently into his arms; taking care not to harm her shoulder. "Good morning, my love." Chogan kissed her and held her close.

Amelia cuddled as close as she could with the brace. "What time is your flight?" Amelia asked.

"My flight leaves at 3:00 p.m." Chogan walked with Amelia to the swing in the sunroom. He fluffed the pillows and helped her to sit. "I would love to have attended your church while I was here."

Amelia smiled as she took his hand in hers. "I can't go to church until I can sit through a service with this brace so pastor is sending me the service on DVDs so I can watch them."

Chogan stroked her hand with his. "I wish I didn't have to leave you," he whispered.

Amelia smiled and spoke with encouragement. "Chogan, before you arrived this weekend, I was feeling pretty low. I didn't know if we were ever going to see one another again and it was killing me. Now, I've got our wedding to plan and I know we'll be together very soon."

"What can I do to help?" Chogan asked.

"We can plan it together, online." Amelia sat quietly for a few moments. "We need to set a date."

"Do you have a calendar?" Chogan looked around the room as he spoke.

"There's one in the kitchen, on the wall." Amelia directed.

Chogan brought the calendar from the kitchen and flipped it to December. "What do you think about the seventeenth of December?"

"That's perfect," Amelia agreed. "That way it won't interfere with anyone's Christmas holiday."

Chogan grinned mischievously. "It also gives us a week for a honeymoon before Christmas. Do you want to have a ceremony here in Florida or in Colorado?" Chogan asked.

"I don't know if Myron's family can make it to Colorado that close to Christmas. If you wouldn't mind, let me ask them and if they can make it to Colorado, we'll plan our wedding in Frisco."

"If they can't make it; I'll fly here and we'll have a ceremony here." Chogan grinned before he continued. "Then we can take a week for a honeymoon and be home in time for Christmas."

Amelia squeezed Chogan's hand and spoke softly. "That sounds wonderful. I want Topanga and Lovella to be in the wedding."

"They will love that!" Chogan laughed. "Of course they will compete to see who can be the star of the show."

"Chogan, are you sure the girls won't mind having me as a step-mother?" Amelia asked worriedly.

Chogan squeezed Amelia's hand. "Let me put your mind at ease. Topanga asked me if I was bringing Mia home with me."

Amelia was pleased. "Chogan, I promise to be a good mother to the girls."

"That's one of the things that made me fall in love with you, Amelia; your bond with my girls." Chogan's eyes filled with tears. "When I lost Samantha, I thought I'd never find another woman to take her place. You walked into my life and my heart hasn't been the same since the first time I laid eyes on you."

Amelia felt blessed. "I came to Frisco trying to get over a broken heart. I had lost my faith in relationships and I just wanted a week to be with my friend and forget the whole mess." Amelia smiled as the memories of the barbecue ran through her mind. "I'll never forget Lovella saying 'I want to hold you,' she stole my heart that moment." Amelia looked directly into Chogan's eyes. "When you kissed me the first time, I was stunned. I felt something that I had never felt with Liam and it terrified me."

"You were afraid of me?" Chogan asked in concern.

Amelia laughed. "No, I was afraid of what I felt. I wanted you to hold me and never let me go. I found my faith in Frisco, Chogan."

"We will be happy, Amelia. I'll be a good husband to you," Chogan promised.

Amelia smiled. "I am so grateful to God that you are part of my life, Chogan."

Before Chogan left for the airport, he helped Amelia to her feet and held her gently in his arms. Chogan bent his head and kissed her carefully. "That kiss will have to hold me until I can be with you again."

Amelia touched his face, "It will seem like a very long time to me too."

Chogan held her face in his hands and kissed her forehead gently. He ran his finger tenderly down her damaged face. "Please take care of yourself. If you need me, I promise I'll be here." Chogan kissed her again tears filling his eyes as he spoke. "Thank you for forgiving me, Amelia."

Amelia smiled. "There's nothing to forgive; I love you. Thank you for coming, Chogan. You take care of yourself and my girls."

"I like the sound of that," Chogan whispered. "Topanga and Lovella will be your girls as much as mine."

Amelia stood at the door and watched Chogan drive away. She felt the loss immediately. Amelia walked to her room and eased into the bed to rest until everyone arrived home from church.

"Mia? Where are you?" Hilary shouted from the open door.

Amelia eased herself from the bed. "I'm in my room, Hilary."

Hilary ran down the hall and stopped in her tracks. She looked at Amelia's bruised face full of stitches and the shoulder brace and burst into tears. "Daddy! Somebody hurt Mia!" she wailed.

Anne came running down the hall and picked Hilary up. "Shhhh, honey it's ok. Mia had a car accident."

Amelia was crying as she spoke. "I'm sorry, Hilary, I didn't mean to scare you."

Anne whispered gently. "Mia can't hold you right now, but you can give her a kiss to make her feel better."

Hilary turned tear-filled eyes to Amelia and extended her arms. "Can I kiss you, Mia?" she asked in her little girl voice.

Amelia stepped closer and stood still so that Hilary could look closely at her injuries. "I promise I won't break," Amelia whispered.

Hilary leaned from her mother's arms and kissed Amelia softly on her cheek. "Does that hurt?" Hilary asked as she pointed to Amelia's stitches.

"A little," Amelia confessed, "It itches more than anything." Amelia took her hand and gently scratched her cheek for effect.

Hilary giggled. "Your face looks like my paint set when I mix the colors together."

Amelia laughed out loud. "That's the best description I've heard yet. Come on; let's go see what we are having for lunch."

Henry waited until Amelia was seated in the swing. He walked over slowly and sat down beside her. "Can I hug you if I'm really careful?" he asked.

Amelia extended her right arm as she spoke. "I'd love a hug, honey."

Henry hugged her close. He sat back and touched her stitches. "Does that hurt, Mia?"

Amelia smiled at Henry as she spoke. "Hilary asked me that same question. It hurts a little but it itches like crazy."

Henry turned his head sideways and looked at her shoulder. "What is that?" he asked pointed to her shoulder brace.

Amelia lifted her hand and pointed to her collar bone. "I broke this bone and they had to put a brace on my shoulder so it will heal properly."

Henry seemed to accept that. "I'm glad you're ok." He spoke seriously. "Are you going to move to Colorado and marry Chogan?"

"Yes, I am going to marry Chogan before Christmas and I'll be moving to Colorado. Are you ok with that?" Amelia asked.

Henry thought for a moment and then he grinned. "Can we come for a visit and ride the horses again?"

"Absolutely," Amelia assured him. "You'll have two new cousins too."

Henry rolled his eyes and threw his hand against his forehead. "Topanga and Lovella are girls! Couldn't you have a boy and then we'll have three of each."

Amelia laughed. "I promise to work on that for you."

Henry seemed satisfied with that answer and ran off to swim before lunch.

Harmon watched Amelia but wouldn't come close to her. He wasn't quite sure what to think about Amelia's injuries.

After lunch, the children returned to the pool. Amelia was situated on the chaise lounge to rest.

Myron and Anne joined her in the sunroom while the children were under the protective eye of Reggie and Cecilia. "So when is the wedding?" Myron asked.

"December seventeenth," Amelia smiled as she spoke. "I wanted to talk to you both about the wedding."

Anne was concerned. "Amelia, we don't want to miss your wedding; I just don't think we can make another trip to Colorado by Christmas."

Amelia smiled at her sister-in-law. "I totally understand; that's why Chogan and I have made an alternate plan."

Myron looked suspicious. "What do you have in mind?"

Amelia grinned. "Chogan is going to fly to Florida and marry me here with my family and friends."

Anne was surprised. "What about Chogan's family?"

"That's the best part," Amelia assured her. "Chogan is bringing his family with him."

"What can we do to help?" Myron asked.

"I want you both to stand up with us and of course I want the children to be in the wedding." Amelia responded.

"We've got three months to get you better and get this planned," Anne mused.

"Exactly," Amelia agreed. "I've got some ideas but I can't do much right now. Anne, I'm going to need your help."

Anne squeezed Amelia's hand gently. "I'm happy to help."

"I wanted to talk to you about something, sis." Myron made sure the children were still in the pool and out of ear shot. "I got a call from the company that owns the truck that Liam hit you with."

Amelia's face turned sad. "I still can't believe he's gone. No matter what he did to me, I feel sorry for him. I hope he made peace with God before he died."

Myron chose his words carefully. "Amelia, you had no way of knowing that Liam had started abusing alcohol and drugs."

Amelia was shocked. "I am so grateful that Liam dumped me before the wedding. I do feel bad for Courtney."

"Well if it's any consolation, Courtney has found someone else; the doctor that treated her for the beating Liam gave her." Anne said.

Amelia smiled. "I'm glad. She deserves to be happy."

"There won't be a trial for the accident since Liam died." Myron took Amelia's hand. "The company has reached a settlement with your insurance."

"Please tell me they are going to replace my car." Amelia said.

Myron smiled. "They are replacing your car at full value so you can buy whatever you want. They are also offering you a settlement for the accident."

Amelia was stunned. "A settlement? Why?" she asked.

Anne spoke softly, "Amelia, you were injured by a corporate vehicle. Most accident victims would have filed a lawsuit for the damages."

Amelia looked troubled. "I can't imagine doing that."

"God knows your heart, Amelia." Myron assured her. "The company has reached a settlement with your insurance that I think will help you in your new life."

"Do you know how much money they are talking about?" Amelia asked.

Myron winked at Anne. "They are writing you a check for $750,000."

Amelia was shocked. "You're kidding right?"

Myron shook his head. "I'm totally serious. They were more than willing to pay that amount to keep this case out of court."

Chapter Twenty-Five

Amelia wore her brace for six long weeks. She worked on the wedding plans with the help of Cecilia and Anne. Amelia had received the settlement check and deposited it in a special account until she could make a final decision about how to invest it.

Chogan worked on the travel plans for his family to take part in the wedding at Amelia's church in Florida.

Patricia and Geoff were helping with the details and would be flying to Florida to be part of the ceremony.

Loneliness filled Chogan's nights. Chogan fixed his mind on the fact that Amelia would be his wife very soon and that God had given him a second chance.

Cecilia was driving Amelia to the doctor to have her brace removed. Anne would be meeting them at the bridal shop for their fittings. "Today's the big day," Cecilia encouraged Amelia as she drove. "I know you're ready for that brace to come off."

Amelia grinned. "Mom, I really appreciate all that you and daddy have done for me; but I can't wait to take my own showers and get dressed by myself!"

Cecilia laughed. "You've been a marvelous patient, Amelia. I'll miss you when you get married."

"I'll miss you and daddy, too; but I'm ready to start my own life with Chogan and the girls." Amelia dug in her purse for a notepad. "After our fitting today, can we make another stop? I've got some Christmas shopping to do and I need to get it done early."

"Sure honey, I'll take you any place you'd like." Cecilia turned into the medical building parking lot. She helped Amelia from the car and smiled. "This is the last time you'll have to sit uncomfortably in that brace."

"Hallelujah!" Amelia shouted.

Cecilia was still laughing as she followed Amelia through the door.

Anne was waiting in the foyer of the bridal shop when Amelia and Cecilia arrived. "Wow, you look great, Amelia."

Amelia hugged her sister-in-law. “I feel like I’ve lost twenty pounds. Oh wait; I did!” she teased.

Anne hugged Cecilia. “Are you ready for our fittings?”

“Yes I am. I feel privileged to be with my two beautiful daughters.” Cecilia spoke with pride.

“Ladies, if you’ll follow me,” the bridal shop attendant led them to their dressing rooms.

Cecilia emerged first. She was dressed in a beautiful champagne colored gown with a glittering jacket that fell just above her hips. The skirt was shimmery and full and fell to her ankles where she wore matching satin heels.

Anne joined Cecilia in front of the mirrors. “Mom, you look beautiful!” Anne hugged Cecilia as she spoke.

Cecilia held Anne at arm’s length and spoke with love. “My beautiful Anne, you will take Myron’s breath away in that gown!”

Anne peered at herself in the mirror. “I hope so. This dress is so beautiful.” Anne’s dress was made of red satin with a chiffon skirt that fell from a high waist to the floor. The bodice and long sleeves shimmered with glitter. The neckline fell in a soft v-neck. Anne’s shoes were high heeled red satin that were dyed to match the dress perfectly.

Amelia walked slowly to the mirrors and smiled at her mom and Anne. “What do you think?” she asked.

Cecilia’s eyes filled with tears of happiness. “You are beautiful!”

Anne was crying too. “I think you’re the prettiest bride I’ve ever seen!”

Amelia stepped up to the mirrors and turned slowly. Her gown was White velvet and chiffon. The bodice was form fitting with long sleeves. The entire bodice was covered in shimmering glitter that looked like snow in the sunlight. The skirt was full and fell like a bell behind Amelia. The bustle had been added so that Amelia could clip the train up during the reception. Amelia stood still while the bridal attendant slipped her veil on. The cap of the veil fit like a tiny cap with a blusher and four layers of chiffon that fell to Amelia’s waist. Each layer of the veil was trimmed with a tiny glittering edge that perfectly matched the shimmer of the bodice. It was beautiful and elegant in its simplicity.

Amelia smiled as she spoke. “I can’t wait to see Chogan’s face.” Amelia stepped closer to the mirror and her smile froze. She ran her finger down the scar on her face and her eyes filled with tears.

Cecilia spoke softly. “Chogan will think you are the most beautiful bride in the world. He loves you, Amelia. That scar only makes you more beautiful.”

Anne spoke quickly. “Amelia, that scar is just a scar. You are a beautiful bride and nothing can take away from that.”

Amelia turned and hugged Cecilia and then Anne. “I love you both, so much!”

“Has Hilary’s dress arrived?” Amelia asked.

“Not yet, it will be here by Friday.” Anne assured her. “Hilary is so excited that her dress is identical in color and material to mine.”

Amelia asked the attendant. “Have you received the dresses for my step-daughters and my matron-of-honor?”

The attendant grinned. “Yes ma’am. We shipped the matron-of-honor dress to Denver and Patricia is being fitted today. The dress will then be shipped back here to be steamed and delivered to the church with the other dresses.”

“Perfect; thank you so much for all your help with these dresses. They are perfect.” Amelia grinned. “We need a picture!” She handed her camera to the attendant and posed with Anne and Cecilia. “You both look beautiful,” Amelia praised. “I think my daddy and my brother are going to be very happy to escort you to the wedding.”

“What did you pick for Patricia, Lovella and Topanga to wear?” Anne asked.

“Patricia’s dress is identical to yours,” Amelia responded. “Do you have the other two dresses?” Amelia asked the bridal attendant.

“Yes, we do,” the attendant replied as she slipped into the back room. She returned with two small dress bags and gently pulled out the dresses that Amelia had ordered for Lovella and Topanga. They were identical to Hilary’s in style; but they were winter white to match Amelia’s dress.

"They are lovely," Anne touched the material tenderly. "You are matching your girls just like you matched mine; to their mama."

"You're going to be a wonderful mother," Cecilia whispered. "I'm not just gaining another son; I'm gaining two new granddaughters."

October quickly passed. Amelia had resigned her teaching position to focus on the wedding plans and her rehabilitation. She worked diligently to regain her mobility in her shoulder.

Amelia helped her mother select the caterer and worked with the pastor's wife to arrange the fellowship hall for the reception. She had ordered huge baskets of red and white poinsettias for the altar and had the florist make bouquets of red and white roses with tiny twinkling lights intertwined, for the attendants. A brass arch had been rented and would be decorated with white crinoline and tiny flickering white Christmas lights. Red roses with ribbons would adorn the crinoline and attach it to the brass.

Amelia and Chogan talked every day online or by phone. Amelia smiled at the words of love that Chogan would type in his messages. She laughed at the funny things Lovella and Topanga would say to her on the phone. Each day she grew more excited at the prospect of becoming Chogan's wife.

Thanksgiving dinner was set up on the sun porch. Amelia was setting the table when the phone rang. "I'll get it, mom." Amelia spoke as she grabbed the cordless phone. "Hello, Happy Thanksgiving."

"Happy Thanksgiving to you, Mia," Topanga giggled into the phone. "When are you coming home?"

Amelia smiled. "I'll see you in three weeks, my love."

"Hold on, Lovella wants to talk to you, I love you, Mia!" Topanga spoke quickly before she handed the phone to her little sister.

"When are you going to marry us?" Lovella asked.

Amelia laughed. "Very soon, sweetie, I love you."

Lovella giggled. "I love you, Mia." Lovella held the phone out and yelled. "Daddy, Mia is on the phone."

Chogan took the phone and laughed. "Hello my love, Happy Thanksgiving."

"Happy Thanksgiving, I love you," Amelia spoke from a grateful heart. "It will be just three more weeks; until I see you again."

Chogan sighed and took the phone to the den and closed the door for privacy. "I miss you so much, Amelia. We will be arriving Thursday, December fifteenth."

"What time does your flight arrive?" Amelia asked.

"We are scheduled to arrive in Orlando at 11:00 a.m." Chogan sighed. "I've booked our rooms at the hotel and I've rented a mini-van for the family."

"I've got the rehearsal set up for Friday evening and the dinner will be immediately following." Amelia paused. "I won't see you after that until I meet you at the altar," her voice was filled with longing.

"I can't wait," Chogan interjected. "We will be married at noon and after the reception, we head for the airport and our honeymoon."

Amelia's cheeks turned crimson. "Are you going to tell me where we are going?"

Chogan laughed softly. "I will tell you when we get on the plane," he teased.

"Daddy, Topanga is getting into the pie!" Lovella yelled through the door to the den.

Chogan groaned. "I have to go, before my daughters devour dessert. I love you, Amelia. I'll see you very soon."

"Give the girls a hug for me. I love you, Chogan." Amelia hung up the phone.

Dinner was over and Amelia watched as Henry; Harmon, and Hilary helped Reggie and Cecilia put up the Christmas tree.

"Anne, can I talk to you and Myron in the kitchen please?" Amelia spoke softly so the children wouldn't hear.

Myron slipped out of the room behind Amelia and Anne. "What's up sis?"

"I have something for you." Amelia pulled out a large envelope from the bank.

Myron looked at Anne and then opened the envelope slowly. He pulled out the statement and the three tri-fold documents. Myron read them in disbelief and then handed them to Anne.

Tears formed in Anne's eyes. "Amelia, this is too much."

Myron agreed. "Amelia, you were supposed to use this money to start your new life with Chogan."

Amelia smiled and hugged Anne and then Myron. "I prayed and asked God for guidance on what to do with this money. Making sure that my nephews and my niece have a start on their college is important."

Myron spoke quietly. "Amelia, these portfolios show a $50,000 deposit for each one of the children."

Amelia smiled. "That's exactly what it says. You also need to open this." Amelia handed Anne another single envelope from the bank.

Anne opened it and hugged Amelia crying. "I can't believe you did this."

Myron looked from his wife to his sister. "What is in that envelope?" Myron opened the form that Anne passed to him with shaking hands. "Are you serious?"

Amelia hugged Myron. "Big brother, you have always watched out for me. You've been the best brother a sister could have. I know how hard you and Anne work to care for your family; I hope this helps."

Myron read the document again. "$100,000 to be used at our discretion; if I add that to the college funds you've started for our children, that's one third of your settlement."

Amelia spoke with sincerity. "You took care of my accident from the investigation to the settlement. This is my way to say thank you."

Myron hugged Amelia close. "That's an answer to prayer, Amelia."

Amelia was surprised, "What prayer is that?"

Anne smiled. "I've wanted to quit work, to stay home with the children. This money is enough to pay off the house and buy a new, larger vehicle for the family."

"I had no idea you were thinking of being a stay-at-home mom," Amelia responded. "Why do you need a larger vehicle?"

Myron laughed. "You're the first person we've told; Anne is pregnant."

Amelia laughed aloud and hugged Anne close. "I am so happy for you! See how God works? Now I know why God directed me this way. You have to accept this, Myron. God sent it and you can't deny a gift from God."

Myron agreed.

Chapter Twenty-Six

Chogan and his family boarded the plane in Denver on December fifteenth; headed to Orlando. Chogan had ordered his tux in Frisco at a shop that also had connections with a location in Orlando. Chogan allowed his mind to wander as he stared out the window into the sky filled with clouds. He thought back to the day he married Samantha. Her soft smile, gentle ways, and the love he shared with her; would never be forgotten. Chogan remembered the first time he saw Amelia, he felt his heart start to beat again, painfully. God had sent him a woman to love and fill the void that Samantha's death had left. Chogan turned cold when he thought about how close he came to losing Amelia forever. The thought of her accident had haunted his dreams for weeks. Chogan thanked God daily for sparing Amelia's life and for giving them another chance to be husband and wife.

"Daddy, look at that cloud; it looks like a marshmallow," Topanga exclaimed.

"I want to see," Lovella struggled to peer out the window. "I don't see a marshmallow," she argued.

Topanga rolled her eyes, "It's not a real marshmallow, it's a cloud."

Lovella grew bored with the clouds and returned to her coloring book. "Daddy, will Mia be waiting for us?" she asked.

"I told her we would meet her after we check into the hotel," Chogan explained. In his heart he hoped she was at the airport. The last time he'd seen her, she was broken and bruised.

Chogan smiled when the flight attendant announced the arrival into Orlando International Airport. He watched Lovella and Topanga strain to get their first glimpse of Florida.

Amelia was pacing the waiting area for arriving passengers. She had arrived an hour early, anxious to see Chogan and the girls. Amelia looked through the passengers walking up the aisle and saw Chogan. She smiled and her heart began to beat faster.

Chogan felt Amelia's presence. He looked up and made eye contact with her. She was wearing a soft yellow sweater and black slacks. Her hair was pulled up into a pony tail with a yellow ribbon. Amelia's eyes were dancing with excitement that matched the excitement in Chogan's heart. Chogan cleared the secure area and dropped his bag to his feet; he swept Amelia into his arms and kissed her.

Amelia smiled as they pulled apart. "I've missed you so much, Chogan," she whispered.

Chogan felt the same way. "I've missed you too, Amelia."

"Mia!" Topanga ran from her grandparents and threw herself into Amelia's open arms. "I missed you, Mia!"

Lovella walked up shyly and when Amelia held out her arms, Lovella turned her face into Uda's skirt and clung to her grandmother.

Amelia was crushed.

Uda hugged Amelia over Lovella and touched her face. "Hello Amelia. I'm so happy to see you."

"Uda, thank you for coming all this way," Amelia offered her thanks as she smiled at Dakota.

Dakota hugged her close. "Hello Amelia."

Uda bent down and whispered to Lovella trying to convince her to talk to Amelia.

"No," Lovella whispered, "She scares me."

Amelia's eyes filled with tears but she held them as she put on a smile for Topanga and led the way to baggage claim.

"Are you coming to live with me, Mia?" Topanga asked.

"Yes sweetheart, we will have our first Christmas together next week," Amelia explained.

"I asked Jesus for a new mommy this year," Topanga whispered.

Amelia was speechless.

Topanga grinned. "I got my wish, I got you, Mia." She rushed off to Dakota's side.

Amelia waited while Chogan gathered their luggage and Dakota rented their van. She led the way to the parking garage and the rental cars. "Do you want to follow me?" she asked Chogan.

Dakota spoke first, "Uda and I will follow you in the van; I'm sure Chogan would like a few minutes alone with you," he smiled knowingly.

Chogan grinned. “Thanks dad. I think I’ll let my fiancé drive so I can admire her.”

Amelia blushed. She unlocked the doors and smiled as Chogan got in the passenger side and sat staring at her.

Chogan reached over and covered her hand with his; stopping her from turning on the ignition. He leaned across the console and slid his hand behind Amelia’s neck drawing her closer. Chogan covered Amelia’s lips with his speaking softly between kisses. “I’ve missed you so much; you look beautiful.”

Amelia savored the kisses from Chogan and clung to his jacket; keeping him close. “I’ve been waiting for this day; I am so glad you’re here.”

Chogan kissed her one last time. “Just two days, my love; and we won’t have to be apart again.”

Amelia drove carefully to the hotel, watching for Dakota in her rear view mirror.

“Whose car is this?” Chogan asked.

“It’s Myron’s, he loaned it to me to drive to the airport.”

“Have you replaced your car?” Chogan asked.

Amelia reached over and took Chogan’s hand as she drove. “I haven’t done that. I wanted my new husband to help me pick out a vehicle that would be appropriate for Colorado driving.”

Chogan squeezed her hand. “Your husband; I love the sound of that, Amelia. I’ll help you pick out something when we get home.”

“There is something I need to tell you, Chogan.” Amelia said.

“I’m listening,” Chogan replied. “Tell me what it is.”

Amelia took a deep breath. “I received a settlement from the accident. I’ve got enough money to buy a new vehicle.”

“I’m glad; we’ll find you a new vehicle that you’ll be happy with.” Chogan assured her.

“There’s more,” Amelia whispered.

Chogan waited for her to continue.

“I prayed about the money I received, and I followed my heart in spending it.” Amelia took a deep breath. “I started a college fund for my nephews and my niece.”

Chogan smiled. "I'm glad Amelia, that's one of the things I love about you; your generosity."

"That's not all," Amelia continued. "I also gave Myron and Anne a check."

Chogan laughed softly. "How did they react to that?"

"They tried to tell me it was too much, then I found out they are expecting a new baby and Anne had been praying about quitting her job to be a full-time mom." Amelia explained.

"A new baby," Chogan whispered softly. "I'm very happy for them. Children are such a blessing. Your brother and sister-in-law are amazing together."

Amelia glanced over at Chogan. "I've also started a college fund for Topanga and Lovella. Please don't be offended."

Chogan was stunned. "Amelia, that's wonderful. You have already become a mother to the girls."

Amelia relaxed. "I was afraid you'd be angry or offended with me."

"Why?" Chogan asked.

"Because we aren't married yet and I don't want you to think I'm trying to buy Topanga and Lovella's love." Amelia explained.

Chogan squeezed her hand. "Amelia, in two days you become my wife. I plan to share every aspect of your life and have you share every aspect of my life with love and respect for one another's opinions."

Amelia's smile turned sad. "Chogan, why is Lovella afraid of me?" she asked.

Chogan squeezed her hand. "I don't know, unless it's the scar."

Amelia's eyes filled with tears. "I'm sorry, I know it's ugly. What am I going to do?"

"Amelia, that scar is a reminder of how close I came to losing you forever," Chogan's voice choked up with emotion. "When I see that scar, I thank God for giving me another chance to share your life." Chogan ran his finger gently down her cheek, "It only adds to the beauty I see when I look at you."

Amelia didn't reply, she held Chogan's hand and drove on to the hotel.

Uda and Amelia waited with the girls, while Chogan and Dakota unpacked the luggage and checked them in.

The elevator took them to the sixth floor and the door opened into a two bedroom suite with two bathrooms.

Lovella stayed with Uda and wouldn't leave her side.

Topanga pulled Amelia by the hand from one end of the suite to the other, checking every aspect of the room.

They rode the elevator back down to the lobby and had lunch in the restaurant at the hotel. Lovella and Topanga were yawning by the time lunch was over. Their early morning ride to Denver and the flight to Orlando had exhausted them.

Dakota spoke softly to Chogan, "Why don't you let your mother and I put the girls down for a nap. I'm sure you and Amelia need some time alone."

Chogan squeezed Amelia's hand. "Thanks dad. I promised the girls they could swim this afternoon at the indoor pool."

Amelia grinned, "Don't forget we're having an early Christmas at my mom and dad's house tonight with the whole family. Chogan and I will come back to the hotel and you can follow us."

Uda pulled a sleeping Lovella into her arms. "What time should we be ready?" she asked.

Amelia checked her watch. "We'll be back by 6:00 p.m., will that be enough time?"

"That will give the girls time for a nap and a swim and then they will be ready for the evening," Uda agreed.

Chogan paid for lunch and wrapped his arm around Amelia's waist as they walked to the car. "Where are we going?" Chogan asked as he fastened his seat belt in the car.

"I've got some last minute things to pick up at the mall; do you mind going there?" Amelia asked.

Chogan leaned across the console and kissed her. "I don't mind going anywhere, as long as we are together," he whispered.

Amelia finished her list and walked with Chogan to the tux shop. She waited while Chogan was fitted for his tux to make sure everything was in line for the ceremony.

"All done," Chogan said as he emerged from the back of the shop. "Where would you like to go next?" he asked.

Amelia checked her list and then her watch. "I've got one more stop to make," she spoke softly. Amelia drove a short distance from the mall to the park. The weather was sunny and cool in the low sixties. "I thought we'd take a walk," Amelia suggested.

Chogan wrapped his arm around Amelia's waist and they walked along the path until they reached a gazebo at the center of the park. Chogan pulled Amelia into his arms and slowly lowered his head to kiss her.

Amelia held him close and whispered. "This feels so right."

"I think so too," Chogan agreed. "I hated to leave you after the accident. You were so broken and every night I've thought of you standing there bruised and trapped in that brace." Chogan pulled back and held Amelia at arm's length. "You look beautiful; how is your shoulder?" he asked softly.

Amelia lifted her arms above her head and then slowly brought them down to Chogan's shoulders. She pulled him slowly to her and smiled, "I'm fine Chogan; physical therapy and swimming have given me back my mobility." Amelia felt Chogan's arms circle and pull her closer. "Now I can hold you and kiss you the way I want," she whispered as he claimed her lips once more.

Chogan and Amelia arrived at the hotel at 6:00 p.m. as planned. Dakota and Uda were in the lobby with the girls. They drove to Reggie and Cecilia's. Myron and Anne arrived at the same time. Lovella and Topanga were quickly included with Henry, Harmon and Hilary checking out the Christmas tree in the sun room.

Amelia, Anne and Uda joined Cecilia in the kitchen to help set up the dinner. Dakota, Reggie, Chogan and Myron were in the sun room with the children.

The doorbell rang. "Amelia, will you answer that sweetheart?" Cecilia asked.

"Sure, mom," Amelia answered. She opened the door and let out a squeal, "Patricia!"

Patricia grabbed Amelia and hugged her tight. "I have missed you so much!" Patricia spoke quickly holding Amelia tight. "Let me look at you," she pulled back and tears filled her eyes. "I'm so glad you're okay, Amelia, don't you ever scare me like that again," she scolded.

Amelia was laughing and crying with Patricia while Geoff stood behind them waiting to be invited in. "Geoff, get in here," Amelia spoke over Patricia's shoulder. Amelia grabbed Geoff and hugged him tight. "Thank you both for coming."

Geoff hugged Amelia as he spoke. "We wouldn't miss our best friends' wedding for love nor money."

Chogan joined Amelia and shook hands with Geoff. "Hey Geoff, I'm so glad you all are here." Chogan looked at Patricia and smiled. "Am I forgiven yet?" he asked.

Patricia hugged him and whispered. "I forgive you Chogan, but you better take really good care of my best friend."

Chogan whispered, "Patricia, I promise you, I'll protect Amelia with my life."

Cecilia spoke from the kitchen doorway. "Patricia, it's so good to see you honey."

Patricia let out a squeal and hugged Cecilia tight. "Cece, I smell zucchini bread!"

Cecilia laughed. "Yes you do, come join the ladies in the kitchen."

Hilary, Topanga and Lovella were playing with a dollhouse that was set up in the corner of the sun room. "My aunt Mia is going to marry your daddy," Hilary whispered.

"She's gonna be my new mama," Topanga giggled. "I asked Jesus for a new mommy for Christmas, and I got one."

Lovella frowned. "No, she scares me."

Hilary put her hands on her hips and scowled at Lovella, "You take that back. My aunt Mia is the bestest aunt in the whole world, she's not scary."

Topanga joined the argument, "Why are you scared of Mia? You said you loved her too?" she asked.

Lovella's eyes filled with tears, "Her face has a boo-boo; it scares me," she whispered.

Hilary smiled and spoke with the wisdom of a four-year-old. "Aunt Mia was in an accident, mommy splained it to me." Hilary used her hand to draw a scar on her own face from her eye to her mouth. "That scar on Aunt Mia's face is a smile."

Lovella looked confused. "A smile?" she asked.

Hilary sighed, "God wanted me to remember that Aunt Mia is so special that he protected her in the accident. He put a smile from her eye to her mouth to show me how much he loves her."

Lovella sat quietly for a minute. "God put that on Mia's face?" she asked.

Topanga smiled. "Mia is pretty, I'm glad she's gonna marry us and be our new mama." Topanga turned to Lovella, "You need to love Mia so she will be happy and God will be happy too."

Lovella's eyes filled with tears, "I love Mia; her face scared me, but not anymore." Lovella stood and walked to the kitchen. She maneuvered her way between the adults and pulled on Amelia's sweater.

Amelia looked down and smiled softly. "Lovella, what do you need sweetie?" she asked.

"I want to hold you," Lovella whispered.

Amelia picked Lovella up and waited while Lovella traced the scar from her eye to her mouth.

"Does that hurt, Mia?" Lovella asked.

Amelia smiled as she spoke, "No sweetie, it doesn't hurt at all. I'm sorry I scared you with my scar."

Lovella's eyes filled with tears. "I'm not afraid no more. Hilary told me about God's smile," she wrapped her arms around Amelia and hugged her tightly. "I love you Mia," she whispered.

"I love you too, Lovella," Amelia hugged her new daughter close as she spoke. She didn't understand but was so grateful that Lovella was no longer afraid that she didn't question it. When the other children yelled for Lovella, Amelia sat her down and watched as she ran to the sun room laughing.

"Amelia, I can explain what Lovella was trying to tell you," Anne commented. "When Hilary first saw you after the stitches were removed, she didn't understand why you had the scar." Anne smiled as she recalled that conversation. "I explained that God loved you so much that he spared your life in that accident and placed his smile on your face from your eye to your mouth to remind us how special you are."

Cecilia hugged Anne. "That's a beautiful explanation Anne."

Uda spoke softly, "I tried to explain the scar to Lovella today but I had no success. Your explanation was perfect."

Amelia hugged Anne. "Thank you, I didn't want my new daughter to be afraid of me."

After dinner, everyone moved to the sun room and celebrated Christmas. The children tore into their gifts with great excitement. Myron took photos around the tree and captured Amelia & Chogan's first Christmas as a family.

It was after 10:00 p.m. when everyone headed home for the night. Dakota and Uda followed Amelia and Chogan back to the hotel and carried a sleeping Lovella and Topanga to their beds.

Chogan walked Amelia back to her car. Chogan leaned against the car and held Amelia in his arms. "This has been a wonderful day," he whispered.

"Yes it has. Lovella isn't afraid of me anymore," Amelia said.

"Myron and Anne are amazing parents," Chogan offered. "Myron told me how Anne explained your scar to Hilary." Chogan ran his finger down Amelia's cheek. "I believe Anne was right, you are so special to all of us that God gave us a permanent reminder."

Amelia kissed Chogan softly. "Thank you, I think you're pretty special too."

Chogan kissed her slowly and held her close. "I need to say goodnight so you can get some rest. Tomorrow is a busy day." Chogan opened the door and waited until Amelia was buckled in. He leaned into the car and kissed her softly. "Drive safely my love, text me when you get home so I'll know you're safe."

Amelia touched his cheek. "Goodnight Chogan. I love you; I'll see you in the morning."

Chogan watched her drive away and took the elevator back up to the suite. He couldn't rest until he received the text message from Amelia that she was home safe. Chogan went to bed with a smile on his face. "One more day my love, and then you'll be with me," he whispered into the darkness.

The church was full of volunteers, decorating the sanctuary and the fellowship hall for the wedding. Chogan and his family were greeted warmly and introduced to Amelia's church family.

The rehearsal was held at 6:00 p.m. and by 8:00 p.m. the entire wedding party headed for the rehearsal dinner. Amelia's mom and dad had reserved a room at the local steakhouse.

Pastor Greene was the first to greet Chogan and Amelia. "Chogan, you are about to marry one of the most precious members of my flock. I dedicated her as a baby; I baptized her as a new convert; and now it's my honor to perform her wedding. Take care of one another; your marriage is a gift from God."

The entire room applauded as Chogan stood and shook Pastor Greene's hand.

Myron took the floor next lifting his iced tea glass in a toast as he spoke. "To Chogan and Amelia; I pray God's blessing on your life together. I pray you have compassion, faith, and most of all love that will bind you together for now and forever."

Myron hugged Amelia and Chogan as the room applauded.

Reggie took the floor next. "Chogan, the first time we met you; we knew you were not going away."

The room erupted in laughter.

Reggie continued. "If I had any doubt that you loved my daughter, the doubt was removed, when you showed up in Orlando to check on her after the accident." Reggie paused while he cleared his throat in an effort to get his emotions under control. "Amelia is a very special gift from God and I pray that you will always treat her as a precious, priceless jewel." Reggie hugged Amelia and then hugged Chogan too.

Patricia stood and raised her glass. "To Chogan and Amelia, I love you both and I pray that God blesses you both with love, laughter, and many children that will be as mischievous as Amelia and I were, growing up." The room erupted in laughter again.

Dakota stood and raised his glass. "Amelia, the first time we met you; we knew God had sent us a special gift. Welcome to the family." Amelia hugged Dakota and Uda.

Chogan took the floor last. "Amelia, I will forever be grateful to God for bringing you into my life. I love you, and I promise you before God and this gathering of friends and family that I will cherish you, and never take for granted our life together, but honor it as a gift from God."

Amelia stood and kissed Chogan; wrapping her arms around him and holding him close to her heart. Amelia gave the final toast. "Chogan, you are my love, my life, and I give you my heart. Thank you friends and family for sharing our special day. Pray for us that God will bless us in our life together as we serve Him."

The rehearsal dinner broke up at 11:00 p.m. and Amelia drove Chogan back to his hotel. She parked the car and turned off the ignition.

Chogan held her hand in his as he spoke, "I don't want to say goodnight to you."

Amelia squeezed his hand. "I'm having the same problem. It's kind of like being a little girl and waiting for Christmas morning; I knew the sooner I went to sleep the sooner Christmas would be here."

Chogan laughed and turned to kiss Amelia. "Drive safely, Amelia. Tomorrow I will marry you."

Amelia touched Chogan's face with her hand. "Sweet dreams, Chogan."

Amelia was up at 6:00 a.m. and sipping a glass of tea at the dining room table.

Reggie joined her at the table. "Today's the big day, how do you feel?"

Amelia sighed. "I'm feeling loss that I will be leaving my family; but I'm feeling excited that I'm about to start a new chapter in my life."

Reggie squeezed her hand. "I am so proud of you. If you ever need us, we are just a phone call away."

Amelia stood and hugged her father. "Daddy, I love you and mom so much. I wish you all would let me share some of the settlement with you."

"Amelia, your mother and I have everything we need. The fact that you made a way for Myron and Anne to have their prayer request answered was enough." Reggie spoke with pride in his children.

Anne arrived with Hilary. "Ok Amelia, let's go!"

Cecilia joined the girls in the car. "I confirmed with the florist, the flowers have been delivered." Cecilia tapped the screen of her cell phone as she spoke. "The cake will be set up by 10:00 a.m. and the photographer is meeting us at the church by 10:30 a.m."

Amelia laughed. "Mom, you and Anne are amazing. I could never have pulled off this wedding without your help."

"I think this wedding proves that our family is awesome." Anne teased. "Amelia, what time are Uda and the girls coming to the church?" Anne asked.

Amelia grinned. "They should be there about the same time as we get there. Patricia is bringing them."

The hairdresser spent three hours preparing the bridal parties' hair. Cecilia had brought her camera and made sure they documented the entire experience. Cecilia's hair was pulled up into a soft curls; the hairdresser accented the style with rhinestone pins.

Hilary's hair was pulled up into a princess style with a tiara and tiny tendrils framing her face. "Mommy look, I'm a princess!" Hilary spoke in awe of her reflection.

"Hilary, you will always be my princess." Anne assured her. Anne's hair was curled loose and full and she wore a headband of rhinestones that picked up the iridescent sparkles of her dress.

Patricia's hair was styled like Anne's, loose and full and she also wore a headband of rhinestones. "Amelia, these dresses are beautiful," she exclaimed.

Uda's hair was pulled up into a twist with rhinestone pins tucked into the style. She smiled as she watched her granddaughters twirl in their dresses.

Lovella and Topanga wore tiaras like Hilary and the three girls giggled and spun as they waited for the ceremony to start.

Amelia's hair was styled to support her veil. Her long blonde hair was pulled up and curled in an abundance of tendrils that fell down her back.

Cecilia watched the hairdresser place the finishing touches on Amelia's hair. "Amelia, you have never looked more beautiful."

Amelia sobered as she ran her finger down the scar on her face. "This scar kind of flaws the overall effect."

Anne stood behind Amelia and spoke softly. "Amelia, you are the most beautiful bride I have ever seen. Remember, that scar represents God's smile."

Amelia grinned. "Thanks Anne, I needed that!"

The photographer took photos of the bridal party without the bride and groom so that Chogan would not see Amelia before the wedding.

The sanctuary filled quickly and by 11:45 a.m. there were no seats left. Geoff served as Chogan's best man and he lit the candles on the stage. Geoff then escorted Uda to the platform to light the groom's mother candle. He seated her and then moved to the groom's room.

Myron escorted Cecilia to the platform to light the bride's mother candle and seated her, before joining the men in the groom's room.

The music started and Pastor Greene, Chogan, Geoff, Myron, and Henry walked to the altar and took their places.

All eyes turned to the aisle as Anne walked slowly down the aisle. Her red dress sparkled in the candlelight. Anne stared at Myron as she walked; she wore a lovely smile of contentment.

Myron watched Anne walk from the back of the church to take her place at the altar and he winked at her. After three children, another on the way, and many years of marriage; Myron was proud of his wife and the love they shared warmed his heart.

Patricia came down the aisle next. She smiled at Geoff, grateful for the opportunity to introduce her husband to her church family in Florida. She joined Anne at the altar.

Geoff watched Patricia move down the aisle, thankful that she was his wife, and grateful that Amelia had decided to marry in Florida so Patricia could be home with her family.

Hilary followed Anne down the aisle; she carefully dropped her red rose petals along the path. When she reached the front of the church, she turned and waved at her daddy, waved at her mamaw, and then curtsied for the congregation. Laughter rolled across the sanctuary.

Harmon came up the aisle carrying the ring pillow. He avoided the rose petals that Hilary had dropped, exaggerating his steps as he walked around them. Again, laughter filled the sanctuary.

Lovella and Topanga started down the aisle side-by-side. They dropped white rose petals as they walked slowly down the aisle. Once Lovella reached the pew that held Dakota and Uda she stopped and spun slowly in a circle. “Papaw, I’m a princess!” she declared.

The congregation laughed as Topanga rolled her eyes and tugged her baby sister to the altar.

Chogan stood waiting and watching. He didn’t think he would breathe again when Amelia entered the sanctuary on the arm of her father. She was breathtaking. The winter white velvet dress sparkled like snow and she looked like a princess from a fairy tale.

Amelia stood holding Reggie’s arm as Pastor Greene spoke. “Who gives this woman to be married to this man?”

“Her mother and I do,” Reggie hugged Amelia gently and placed her hand in Chogan’s.

Chogan led her up the stairs to stand beneath the arch. The tiny flickering white lights cast a gentle glow over the couple waiting to be wed.

Pastor Greene performed the ceremony and had Amelia and Chogan walk to the mothers’ candles. They stood facing one another while the soloist sang ‘Forever and Ever Amen.’

Chogan stared into Amelia’s eyes and stroked the back of her hands with his thumbs.

When the song ended, Chogan and Amelia lit the unity candle and extinguished the mothers' candles. They moved back to the arch and knelt facing one another to take communion.

Pastor Greene prayed over the couple and then had them stand. He led them in their vows and then asked for the rings.

Chogan slid the bride's wedding band on Amelia's left hand and spoke his final vows. "In token and in pledge, of the vows between us made; with this ring, I thee wed."

Amelia slid the groom's wedding band on Chogan's left hand as she spoke her final vows. "In token and in pledge, of the vows between us made; with this ring, I thee wed."

Pastor Greene smiled as he completed the ceremony. "In as much as Amelia and Chogan have confessed their love to one another; and have taken the holy vows of matrimony; with the power vested in my by the State of Florida and almighty God; I now pronounce them husband and wife. Chogan, you may kiss your bride."

Chogan gently lifted Amelia's blusher veil. He folded it back softly and pulled Amelia into his arms. He kissed his new bride with passion.

Amelia slid her arms around her new husband and returned his kiss in kind.

Pastor Greene waited patiently until Amelia and Chogan's kiss ended. "Ladies and gentlemen, it is my pleasure to present to you Mr. and Mrs. Chogan Hawk."

The congregation erupted in applause as the wedding recessional started and Chogan took Amelia's hand and led her to the back of the church. Chogan pulled Amelia into his arms and kissed her slowly; while the wedding party joined them in the foyer.

The photographer took final photos of the bride and groom and the wedding party quickly. By the time the wedding guests were seated in the fellowship hall; Chogan and Amelia entered the room with the bridal party and the children.

The reception was lively and entertaining. Chogan sat next to Amelia at the bridal table and kissed her every time the customary glasses were struck. When it was time to cut the cake, Chogan stood beside Amelia and wrapped his arm around her waist as they posed for the photo.

The wedding cake was a three tier traditional cake with red and white sugar roses. The bride and groom stood beneath a tiny brass arch; decorated to match the arch from the sanctuary."

After the cake, Amelia tossed her bouquet to the single females in the crowd.

Chogan knelt before Amelia and slid his hands up her leg in search of the traditional garter. Chogan's hand caressed Amelia's leg, under the cover of her dress; and made her blush. Chogan tossed the garter to the single males in the crowd.

It was after 1:30 p.m. when Chogan and Amelia were able to slip away. They ran from the fellowship hall beneath a shower of birdseed. Chogan helped Amelia into the back seat of the limo he had rented and slipped in beside her. The driver headed for the airport as Chogan pulled Amelia into his arms.

Amelia was flushed when the kiss ended and she looked up into Chogan's eyes. "Can you tell me now where we are going for our honeymoon?" she asked.

Chogan took her hand in his and lifted it to his lips. "We are catching a flight to Hawaii," he said. Chogan saw the look of surprise on Amelia's face and smiled. "I can't imagine a more romantic place to spend our honeymoon than Kauai."

"Chogan, I have always wanted to go to Hawaii. How did you do this?" she asked.

Chogan laughed. "One of the guys at the fire house has a time share on Kauai and he rented us his week."

Amelia pulled Chogan to her and kissed him passionately. "I can't believe you did this, a limo to the airport, and a honeymoon in Hawaii; how can I say thank you?" she whispered.

Chogan stroked her face with his hand and spoke solemnly. "You married me today, Amelia; that's all the thanks I need."

Once they reached the airport, their luggage was checked curbside and they were directed to their departure gate. The flight to Lihue left on time and was scheduled to arrive at 8:30 p.m. Chogan had booked them in first class and they cuddled and watched Christmas movies.

They fell asleep during the last leg of their flight and didn't wake until the pilot announced they were making their final descent into Lihue.

Amelia watched for their luggage while Chogan picked up their rental car. They were on the way to their condo by 9:15 p.m. Chogan parked the car and walked with Amelia into the registration office.

"Aloha, you must be Mr. and Mrs. Hawk; we've been expecting you," the night clerk greeted.

"Aloha, yes we are very happy to be here," Chogan smiled at Amelia as he spoke.

They were given directions to their room and a folder with information for the week. Chogan carried their luggage to the elevator and walked with Amelia to their room facing the ocean on the top floor of the building. Amelia slid the key card and unlocked the door.

"Wait here," Chogan asked.

Amelia stood waiting and watched as Chogan flipped on the lights and sat their luggage just inside the door, against the wall.

Chogan returned to the door and picked Amelia up in his arms and carried her across the threshold. He allowed the door to shut behind them and carried Amelia through the unit to the living room. Chogan sat her gently on her feet and opened the sliding glass doors to allow the trade winds to blow through the unit. He pulled Amelia into his arms and kissed her slowly. "I love you Amelia, my beautiful wife."

Amelia trembled, "Chogan, I love you, too." She kissed him gently and then slowly moved to the entryway and picked up her bag. She turned and saw Chogan watching her, "I'll be just a few minutes, my love."

Chogan watched the door to the bathroom close and he removed his jacket and hung it in the closet of the bedroom. Chogan has requested a shopper for their trip and he found cokes and chocolate covered strawberries in the refrigerator along with groceries; champagne glasses for the cokes waited on the counter. Chogan carried the strawberries into the bedroom and filled the ice bucket with ice and glass bottles of coke. He placed the ice bucket and champagne glasses next to the strawberries on the nightstand for later.

Chogan walked out to the balcony of the unit and stood in the moonlight listening to the waves slap against the shore. He breathed in the salt air and whispered a prayer. "Thank you, Lord, for bringing us safely to this beautiful island. Thank you, for blessing my life with Amelia, I will forever be grateful."

Amelia spoke from living room, "Chogan?"

Chogan turned slowly and sucked in his breath at the vision Amelia presented.

Amelia was wearing a white spaghetti strap gown of satin. The overlay was sheer and only the edge was adorned with glitter from the neckline to the bottom edge as well as around the cuff of the bell shaped sleeves. Amelia still had her hair pulled up from the ceremony with a white satin ribbon holding her hair back from her face.

"You look like an angel," Chogan whispered.

Amelia walked slowly to the balcony and stood before her husband. "I'm not an angel, but I am your wife," she whispered softly.

Chogan pulled Amelia into his arms and kissed her slowly. Chogan swept Amelia off her feet and carried her into the bedroom and sat her on the bed. He knelt before her and kissed her lips. Chogan ran his finger down the scar on Amelia's face as he spoke. "My beautiful, Amelia; you took my breath away in your wedding gown and now seeing you like this…" Chogan's voice trailed off as he kissed the top of her scar where it touched her lower eyelid. He continued to kiss the scar from top to bottom, ending at her lips. "I love you, so much," Chogan's voice was hoarse as he spoke. He reached up and released the satin ribbon that held Amelia's hair and allowed the long tresses to spill down and around her shoulders. Chogan slid his hands up under Amelia's hair and pulled her gently to him; kissing her softly and tenderly.

Amelia slid back into the bed and propped herself up on the pillows. Amelia held her hand out in invitation to Chogan; he laid down beside her and drew her into his arms. "I love you Chogan," Amelia spoke as she traced his face with her hand. "I am so glad that we are husband and wife." Amelia smiled as Chogan ended her speech by pulling her into his arms.

Chapter Twenty-Seven

Amelia was awaked by feathery kisses across her forehead. She had fallen asleep in Chogan's arms with her head on his shoulder. "Mmmm, this is nice," she whispered.

Chogan shifted and pinned Amelia on her back and kissed her slowly.

Amelia slipped her arms around Chogan and ran her hands through his hair pulling him closer still. Amelia returned Chogan's kisses until he was breathing heavily.

Chogan pulled back and grinned, "Wow, do you always wake up like this?" he asked.

Amelia rolled him to his back and pinned him against the pillow. "I don't know, I've never woke up with a husband before," she teased.

Chogan twirled a strand of her hair around his finger. "What do you want to do today, my love?" he asked.

Amelia wiggled her eyebrows up and down suggestively and she teased Chogan with kisses. "I'm sure I can think of something…" her words ended as she trailed kisses from Chogan's lips to his cheek.

An hour later, Amelia and Chogan ate breakfast on the balcony overlooking the ocean. Amelia had made omelets with the eggs, cheese and tomatoes that were in the fridge, while Chogan sliced fresh fruit and made toast.

Amelia leaned her head back and soaked in the sun's rays. "Chogan, what time is it?" she asked.

Chogan checked his watch. "It's only 8:30 a.m. here. I reset my watch last night when we arrived, to island time."

Amelia reached across the table and took Chogan's hand. "Do you think we could find a church to go to this morning?" she asked softly. "I'd like to start our first full day as husband and wife in God's house."

Chogan interlaced their fingers. "I found an Assembly of God church not too far from here. They start morning worship at 11:00 a.m." He watched the sunlight play off Amelia's hair, loving her. "Let's go there this morning, okay?" he asked.

Amelia stood and came around to Chogan's side of the table. She sat down on Chogan's lap and wrapped her arms around him. "That sounds wonderful. That gives me enough time to cuddle with you before I take my shower."

Chogan held her close and kissed her as he whispered. "I love you."

Amelia smiled, "I love you, too."

They arrived at the Aloha church ten minutes before morning worship. The greeters presented each of them with a sea shell lei and welcomed them to the service. The music was a mixture of southern gospel and contemporary made unique by the island drums and instruments used.

After church, Chogan and Amelia drove to Waimea Canyon and took photos of the deep colors etched from sky to the valley below. They found a little gift shop and bought T-shirts for the family. Chogan had been given directions to a secluded beach that would give them a beautiful view of the Pacific Ocean and the cliffs of Kauai. Chogan drove through a sugar cane field on a sandy path to the beach.

He parked the car and took Amelia's hand. They climbed the dune and when they reached the other side they were awestruck with the view. The beach was deep in soft sand and to the right it ended at the base of a cliff that reached high to the sky. A beautiful rainbow arched from the ocean across the top of the cliff and into the valley beyond. Amelia captured the scene with her camera.

Chogan spread the blanket he brought across the sand and captured Amelia in his arms. They sat together watching the sun set into the ocean and enjoying the tranquility of the waves slapping against the shore.

Amelia sighed deeply. "Chogan, this is the most beautiful place I have ever seen," she whispered.

Chogan pulled her closer. "I think you are right. This place is pretty spectacular."

Amelia was puzzled. "I don't understand why this beach is so deserted. It's so peaceful."

Chogan explained. “They told me that the islanders believe that when someone dies, their spirit goes into the ocean. This beach is considered sacred.”

Amelia captured the last of the sunset with her camera and stood with Chogan to return to the car. They drove to the condo and unloaded their purchases.

“What do you want to do about dinner?” Chogan asked.

“Let’s eat at the restaurant across the street; their menu looks pretty good,” Amelia suggested.

At the restaurant, they dined on the lanai by candlelight overlooking the ocean and ate shrimp and steak enjoying the local musicians that performed Christmas music in a floor show. After dinner they strolled back to the condo and walked up the path lit by tiki torches.

Amelia stopped Chogan with her hand. “Do you feel up to swimming?” she asked.

Chogan laughed. “That sounds great. The pool looked pretty inviting from our room.”

Chogan dove into the water from the side of the pool and waited while Amelia moved to the diving board. The pool had underwater lights and was warm under the evening trade winds.

Amelia lifted her arms and gracefully dove into the water and came up in front of Chogan. “Fancy meeting you here,” she teased.

Chogan laughed and pulled Amelia into his arms kissing her and then dunking her quickly in the water.

Amelia came up sputtering and giggling. They swam laps back and forth until their energy was spent.

“You love the water, don’t you?” Chogan asked.

“I have been swimming since I was a little girl,” Amelia admitted. “Swimming in December is a real treat.”

“Let’s try out the hot tub,” Chogan suggested.

Amelia smiled. “I like that idea.” She slipped into the hot tub and Chogan joined her.

The hot tub was situated in a grove of palm trees and was lit with underwater lights like the pool. Chogan and Amelia enjoyed the pulsating heat of the water as they watched the wind gently move the palm fronds above them.

"We need a pool," Chogan spoke thoughtfully.

Amelia turned to face him. "Can I make a suggestion without offending you?" Amelia asked.

"Amelia, you don't need to worry about offending me," Chogan looked troubled. "I love you and I will do my best to make you happy."

Amelia realized her mistake. "I'm sorry Chogan, I just have an idea that I hope you will like."

Chogan smiled. "Tell me your idea."

"Would you consider an indoor pool a good investment?" Amelia asked.

Chogan thought for a moment. "If you are talking about putting one in at the ranch; I think it's a wonderful idea."

Amelia laughed softly. "That's exactly what I meant. Is there room without disrupting the layout of the ranch?"

Chogan pulled her into his arms and held her close. "There's plenty of room. If we designed it right, we could attach the building to the house so we could access it without going outside during the winter months."

"How much do you think it would cost?" Amelia asked.

"I don't have any idea," Chogan admitted honestly. "We could contact a contractor and ask them."

Amelia looked deep into Chogan's eyes. "I want to do this for us."

"Amelia, you don't have to do that." Chogan reminded her.

Amelia smiled softly. "Chogan, you've not asked me how much money I received in the settlement for my injuries."

Chogan touched her face with his finger. "It doesn't matter to me, Amelia. That money is yours."

"No Chogan, that money is now ours," Amelia corrected him.

Chogan pulled her to him gently and kissed her. "When we get home," he whispered between kisses, "We'll contact a professional contractor and see about getting started in the spring when the ground thaws."

"I love you," Amelia whispered.

Chogan kissed her and then stood and pulled her out of the hot tub. "Let's head back to the room, and I'll show you just how much I love you, too."

Amelia and Chogan visited Hilo Hattie's on Kauai and bought Hawaiian dresses for the girls and Hawaiian shirts for the boys. They also found Hawaiian items for the rest of the family. They drove to the spouting horn and while they were there, two sea turtles surfaced in the water and Amelia was able to capture them with her camera.

Chogan took Amelia to a traditional luau. They sat under the lights of the tiki torches and cuddled while the entire Polynesian repertoire was re-enacted. The colors were breathtaking. Chogan bought Amelia a lei made of plumeria blossoms and placed it around her neck.

Amelia scheduled a helicopter tour and she and Chogan toured the island of Kauai from the air and captured photos of the coastline and inland areas that could not be accessed by land.

Chogan leaned up on his elbow and watched Amelia sleep early Friday morning. Today was the last full day of their honeymoon; they were flying home early Saturday morning. He smiled at the memories they shared from their week on Kauai. Chogan gently moved Amelia's hair exposing her neck. He rained kisses from her shoulder to her cheek and smiled when she slipped her hand up to his neck and pulled his lips to hers.

"Good morning to you too," Amelia whispered.

"We are taking the catamaran tour today," Chogan reminded her.

Amelia stretched slowly, "I'm looking forward to it."

They showered and changed and took their beach bag to the car. Chogan drove to the dock and they were on the water by the time the sun came up. A school of dolphins chased the catamaran and entertained them. Chogan and Amelia sat on the deck of the boat enjoying the view and the spray of the water.

The catamaran sailed slowly along Hanalei Bay. They sailed along the coastline and back spotting sea turtles, whales and dolphins through-out the day. The tour ended back at the dock and Chogan bought Amelia a Christmas ornament for their tree in Colorado from the gift shop.

Chogan and Amelia wanted to spend their last night in Hawaii relaxing. They picked up a pizza and some bottled cokes and headed back to their room. They ate their pizza on the balcony and sipped their cokes.

"Can we take one last swim?" Amelia asked.

Chogan grinned. "Let's go."

Amelia dived into the water while Chogan watched. He swam over to her and pulled her into his arms. "I love to watch you in the water. Promise me that you will teach Lovella and Topanga to be as comfortable in the water as you are."

Amelia grinned, "Our daughters will be natural born swimmers when I'm done with them."

Chogan and Amelia swam laps and then sat in the hot tub under the stars. They walked hand-in-hand along the path back to their room one last time.

Chogan held Amelia in his arms, savoring their last night in Hawaii. "This week has been amazing," he whispered.

Amelia snuggled closer. "I am so grateful for this week. You are an amazing husband." Amelia leaned up on her elbow so she could look into Chogan's face. "Thank you for making this week so special. I love being married to you."

Chogan kissed her, "I love being married to you, too. The girls will be so glad to see you tomorrow," he assured her.

Amelia laughed softly, "We are going home on Christmas Eve," she whispered. "Did you give any thought to my gift idea?" Amelia asked.

Chogan rolled his eyes and then laughed softly. "I called dad and he found exactly what you wanted. He and mom will deliver your special surprise tomorrow night so you can surprise the girls Christmas morning."

"Thank you Chogan. Lovella told Hilary what she wanted for Christmas and I had to get it for her," Amelia explained.

"What did Topanga want?" Chogan asked.

Amelia's smile turned wistful and she answered. "Topanga told me that she asked Jesus for a new mama for Christmas." Amelia's eyes turned glassy with tears, "She told me I was her Christmas gift."

Chogan kissed her and held her close. "You're my Christmas gift, too."

Amelia kissed Chogan gently, "You are the best gift I could ever hope for. If I haven't said it this week; I'm very happy and so in love with you."

Chapter Twenty-Eight

Amelia and Chogan flew from Kauai to Denver, Colorado on Christmas Eve. Amelia shivered at the change in temperature. Dakota picked them up at the airport and drove them to the ranch.

"So how was Hawaii?" Dakota asked.

"Beautiful," Amelia answered. "Thank you for helping me with the girls' Christmas gift."

Dakota laughed as Chogan rolled his eyes. "You are most welcome, Amelia. Although from Chogan's expression, I don't think he's as thrilled as Topanga and Lovella will be."

Amelia squeezed Chogan's hand. "You don't mind do you?" she asked.

Chogan laughed. "Amelia, if this gift makes you and the girls happy; I don't mind at all."

They arrived at the ranch and left their luggage in the vehicle until after they greeted the girls. Dakota opened the front door and Chogan scooped Amelia up in his arms and carried her across the threshold.

"Welcome home, Amelia my love; welcome home," Chogan whispered as he kissed her slowly and then placed her gently on her feet.

"Daddy!" Topanga ran from the living room with Lovella close behind.

Chogan knelt and captured both girls in his arms holding them close. "Topanga, Lovella, look who's here."

Topanga and Lovella turned and squealed out loud, "Mia!" they reached Amelia as she knelt down and they were captured in her hugs. "You're here, you're finally here," Topanga whispered.

"You stay this time, forever," Lovella instructed.

Amelia hugged them both as she spoke, "Forever and ever, amen!"

Uda stood in the doorway watching, "Girls, there are homemade cookies in the kitchen," she whispered.

Lovella and Topanga ran for the cookies and Chogan helped Amelia to her feet.

Amelia hugged Uda, “Welcome home, my new daughter,” Uda spoke softly as she held Amelia close.

“It’s wonderful to be home,” Amelia agreed. The house is beautiful, I love the decorations.

Chogan wrapped Amelia in his arms, “Our daughters couldn’t wait for us to get back from Hawaii; you’re not offended are you?” he asked.

Amelia laughed, “I think it’s wonderful!”

Dakota spoke from the hallway, “Amelia, why don’t you and Uda join the girls in the kitchen while Chogan and I bring in the luggage?”

Amelia hugged Dakota, “That sounds great, thank you both for everything you’ve done to make me part of this family.”

Dakota laughed, “No thanks necessary, we are happy to have our new daughter home at last.”

Chogan and Amelia tucked the girls into bed shortly after Dakota and Uda left for home.

“I don’t want to go to bed, Mia,” Lovella whimpered. “I wanna stay up with you and daddy.”

Amelia smiled as she tucked the blanket around Lovella’s body. “The sooner you go to sleep, the sooner it will be Christmas morning,” she whispered.

Lovella’s eyes grew wide with excitement. “Santa comes tonight. I’ll be good.” She sat up and hugged Amelia close. “Love you Mia,” she whispered.

“I love you too, Lovella,” Amelia whispered.

Topanga was waiting on the side of her bed for Amelia to tuck her in. “Mia, you aren’t going to leave are you?” Topanga asked softly.

Amelia pulled Topanga into her lap and hugged her close. “Topanga, your daddy and I are now married. I’m not leaving you, I’m here to be your new mama, if you’ll let me,” Amelia explained.

Topanga hugged her close. “I’m glad you’re here. I love you, Mia.”

Amelia hugged Topanga and whispered, “I love you too, Topanga. I ask for two beautiful daughters for Christmas, guess what I got?”

Topanga giggled and crawled into her bed.

Amelia kissed Topanga goodnight and tucked the blankets around her.

Chogan was standing in the doorway watching. "It never ceases to amaze me how natural you are as a mother," he told Amelia.

Amelia walked out of the room and took Chogan by the hand. She led him to the couch in the living room and waited while he sat. Amelia sat down in Chogan's lap and wrapped her arms around him. "I love being a wife and mother, this is what was missing in my life, Chogan."

Chogan kissed her and sighed. "I feel like I'm dreaming," he whispered.

Amelia stroked his face with her hand, "Why?" she asked.

"Because you're my wife, in my home, wrapped in my arms; and my loneliness is gone," Chogan spoke softly. He pulled Amelia's hair back and kissed her neck slowly.

Amelia's senses tingled at his touch. She arched her neck and while Chogan teased her with feather kisses, she placed kisses along his cheek and neck.

Chogan groaned deep in his throat, "Amelia," he whispered her name.

Amelia stood and pulled Chogan by the hand. She peeked into the girls' rooms to make sure they were sleeping and led Chogan to the master bedroom. She closed the door behind them as she spoke softly, "Merry Christmas Chogan."

Chogan was sound asleep two hours later.

Amelia kissed him softly and slid gently out of the bed so she wouldn't disturb him. She filled Lovella, Topanga, and Chogan's stockings and hung them back on the fireplace mantle. Amelia slipped into the room behind the kitchen and checked on her Christmas gift for the girls. She slipped her presents under the tree that she had packed in a special suitcase and sent home with Uda and Dakota from Florida. Amelia slipped back into the bedroom an hour later and eased into the bed.

"Are you finished for the night, Mrs. Clause?" Chogan asked.

Amelia giggled. "Yes Mr. Clause. Did you miss me?" she asked.

Chogan pulled her close and spooned her into his body. “I can’t tell you how many nights I tossed and turned in this bed, wishing you were here as my wife.” Chogan’s voice was low and husky.

Amelia turned to face Chogan and whispered, “I’m here now, and I’m very happy to be your wife. I love you.” She kissed him slowly and deeply.

Chogan woke at 6:00 a.m. and reached for Amelia. Finding her gone from the bed, he slipped on a housecoat and slippers and went in search of her.

Amelia was in the kitchen. Her hair was pulled up and clipped in a banana clip. She was wearing fuzzy socks, and flannel pajamas with snowflakes all over them. Her cheeks were flushed from baking and she had a streak of cinnamon and sugar across her chin.

Chogan walked up behind Amelia and wrapped his arms around her. “Merry Christmas, Amelia,” he whispered.

“Mmmm, Merry Christmas to you too,” Amelia giggled.

“I was lonely; I woke up and you were gone,” Chogan teased.

Amelia turned in his arms, “I had to bake my traditional cinnamon buns for Christmas morning. I thought my family would enjoy them.”

Chogan kissed the cinnamon from Amelia’s chin and smiled. “That’s almost as sweet as you.”

Amelia’s eyes dilated and she kissed Chogan seductively. “You are a distraction in the kitchen, my love.”

Chogan laughed. “What can I do to help?” he asked.

“If you’ll make a pot of coffee, I’ll make a hot pot of tea,” Amelia offered.

They were still in the kitchen when Topanga and Lovella found them. “Santa came,” Lovella spoke in wonder.

Topanga ran to Amelia and threw her arms around her waist. “Mia, you’re here.”

Amelia picked Topanga up and sat her on the stool next to the counter. She touched her forehead to Topanga’s and whispered, “I told you, I’m here to stay.”

Topanga giggled, “What smells good?” she asked.

Lovella had crawled up into Chogan's lap across the counter from Topanga and watched in wonder while Amelia pulled out two large cookie sheets with homemade cinnamon sticky buns on them.

Amelia pulled a bowl of icing from the counter and stirred it one last time. She moved the sticky buns to large platters and then handed Chogan a spatula. Amelia sat the bowl of icing in the center of the counter and picked up a spatula for herself. "This is our new tradition, every Christmas morning we make sticky buns and everyone helps with icing," she explained.

Chogan handed the spatula to Lovella and he wrapped his hand around hers and helped her dip the spatula in icing and apply it to the hot buns.

Amelia gave the spatula to Topanga and helped her with icing the other platter of buns.

Thirty minutes later, the buns were iced and the girls were giggling with Chogan and Amelia.

Dakota and Uda arrived and walked into the house. "Merry Christmas! Anyone home?" Dakota called out.

"We're in here," Chogan yelled from the kitchen.

Uda laughed out loud when she entered the room. Topanga and Lovella had as much icing on their faces and hands as the sticky buns had on them. Chogan and Amelia were also wearing icing on their faces.

Dakota walked over, poured himself a cup of coffee and snagged a sticky bun biting into it and getting icing across his upper lip. "Wow, these are amazing," he offered.

"Papaw, you've got icing on your lip!" Topanga teased.

Dakota exaggerated licking the icing off his lip and the girls each took a sticky bun and tried to mimic his icing mustache.

Amelia and Chogan washed their hands in the sink and watched their daughters with Dakota.

"Let's get changed while the girls are being entertained," Chogan suggested.

Amelia agreed. They slipped into the bedroom and Chogan pulled on blue jeans and a sweatshirt that Amelia had bought him in Hawaii. Amelia pulled on her blue jeans and a pink sweatshirt from Hawaii. They returned to the kitchen as Uda was wiping the girls' mouths and hands with a wet wipe.

"Who's ready for Christmas?" Chogan asked.

"Me, me, me," Topanga and Lovella answered together.

Amelia took down their stockings and gave them out. Topanga and Lovella's stockings had bows, ribbons, fuzzy socks, candy, and small toys. Chogan's stocking held aftershave, cologne, razors, socks, and candy.

Chogan had filled Amelia's stocking and she opened it to find ribbons for her hair, fuzzy socks, cologne and warm gloves.

Amber was sitting beside Chogan and Amelia took down the last stocking and sat beside the collie. She pulled items out of the stocking one at a time and Amber barked between each one.

Chogan sat mesmerized at Amelia's ability to fit so well into the family. Amber hadn't barked or showed emotion since Samantha had died. Now she was acting like a puppy again. Amelia had purchased dog toys, chew bones, and a new brush for Amber's stocking.

Amelia and Chogan took turns giving out the gifts under the tree. Amelia captured photos of their first Christmas with her camera. Dakota picked it up several times and captured Amelia with Chogan and the girls.

Amelia handed her gift to Chogan. "Merry Christmas, my love," she whispered.

Chogan removed the wrapping from the box and pulled out a beautiful ring of Australian opals and diamonds. He slipped it on his right hand, "Amelia, this is beautiful," he exclaimed.

Amelia smiled and kissed him softly. "I found a unique ring to match the wonderful unique man that God blessed me with."

Chogan handed her a box from under the tree, "Merry Christmas sweetheart."

Amelia lifted the lid and took out a photograph. "Is this what I think it is?" she asked excitedly.

"She wouldn't fit in the box," Chogan laughed. Chogan bought Amelia a horse of her own. The mare was deep dark brown with a black mane and tail. "I'll introduce you this afternoon."

Amelia threw her arms around Chogan and kissed him. "Thank you so much!"

Amelia gave her gift to Uda, "Merry Christmas Uda."

Uda removed the ribbon and wrapping paper and lifted the tissue paper. Inside the box was a beautiful embroidered tablecloth with matching napkins. Uda lifted the linen material and gently touched the wildflowers and butterflies that were stitched on each. "This is lovely, Amelia. Who did this embroidery?" she asked.

Amelia blushed, "I did. I wanted you to have something personal from me, as your new daughter-in-law."

Uda sat the box aside and hugged Amelia gently. "I think I've gained another daughter, sweet Amelia. Thank you for the beautiful gift."

Dakota opened his gift from Amelia and smiled. "These are beautiful, Amelia." His box contained a set of ivory inlaid carving knives for woodworking and design.

Topanga and Lovella had opened clothes and toys and were watching the adults open their gifts.

Amelia winked at Chogan, "Topanga, Lovella, I think Santa left one more gift for each of you."

Chogan walked out of the room and returned with two boxes with large bows on top.

Topanga and Lovella sat very still until Chogan sat the boxes in front of them.

Amelia captured the photos with her camera as they lifted the lids simultaneously and squealed as they found their kittens. Topanga's kitten was solid black and Lovella's kitten was solid white.

Amber investigated the boxes and received hisses and slaps from the tiny kittens. She barked at them wagging her tail in joy.

Chogan pulled Amelia into his lap and whispered in her ear. "You have created a monster my love."

Amelia laughed out loud. “I think its chaos, but it’s so worth it. Thank you Chogan for letting me do this.”

“You don’t need to thank me, Amelia; your happiness means the world to me.” Chogan held Amelia in his lap and savored the joy of a wife to have and to hold.”

Chapter Twenty-Nine

Christmas dinner was served at 1:00 p.m. and Amelia loved meeting Onawa and Talise, Chogan's twin sisters. After everyone left at 7:00 p.m.; Chogan and Amelia turned on the TV and watched Christmas movies with Lovella and Topanga. Lovella fell asleep on Chogan's lap with her kitten curled up on her neck in her hair. Topanga was asleep in Amelia's lap with her kitten asleep on her tummy.

Chogan eased off the couch and tucked Lovella into bed with her kitten. Amelia had moved Topanga to her bed and placed the kitten beside her to sleep. Amber followed Amelia as she moved from Topanga's room back to the couch. Chogan stretched out on the sofa and Amelia joined him pulling a blanket from the back of the couch to cover them as they finished watching their movie. Amber stretched out on the floor in front of the couch and Amelia stroked her fur until the dog was snoring quietly.

Chogan removed the clip from Amelia's hair and twirled the strands in his fingers. He pulled it gently away from Amelia's neck and kissed her neck, her cheek and wrapped his arms around her from behind. He whispered in her ear. "This has been a wonderful Christmas, Amelia. I love you so much."

Amelia rolled over and faced Chogan. "I think this has been a pretty special Christmas too. I am so grateful for God's direction in bringing us together. You are the best gift I have ever received. I love you."

Chogan stroked her face and kissed the tip of her nose. "Are you happy, Amelia?"

Amelia slid her hand into Chogan's hair and caressed his neck with her fingers. "I'm beyond happy, Chogan." She leaned up and kissed Chogan slowly, sharing how she felt without words. Amelia sighed and cuddled against Chogan's chest until she fell asleep.

Chogan watched the Christmas tree lights reflect off of Amelia's hair and he held her gently while she slept. "Thank you, Lord for this beautiful Godly woman who is kind, compassionate and loving. Bless our home with love and laughter," he whispered.

Chogan eased himself from the couch and turned down the bed. He returned to the living room and gently lifted Amelia into his arms.

Amelia opened her eyes, "Chogan, I'm sorry I must have fallen asleep," she whispered.

"Shhhh, lay still," Chogan whispered as he carried her to the bedroom. Chogan laid her on the bed and smiled as Amber curled up on the rug beside Amelia's side of the bed. Chogan crawled under the covers and pulled Amelia into his arms cradling her warm body against his own. "Sleep tight my love," he whispered.

Amelia and Chogan took the girls and attended the New Years Eve celebration at the church. Patricia and Geoff joined them at their table in the fellowship hall for the dinner.

"Amelia, I'm so glad you're married to Chogan," Patricia teased. "Now I have a wonderful husband and my best friend close by. God is good all the time!"

Geoff laughed. "I'm glad you're married to Chogan, too. Now my wife is very happy and if Patricia's happy, I'm happy," he teased.

Patricia kissed him gently. "I hope you're happy, you've made me very happy."

"How is your job going?" Amelia asked.

Patricia grinned, "I love it. Fourth graders are the same no matter where you are. What about you, Amelia, are you going to teach?"

Amelia squeezed Chogan's hand. "I think for now, I'm going to focus on caring for my family. I want to spend time with the girls before they start school."

They spent the evening catching up on news from home. At midnight, pastor prayed and all the children opened bubbles and celebrated the New Year giggling and laughing.

Topanga and Lovella fell asleep in the truck on the way home. Chogan and Amelia carried them to their rooms and put them in bed. The kittens were not in the girls' rooms and Amelia was very concerned. She started to panic until she walked in the living room. Amber was asleep on the rug in front of the fireplace. The two kittens were curled up in Amber's fur and sleeping soundly.

"Looks like the enemies have made friends for the new year," Chogan whispered as he spied the animals.

Amelia laughed softly. She slipped into her gown and crawled under the covers. "Chogan, are you ok with me not working?" she asked.

Chogan smiled, "Amelia, you can stay with the girls, or you can work. I want you to be happy."

Amelia smiled. "I never thought I'd be happy being a stay-at-home mom, but I have to admit; I love it."

Chogan spoke softly, "I love the idea of you being here when I get home every day."

Winter was long and cold but Amelia found plenty to keep her busy. She was working with Topanga and teaching her to read. Lovella was learning her numbers and the alphabet. Each night the girls were in the kitchen watching Amelia cook when Chogan arrived home.

March blew in cold and harsh. Uda and Amelia had been planning a special dinner for Chogan's twenty-eighth birthday.

Lovella and Topanga had made birthday cards for their daddy using construction paper, glitter and glue. Amelia had allowed the girls to help decorate the homemade birthday cake for their daddy also.

Uda prepared a glazed ham and Chogan's sisters each brought a casserole. Geoff and Patricia were bringing a veggie tray and Amelia made homemade yeast rolls and beef roast.

When Chogan walked through the door he was greeted with a very loud "SURPRISE!"

Amber barked and wagged her tail wildly while Lovella and Topanga rushed to hug their daddy.

After dinner Chogan was presented with his birthday gifts. Topanga and Lovella waited impatiently while Chogan read their cards. "These are the prettiest cards I've ever seen," Chogan praised.

"I did it all by myself," Topanga bragged. "Mia said I did good."

Lovella was not to be outdone. "I wrote mine too daddy, Mia showed me how and I did it," she proclaimed.

"I am so proud of both of you," Chogan whispered as he hugged them to him.

Dakota carried in a large box and sat it before Chogan. "Son, this gift is from your mother and me, happy birthday."

Chogan lifted the lid and gasped audibly. "Dad, did you do this?" Chogan asked.

Uda wrapped her arms around Dakota. "Your father is a man of many talents, Chogan," she said.

Chogan pulled out a saddle that was hand-made. The leather had been weaved to form Chogan's name and the image of a black bird in flight. Chogan stroked the leather lovingly and stood to hug his father. "Dad, I don't know what to say, it's beautiful."

Talise handed Chogan another box. "Big brother, this gift is from Onawa and me," she spoke with quiet pride.

Chogan lifted the lid and smiled. "Mom, you should be proud. My sisters have mastered your weaving ability." Chogan carefully opened the saddle blanket displaying the beautiful Native American design.

Amelia touched the blanket and ran her fingers along the pattern. "This is so beautiful. Can you teach me to do this?" she asked.

Onawa hugged Amelia, "We would love to teach you," she promised.

"Open Mia's next," Topanga was barely able to contain the secret. "Please daddy, open Mia's present."

Chogan grinned at Amelia and pulled the ribbon slowly from the box. He lifted a smaller box and pulled the ribbon. Chogan laughed as he lifted yet another box from inside. By the time he reached the actual center, he had opened seven nested boxes. The final box held a piece of paper with Amelia's handwriting. The note simply said, "Happy Birthday my love, your gift is in the bedroom."

Amelia's eyes were twinkling with mischief as everyone watched Chogan walk slowly to the bedroom. She winked at Uda as Chogan let out a slow whistle.

Chogan returned to the living room carrying a beautiful guitar. The body of the guitar was ebony black and the edge of the face had a thin band of mother-of-pearl. The guitar had been autographed by Randy Travis, Chogan's favorite country singer. "How did you know?" he asked Amelia.

"Your mother told me how you have always loved Randy Travis' music. That's why we had Forever and Ever Amen as our wedding song. She also told me that you are a really good musician, so would you favor us with a song?" she asked.

Chogan took a deep breath. "I haven't played since…" his voice trailed off as his eyes turned glassy. "Let's see if I can still play this," he added. Chogan sat on the edge of the couch and gently ran his fingers across the strings. He felt the music deep in his soul. Chogan closed his eyes and began to pick out the song that had played at their wedding. When he finished the room erupted in applause.

Amelia felt the tears roll down her cheeks. "That was amazing," she whispered as she clapped.

Chogan grinned and passed the guitar to Geoff, "Let's see if you can still play, my friend." Chogan walked over to Amelia and hugged her. He whispered in her ear, "Thank you Amelia, I love it."

Amelia moved to the kitchen to serve the cake and ice cream; Patricia followed her.

"Amelia, this was a wonderful party," she commented.

Amelia grinned. "I couldn't have done it without everyone helping. So how are you? You look tired," she worried.

Patricia touched Amelia's arm. "Amelia, I'm pregnant," she whispered.

Amelia hugged her. "I'm so happy for you." Amelia pulled back and looked into Patricia's face. "What's wrong? Is Geoff not happy?" she asked in concern.

Patricia lowered her voice in case anyone could hear. "I haven't told him yet, I'm afraid."

Amelia was stunned. "Afraid of what?" she asked.

Patricia took a deep breath. "What if he isn't ready for children? We didn't really discuss when we would start a family and I'm so emotional right now I don't know what to do." Her eyes filled with tears as she spoke.

Amelia laughed softly and pulled her friend into her arms. "Patricia, Geoff will be ecstatic that you are pregnant. He loves you my friend, he will love this baby that you created together, tell him," she encouraged.

Patricia laughed and wiped the tears from her eyes. "Whew, I hope this is just hormones and not the real me coming out," she teased.

"Patricia, are you sick?" Geoff had come into the kitchen for a coke and saw Patricia crying.

Amelia whispered, "That's my cue," as she excused herself from the kitchen.

Geoff walked over to Patricia and lifted her chin. "Honey, what's wrong?" the concern was evident in his voice.

Patricia looked up into Geoff's eyes and spoke softly. "I need to tell you something and I'm afraid," she confessed.

Geoff was shocked. "Patricia I'm your husband, I love you. You never need to be afraid to tell me anything. What's wrong?" he asked, his voice filled with worry.

Patricia looked up into Geoff's eyes and tears began to fall. "I'm pregnant, Geoff. We're going to have a baby," she whispered softly.

Geoff let out a loud yell and wrapped his arms around Patricia lifting her feet of the floor he spun around with her.

Patricia spoke firmly, "Geoff , unless you want me to toss my cookies, please don't spin me around."

Geoff stopped abruptly and sat Patricia gently down. He placed his hands on either side of her face and pulled her close, kissing her softly. "Why would you be afraid to tell me this?" he asked confused.

Patricia looked up into his eyes. "We never talked about when we wanted to start a family. I was afraid you would be angry with me."

Geoff kissed her again and again, the smile on his face showing his true feelings. "I love you Patricia, you've made me happier than I've ever been in my life. This baby is a product of our love and a wonderful gift from God."

Patricia laughed and kissed Geoff. "So should we tell the others?" she asked.

Geoff laughed. "Oh yeah, we need to share this news," he teased.

Geoff took Patricia by the hand and walked into the living room. "Friends, we have an announcement," Geoff's voice stopped all conversation as all eyes turned to him and Patricia.

Geoff hugged Patricia close. "My beautiful wife has just informed me, we are going to have a baby."

The room erupted in applause again. Everyone congratulated Patricia and Geoff and Amelia watched her friend's emotions move from fear to blissful joy.

Chogan walked over to Amelia and hugged her. "Geoff's life will never be the same," he whispered.

Amelia agreed.

Chapter Thirty

Spring thaw meant the start of construction at the ranch. Amelia was overseeing the construction of their indoor pool and hot tub and preparing for Topanga's fifth birthday in May.

The pool was completed by the last weekend in April, and Topanga's birthday party was scheduled for Mother's day weekend. Amelia had invited the children from Topanga's Sunday school class and expected a total of ten children for the party.

Amelia had decorated the pool house with a theme of the mermaids and had planned the party to the smallest detail. The children swam for over an hour and played games with prizes for every winner. The piñata shaped like a dolphin kept the children busy with Dakota and Chogan while Amelia and Uda prepared the cake and ice-cream.

Topanga opened her gifts and laughed and played until every last friend said goodbye.

Amelia was cleaning up the kitchen when she felt a hug from behind. She turned to see Topanga standing with her arms raised. Amelia dried her hands and lifted Topanga into her arms. "Happy birthday my darling daughter," Amelia whispered.

"Thank you mama," Topanga whispered as she hugged Amelia close.

Amelia's eyes filled with tears of joy. She hugged Topanga close. "You are welcome, honey. Daddy and I have a special birthday gift for you," she whispered.

Topanga pulled back and looked into Amelia's eyes. "Another present for me?" she asked.

Amelia kissed Topanga's forehead and whispered, "Go see if daddy is ready to give you the special gift we bought for you," she prompted.

Topanga slipped out of her arms and ran outside in search of Chogan.

Chogan held Lovella as Topanga pulled him into the house. "Topanga seems to think there is another birthday gift from us," Chogan teased.

Amelia lifted Topanga to the stool and pulled a box wrapped in mermaid paper with a large iridescent teal bow from under the counter. "Happy Birthday, Topanga."

Topanga pulled the bow off the box and lifted the lid. She lifted the card from inside the box and her eyes widened in surprise.

Lovella couldn't stand the suspense, "Sissy, what is it?" she asked impatiently.

Topanga read the words on the card, "Let's celebrate your birthday at Disneyworld," she read. Topanga looked at her daddy, "Are we going to Disneyworld?" she asked.

Chogan laughed and swung Topanga in a circle, "Yes ma'am. Your mama and I are taking you girls to Disneyworld and because you're five we are staying in Cinderella's castle."

Topanga hugged Chogan tight and then ran for Amelia. "Mama, you are the best!" she yelled.

The girls carried Topanga's gifts to her room and Chogan watched as their kittens, now half grown hid and attacked them each time they passed by. They giggled and played with the kittens while Amelia wiped down the counter tops and restored the kitchen to order.

Amelia tucked the girls into bed and helped Topanga mark the calendar for their trip to Florida, in July. She joined Chogan on the porch swing and cuddled into his arms.

Chogan kissed the top of her head and pulled her closer. "Thank you, Amelia."

Amelia smiled in the darkness. "You're welcome, but what are you thanking me for?" she asked.

Chogan's voice was filled with emotion. "For being a mother to our daughters," he spoke huskily.

Amelia sat up and turned in the swing to face Chogan, "Topanga called me mama today," she whispered.

Chogan stroked her cheek. "I heard that too," he whispered. "Tomorrow is Mother's Day and I can't imagine anyone who's earned the title, more than you."

Amelia kissed him, "You made me their mother, Chogan, thank you for making my life complete."

June rolled in and the meadows were filled with wildflowers. Amelia didn't feel well but didn't want to worry Chogan. She had lost weight and she was tired often.

The phone rang in the middle of the night and Amelia snatched it up, "Hello?"

"Amelia, it's a girl," Myron spoke quickly and excitedly.

"Myron, congratulations, how is Anne?" Amelia asked.

"She's great, sis. The baby is healthy and beautiful," Myron's voice broke with emotion.

"What's her name?" Amelia asked, smiling at Myron's reaction.

"We named her Hannah; Amelia when are you coming home for a visit?" Myron asked.

Amelia smiled in the darkness. "We're coming the first week in July, Myron. We're taking the girls to Disney and I can't wait to see you and the kids."

They talked for several minutes before Myron had to disconnect. "I love you, Myron. Give my love to Anne," Amelia spoke softly. She hung the phone up and laid back down in the bed.

Chogan pulled her gently into his arms. "Congratulations Aunt Mia," he said softly.

Amelia cuddled against Chogan. "Another girl, poor Henry," she giggled.

"Poor Henry?" Chogan asked confused.

Amelia explained, "Henry said that with our two girls, the boys were outnumbered. He wanted a boy."

Chogan laughed softly. "I'm looking forward to our trip, I like spending time with your family."

Amelia didn't respond. She was sound asleep in Chogan's arms.

Chogan kissed her softly and pulled her closer in his arms. She had lost weight and he was worried. She looked tired and had fallen asleep as soon as her head hit the pillow each night. "Please God, protect Amelia, strengthen her body," Chogan prayed. Tears fell from his eyes as he thought of how lost he would be without her.

Amelia prepared for their trip to Florida and had to struggle to find the energy to pack.

Patricia had finished the school year and was enjoying her pregnancy. She sat on the edge of Amelia's bed watching her friend pack the suitcase. "Amelia, what's wrong with you?" she asked.

Amelia looked up in surprise, "Nothing, I'm fine. Why do you ask?"

"I've known you my entire life. You're always full of energy and lately you look exhausted. How much weight have you lost?" Patricia asked growing concerned.

Amelia sat down beside Patricia. "I weighed myself this morning. I've lost ten pounds since Mother's day and I don't know why. I eat all the time and all I want to do is sleep," she offered.

Patricia looked at Amelia and smiled. "Amelia, are you pregnant?" she asked.

Amelia looked up in surprise, "I couldn't be," she spoke softly.

Patricia grinned, "You have no energy, you're eating more than usual, you want to sleep," do you see a pattern here?

Amelia's eyes misted over. "Wouldn't that be wonderful," she whispered.

Patricia stood, "Where are the girls?" she asked.

"They are spending the night with Uda and Dakota, tonight," Amelia explained.

"Come on," Patricia offered Amelia a hand up.

"Where are we going?" Amelia asked.

Patricia grinned. "I'm taking you to see my doctor."

"I don't have an appointment," Amelia said.

"You don't need one, they have walk-in appointments for this," Patricia explained.

Amelia was cooking dinner when Chogan arrived home. He walked into the kitchen and gently hugged her from behind. Amelia was dangerously thin and Chogan knew he wasn't imagining it. "Hello my love," Chogan spoke into her ear.

"Hello to you too," Amelia smiled as she spoke. "Could you set the table?" she asked.

Chogan moved the plates and silverware to the table and filled their glasses with iced tea. He tried to find a way to broach the subject of Amelia having a check-up. His concern for her health was growing each day as she looked pale and continued to lose weight.

Amelia sat the food on the table and sat quietly while Chogan said grace.

Chogan filled his plate and watched Amelia push the food around with her fork. He couldn't wait any longer. "Amelia, I need to ask you to do something for me," he spoke softly.

Amelia looked up and smiled, "What do you need?" she asked.

Chogan pulled his chair closer to hers and took her hands in his. "I want you to see a doctor. I'm worried about you, you've lost a lot of weight and you're pale and tired all the time."

Amelia leaned forward and kissed Chogan softly. "I love you," she whispered.

Chogan's heart filled with fear, "What's wrong, you're sick aren't you, tell me Amelia, I'll find the best doctors, what's wrong?" the pain on his face was Amelia's undoing.

Tears fell from her eyes and she covered his lips with her fingers. "Shhhh, Chogan it's not what you think. I went to the doctor today," she began.

Chogan sat very still. His worst nightmare was that Amelia was very sick, he couldn't lose her.

Amelia stood and moved to Chogan's lap. She waited until his arms were wrapped securely around her and she lifted his face so she could look directly into his eyes. "I've lost ten pounds since mother's day and I've been exhausted and had no energy." Amelia took a deep breath. "Patricia took me to the doctor today. Chogan, we're going to have a baby." Amelia watched his face for a reaction.

Chogan stared into her eyes. A baby, Amelia was going to have a baby. That explained the tiredness and the weight loss could be explained by her constant activity and the new life growing inside her. His thoughts were racing through his head as the realization sank in. Chogan moved his hand to Amelia's abdomen. "A baby?" he whispered.

Amelia nodded slowly, "Are you happy?" she ask, the worry evident in her eyes.

Chogan kissed her softly and leaned his forehead against hers. "A baby," he sighed. "I was so worried, I thought you were…" He choked back the tears.

Amelia kissed him and smiled. "Chogan, I'm fine. The doctor said I'm anemic and that's why I'm tired and losing weight. She gave me prenatal vitamins and told me I had to eat more."

Chogan looked at her and stroked her face. "When?" He asked.

"When what?" Amelia was confused.

Chogan laughed, "We've had this conversation before. When is our baby arriving?"

Amelia laughed softly, "We can expect our baby in January," she responded.

Chogan hugged her close, "I am so glad you're okay, I was worried sick about you."

Amelia pulled his hand back over her abdomen. "I'm very happy about this baby, Chogan. I want you to be happy too."

Chogan kissed her and lingered until she was clinging to him. "I'm thrilled that we are having a baby. That's the greatest gift you could ever give me. Maybe we'll have a boy, for Henry," he teased.

Amelia laughed.

Amelia started feeling stronger within a week of starting her prenatal vitamins. Her energy was starting to match her appetite. They arrived in Florida and drove straight to Reggie and Cecilia's house.

Myron and Anne were at the house with the baby. The children swam in the pool while the men kept an eye on them. Amelia, Anne and Cecilia were in the sun room enjoying the new baby.

Cecilia went to the kitchen to start preparing lunch and Anne whispered to Amelia, "When are you due, Amelia?"

Amelia was stunned, "Is it that obvious?" she asked.

Anne grinned, "I just gave birth to my fourth baby, I know a pregnant woman when I see one."

Amelia squeezed her hand. "We're going to tell everyone at lunch."

Cecilia called everyone to the table for lunch. Everyone bowed their heads while Reggie prayed. "Thank you, Lord, for this food and for reuniting our family around this table. I asked you to bless the food to the nourishment of our bodies and bless our bodies to your service. Amen."

Everyone filled their plates and Chogan lifted his glass of iced tea. "I'd like to propose a toast," he raised his glass and continued. "To Anne and Myron, congratulations on your beautiful new daughter, Hannah; may she fill your lives with love and laughter. To Reggie and Cecilia, thank you for blessing my life with your beautiful daughter; may the child she carries, fill our lives with love and laughter also."

The room was silent for just a few seconds before Myron, Reggie and Cecilia rushed to hug Amelia.

Henry waited until everyone sat down; he stood solemnly and lifted his glass of tea. "To Aunt Mia, I pray your baby is a boy!" he rolled his eyes as everyone laughed.

The week with family and at Disney invigorated Amelia and bronzed her skin.

Lovella turned three while they were at Disney and Amelia set up a birthday party at the Magic Kingdom with all the Disney princesses. Lovella was thrilled with her party and that she had Hilary, Harmon, and Henry there in addition to her sister Topanga.

Amelia was content and happy as they flew home to Colorado.

Chogan tucked the girls into bed. They were exhausted from their trip and didn't argue when bedtime came. The kittens curled up with the girls, happy to be reunited.

Chogan laughed softly as he watched Amber follow Amelia into the bedroom, tail wagging. He walked into the bedroom and smiled as Amber sat in front of Amelia with her head in Amelia's lap. Amelia spoke softly and stroked Amber's fur giving her the much needed affection she craved. Amber laid down on her rug content that her mistress was home.

Amelia moved to the bathroom and changed into her gown. She let her hair down and stood in the doorway brushing it over her shoulder. "I think my hair has grown an inch since I started these vitamins," Amelia teased.

Chogan walked over to where Amelia stood and took the brush from her hands and placed it on the dresser. He ran his hands through her hair and smiled. “I love your hair; the way it feels across my skin is like satin. You are beautiful, Amelia.”

Amelia stood on her tiptoes and kissed him gently. “You make me feel beautiful, even with this scar. Do you realize what today is?” she asked.

Chogan looked confused. “I don’t think so, what am I missing?” he asked.

Amelia smiled and led him to the bed; she pushed him gently until he was sitting in front of her. “One year ago today, I walked into the Butterhorn Bakery and saw a gorgeous fireman sitting across the restaurant from me with haunting blue eyes.” Amelia’s smile was wistful as she placed her hands on her abdomen. “Just two months later that same man came to Florida and woke me with a gentle kiss. He looked at my bruised and broken body with love in his eyes.” Tears fell slowly as Amelia continued. “He offered me his heart and shared his life with me. I will forever be grateful for this day,” she spoke softly.

Chogan’s eyes were glassy with unshed tears. He leaned forward and kissed Amelia’s abdomen gently through the satin of her gown. “I had no idea that day we met that you would fill my life with so much joy.” Chogan pulled her into his lap and kissed her caressing her abdomen with his hand. “I love you, Amelia.”

School started the Tuesday after Labor Day and Amelia drove Topanga to kindergarten with a bittersweet heart. “Do you want me to stay with you today?” Amelia asked.

Topanga hugged her tight. “No mama, I’m fine. You and Lovella have a good day and I’ll see you after school.”

Amelia watched her little girl settle into the classroom and smiled as two of the children from her Sunday school class joined her.

Chapter Thirty-One

Patricia had taken a semester off of school to have the baby. Geoff was protective as a mother hen and Patricia was growing stir crazy just sitting in the house. She called Amelia. “I need a friend,” Patricia stated when Amelia answered the phone.

Amelia laughed softly. “I can come now if you like; Lovella is spending the day with Uda.”

Patricia shifted her swollen body to raise her feet on the couch. “Please come, I’m going crazy, Amelia.”

“I’ll be there shortly,” Amelia promised. She hung up the phone and grabbed her purse and keys. At six months pregnant, Amelia was still active but had gained twenty pounds already. Amelia crawled into her vehicle, grateful that the steering wheel tilted above her protruding tummy, and drove to Patricia’s.

Patricia opened the door before Amelia could knock and burst into tears.

Amelia took Patricia by the hand and led her to the kitchen. She sat her in the chair and got them both a glass of tea. “Now, tell me what’s wrong,” Amelia prompted.

Patricia sniffed and wiped her eyes with the Kleenex Amelia handed her. “I’m just a mess; I felt so good yesterday that I cleaned the entire house. Today I am exhausted and bored and just feel like I want to scream.”

Amelia smiled knowingly. “When is your due date?” she asked.

Patricia looked at the calendar as she spoke, “Today is October fifteenth and the doctor said October tenth; I’m past the due date and I’m just miserable.”

“Have you talked to your mom or dad recently?” Amelia asked trying to cheer Patricia up.

“I talk to them every day,” Patricia groaned and shifted, her face contorted with pain. “They are waiting for the baby to arrive before they come for a visit.”

“Patricia, how long have you been hurting?” Amelia asked softly.

Patricia looked puzzled. "I've been having back pain all morning, I'm sure I just overdid it yesterday."

"I think we should call the doctor," Amelia suggested.

Patricia grinned, "Don't be silly, I think I'd know if I was in labor. Let me get us some cookies." Patricia stood and gasped as the floor flooded beneath her feet. "Amelia, I think my water just broke," she exclaimed.

Amelia helped Patricia to the bathroom and handed her the needed items to clean up; she moved to the bedroom and pulled Patricia's overnight bag and a clean outfit from the closet.

Geoff answered his cell on the first ring, "Hello Amelia, did you dial the wrong number?" he asked laughing.

Amelia spoke calmly while keeping an eye on Patricia, "Geoff, you need to come home immediately; Patricia's water just broke."

"I'm on my way, are you with her?" Geoff asked.

"Yes, I'm here," Amelia moved away from the bathroom and lowered her voice, "Hurry Geoff."

Geoff hung up the phone, "Captain, Patricia's in labor, I've got to go," he yelled across the fire hall.

Geoff jumped in his car and drove to the house in record time with his emergency lights blazing. He ran through the door in time to see Patricia emerge from the bathroom. "Honey, I'm here, let's get you to the hospital," he spoke soothingly.

Patricia started to cry, "Geoff, I'm scared," she whispered.

Amelia took Patricia's overnight bag and followed them out the door and to the car. She helped Geoff get her situated and crawled in the back seat to ride with them.

Geoff winked at Amelia and took Patricia's hand as he drove. "We'll be there in just a few minutes, hang on sweetie." Geoff was keeping his eye on Patricia as he drove. "Amelia, did you call the doctor?" he asked.

Amelia smiled. "Yes, she'll meet us in the ER."

Geoff pulled up to the Emergency and tossed Amelia the keys. The staff was waiting with a wheel chair and helped Patricia to sit before rolling her into the hospital.

Amelia parked the car and carried Patricia's bag to the desk, where she was directed to maternity. Amelia was permitted to stay with Patricia and Geoff for just a few minutes while they checked her vitals. She walked over to the bed and squeezed Patricia's hand. "I'll be right outside in the waiting area," she whispered as she kissed Patricia's forehead. "I love you my friend, I'll be praying."

Patricia squeezed Amelia's hand. "I'm so glad you're here. Thanks Amelia, you're always right where I need you, when I need you," she spoke softly.

"That's what friends are for," Amelia acknowledged. She winked at Geoff and headed for the waiting area.

Chogan found Amelia sitting in the waiting room. "Hey there," he whispered softly.

Amelia smiled as Chogan sat beside her and wrapped her in his arms. "I'm glad you're here," she sighed.

"How is she?" Chogan asked.

"She's been in labor for over four hours; I haven't seen Geoff since right after she was admitted," Amelia admitted.

"She's going to be fine," Chogan stroked Amelia's back gently. "How are you? Four hours in these chairs must feel like an eternity?" he asked.

Amelia smiled as she spoke. "I'm getting pretty sore but your baby is having a wonderful time."

Chogan laughed as Amelia placed his hand over her abdomen where a steady kicking and rolling motion were taking place. "Does that hurt?" he asked concerned.

"Not really," Amelia explained. "But when this baby lays on the right spot, it makes me very urgently search for a ladies room." She giggled at her own joke.

"You're amazing." Chogan spoke softly into her ear. He kissed her and took her hand helping her to stand. "Let's walk a bit and see if we can find you some measure of comfort.

Amelia stretched and walked with Chogan's arm around her back, giving her added support. "Are the girls ok with Uda tonight?" she asked.

Chogan laughed. "They are having a slumber party. Mom said to tell you she loves you and to make sure you get some rest."

"Your parents are so dear to me. Having your mom close right now is an added blessing," Amelia admitted. "I miss my family."

Chogan was concerned. "I'm sorry, Amelia. I know this pregnancy is rough with having two daughters to take care of. It has to be even harder without your family close by."

Amelia stopped and turned to face Chogan. "There's no need for you to apologize; sweetie I'm very happy. I talk to my family every few days, I just miss them and that's normal. I love having my daughters to take care for as well as my handsome husband. You all are my life," she assured him.

Chogan pulled her to him and kissed her softly. "I don't think I've told you recently how absolutely beautiful you are, you're glowing."

"Thank you for saying that my love, I feel like a weeble toy," she teased.

Chogan was confused, "What's a weeble toy?" he asked.

"Weebles wobble but they don't fall down," Amelia explained laughing at her own joke.

Chogan couldn't help it, he laughed too. "Come on, let's head back to the waiting area and see if there's been any new developments.

Sabrina Olivia Sandidge arrived two hours later. She weighed in at eight pounds and twelve ounces. Sabrina had big blue eyes and blond hair; mommy was exhausted but very happy.

Amelia and Chogan were permitted to visit for just a few minutes after Patricia was moved to a room. Amelia walked over to the bed and kissed Patricia's forehead, "My friend, I am so proud of you," she said.

Patricia nodded to Geoff, "Amelia, you have to meet our daughter."

Geoff placed the baby in Patricia's arms and stood back with pride watching mother and daughter bond.

"Mommy would like you to meet my dearest friend, Amelia; you can call her Mia," Patricia spoke softly to the baby.

Amelia's eyes filled with happy tears. "She is beautiful, what did you name her?" she asked.

"Sabrina Olivia Sandidge," Geoff spoke the name with pride. "Her initials are SOS because with parents like us, she'll need all the help she can get," he teased.

The four adults laughed at the obvious meaning. "Welcome Sabrina, you are a beautiful addition to the Sandidge family," Chogan spoke softly as he viewed the baby in Patricia's arms.

Geoff came around the bed and hugged Amelia. "Thank you for coming to Patricia today, I am so grateful you were there when her water broke."

Patricia smiled, "I'm grateful too. Amelia has always been there for me."

Amelia blushed. "There's no thanks necessary, that's what friends, and family are for. We're going to go and let you get some rest."

Chogan helped Amelia into his truck and kissed her softly. "You're exhausted my love, I'm taking you straight home and putting you to bed."

Amelia yawned, "I'm sorry, Chogan; Geoff asked me to ride with them to the hospital so I left my car at their house."

Chogan started the truck and patted Amelia's hand. "Not to worry, I'll get your car home tomorrow, you just sit back and relax," he spoke softly and noticed the Amelia had already fallen asleep. Chogan held her hand while he drove through the darkness. He was concerned that Amelia was so tired but with the girls spending the night with Uda, Amelia could sleep in the following morning. Chogan parked the truck and walked around to Amelia's side. He opened the door gently and unfastened her seat belt. "Amelia, we're home," he whispered softly.

Amelia opened her eyes and smiled. "I'm sorry I fell asleep. I'm not much company right now," she apologized.

Chogan chuckled softly, "You are wonderful company, come on let's get you to bed." Chogan helped her from the truck and walked with her to the bedroom. He helped Amelia out of her clothes and into her nightgown.

Amber stood, beside the bed, waiting patiently until Amelia was situated. Amber laid her head on the mattress and waited until Amelia stroked her and talked to her. She was content to curl up and keep watch over her mistress.

Chogan shook his head. "That dog absolutely loves you, Amelia. She watches over you like a guardian angel."

Amelia moved her arm off the bed and stroked Amber's tenderly. "I love her so much, Chogan. She is wonderful company to the girls and to me. Thank you for allowing her to sleep in our room."

Chogan crawled into the bed and smiled down at Amelia as he spoke, "I couldn't break up the relationship that you have forged with that dog. I'm grateful to see her happy again."

Amelia rolled carefully to her side, "Chogan, do you think you could take me to my doctor's appointment next week?" Amelia asked.

Chogan grinned. "I would love to go with you. I didn't want to make you uncomfortable, but I've wanted to go," he explained.

Amelia pulled Chogan to her and kissed him softly. "I am very tired and I don't think the vitamins are giving me the energy they did before." She closed her eyes and was asleep in minutes.

Chogan stroked her face and placed his hand over her tummy. "Bless my wife and this baby, Lord, please help her regain her energy and her strength," he prayed. Chogan's heart began to beat faster as he thought about Samantha and her last pregnancy. "Please God, protect Amelia, keep her in your tender care," he prayed.

Chogan rearranged his work schedule to take Amelia to her prenatal appointment the following week. He waited patiently while the physician examined Amelia and then pulled in a small machine.

Doctor Sarah Kindle was young and friendly and put her patients at ease with her gentle ways. "Amelia, I think we need to do another ultrasound," she suggested.

Amelia took Chogan's hand as Doctor Kindle moved her to a sitting position with her legs stretched out on the table. "Is there something wrong?" Amelia asked.

Doctor Kindle smiled. "You've gained another five pounds and that's a total of twenty-five pounds. That's a bit more than I had hoped for by the end of your second trimester. However, I'm more concerned about the fatigue you're feeling."

Amelia's eyes filled with tears, "Is the baby ok? I've tried to watch what I eat and I am as active as I can be," she said as a tear slid down her cheek.

Doctor Kindle placed a tissue into Amelia's hand and smiled. "Amelia, you are a model patient. If all my new mommies followed instructions as well as you, my job would be much easier," she teased. "I want to make sure that your vitamins are sufficient and that the baby is not in any distress, that's the only reason for the ultrasound."

Chogan stroked Amelia's hand and offered her a smile of encouragement. "Amelia is very concerned that we eat healthy, I'm surprised that she's gained any weight at all," Chogan offered.

Doctor Kindle smeared the gel on Amelia's belly and turned on the ultrasound machine. "Let's just take a look shall we?" she asked.

Chogan was fascinated. As the father of two girls, he should have been ready for the image of his child but he wasn't. His heart was stirred by the sight and sound of their child moving in Amelia's womb.

Doctor Kindle pressed the buttons to record the images as she moved the wand and then she stopped. She turned slowly with a wide smile and spoke slowly, "Amelia, Chogan, I think I have found the cause of Amelia's fatigue and discomfort. She slid the wand slowly and waited for their reaction.

Amelia gasped. "Is that what I think it is?" she asked.

Chogan was confused, "What's wrong?" His fear for Amelia was evident on his face as he asked the question.

Doctor Kindle pointed at the screen with her finger, "This is your son," she moved her finger slowly across the screen, "And this is his twin brother."

Chapter Thirty-Two

Chogan stopped off at the pharmacy and picked up Amelia's new vitamins and two blue teddy bears. He walked back to the truck and tucked the bag in the back seat. Chogan put the key in the ignition but didn't start the truck. He leaned across the seat and kissed Amelia gently. "Thank you my love," he spoke softly.

Amelia was puzzled, "Thank you for what?" she asked.

"For presenting me with not one son, but two," Chogan touched her swollen belly reverently. "You will be taking it easy as the doctor suggested for the next three months." Chogan spoke with a gentle firmness and Amelia smiled.

"I don't know what to think, I'm still in shock," Amelia admitted.

Chogan drove back to the house and helped Amelia to the living room. He whistled once and Amber appeared in the doorway. Chogan tucked a pillow behind Amelia and lifted her legs to the couch. He removed her shoes and massaged her ankles. He turned to Amber and nodded his head once.

Amber moved immediately to Amelia's side and laid her head on the couch next to Amelia, keeping watch.

Chogan stroked Amber's head, "Good dog, Amber. Keep her company while I get dinner ready," he instructed.

Amelia started to object, "Chogan, I…"

Chogan cut her off, "Doctor Kindle said you were to rest," he grinned as he used his authoritative voice, "You will lay on that couch with the remote and your adoring canine admirer while I prepare dinner for the family." Chogan winked at her as he headed into the kitchen whistling.

Amelia turned on the TV and laid her head back onto the pillow that Chogan had placed behind her. She was asleep in minutes.

Chogan returned to the living room and pulled a light quilt from the back of the couch and covered Amelia carefully so he wouldn't disturb her. He walked softly back to the kitchen and finished the meal.

Topanga came through the door like a tornado, "Mama, Daddy, where are you?" she yelled.

Amelia didn't have time to sit up before Topanga spied her on the couch. "Hello sweetheart; how was school?" Amelia asked.

Topanga walked over to the couch slowly. "Mama, are you ok?" she asked quietly.

"I feel wonderful. I was tired and daddy made me take a nap." Amelia opened her arms. "I would feel even better if I had a hug from my daughter."

Topanga tossed her backpack to the floor and hugged Amelia, kissing her on the cheek. "I love you mama," she giggled.

"I love you too darling," Amelia teased.

Lovella came into the house pulling Dakota with her. "Mama, we got enough food for our company?" she asked.

Amelia laughed. "You'll have to ask daddy, he is cooking tonight."

The girls ran into the kitchen and helped Chogan to set the table. Uda kept Amelia company while Dakota helped Chogan with the food.

Dinner consisted of spaghetti and meatballs, tossed salad, garlic bread and for dessert a Boston cream pie that Uda had brought. As everyone was eating dessert, Chogan slipped into the kitchen and carried a bag back to the table. He removed the teddy bears he purchased and gave one to Topanga and one to Lovella.

"Daddy, why are you giving us, a blue teddy bear?" Topanga asked.

Chogan smiled as he knelt between his daughters, "Those bears are a gift from two big sisters to the new baby brother that mommy will soon give us."

Lovella looked at the bear and then at Amelia, "Daddy these bears are the same, why didn't you make them different?" she asked.

Chogan moved to stand behind Amelia, "Daddy made them identical because mommy is having two baby brothers," he explained.

Topanga giggled and jumped from her chair. She ran to Amelia's side, "Mommy is having twins?" she asked.

Amelia grinned, "Yes Topanga, you are getting twin brothers."

Lovella walked over slowly, "Why?" she asked in her three year old inquisitive nature.

Uda laughed and pulled Lovella into her lap. "Lovella, when God loves us he sends us his love in the lives of precious babies like you and Topanga. Sometimes, God has so much love for us that it spills over and he gives us two babies instead of one."

Lovella hugged Uda and grinned. "We must be real special to God, cuz we have four babies for mama and daddy to love."

Amelia called her parents while Chogan tucked the girls into bed. "Mom, it's me," Amelia held the phone close as she listened to her mother's voice. "Can you have daddy pick up the other phone?" she asked.

"Reggie, Amelia is on the phone; pick up the other phone please," Cecilia positioned herself on the swing waiting for Reggie.

"Hi honey, it's dad; what's up?" Reggie asked.

Amelia grinned. "Chogan and I saw the prenatal doctor today to find out why I'm so tired all the time."

"Are you ok?" Cecilia asked immediately.

"I'm more than ok; mom, dad, I'm having twins." Amelia waited for their reaction.

Reggie laughed, "That's wonderful, Amelia. Two more grandchildren, I'm thrilled."

Cecilia was wiping tears of joy, "My baby girl is having two babies. Are you sure you're ok? That's an awful lot to contend with," she spoke with a mother's worry.

"I'm fine mom. Chogan is helping and his mom and dad have been amazing. These babies will be healthy and happy and so will I," she promised.

Chogan stood at the door and listened to Amelia's side of the conversation. His heart constricted at her comment that she would be healthy and happy. The fear of losing her gripped his heart. "Keep her safe, Lord," he whispered under his breath.

Fall quickly turned to winter and Thanksgiving arrived with snow and cold winds. Amelia had learned to conserver her energy but her movements were now limited with the size of the babies she carried. Her body was swollen as she entered her eighth month of the pregnancy and she relied heavily on Uda's assistance.

Onawa and Talise were preparing Thanksgiving dinner at Chogan's for the entire family. Both of Chogan's sisters were in relationships and their boyfriends were joining them also.

Geoff and Patricia were joining them with Sabrina who was now six weeks old.

After Thanksgiving dinner, Geoff, Chogan and Dakota brought in a beautiful blue spruce Christmas tree. Amelia sat with the women stringing popcorn and cranberries to place on the tree. Topanga and Lovella were content to eat the popcorn and chase their cats from the decorations. The entire evening was chaotic and full of laughter.

Amelia waddled to the bedroom, and eased herself gently to the bed. "Chogan, today was wonderful. I don't know what I would do without your family," she sighed.

"They are your family too, Amelia," he corrected.

Amelia smiled. "Do you think I'll ever see my feet again?" she asked absently.

Chogan laughed and crawled across the bed and began to massage Amelia's shoulders gently. "I promise you will see your feet very soon," he teased.

Amelia leaned her head back and whispered, "I miss holding you in my arms," she said.

Chogan kissed her gently. "My love, I miss that, too. I am so proud of you and how well you've done with this pregnancy."

Amelia eased her body into the bed and shifted on her side. "I think I may have overdone it today," she said tiredly.

Chogan was concerned, "Do you need anything?" he asked quickly.

Amelia yawned, "Sleep, I just need sleep," she giggled. Amelia was asleep within minutes.

Chogan covered her with the blankets and watched her sleep. His fears were growing the closer Amelia got to her delivery of the twins. She was now required to see Dr. Kindle every week and his parents were taking her to her appointments.

Patricia came to take Amelia to her appointment the week before Christmas. Lovella and Topanga were spending the night with Uda and baking cookies. Amelia was exhausted but happy that her pregnancy was almost over.

Dr. Kindle came into the room and smiled at Patricia. "Hello Patricia, how are you and Sabrina doing?" she asked.

"Mommy and daughter are doing well; daddy is having sleep issues," Patricia replied.

Dr. Kindle laughed. "Is Sabrina sleeping through the night?" she asked.

Patricia grinned. "Some, she seems hungry all the time."

"Try mixing some rice cereal with her night feeding before you put her to bed. Sounds like your daughter needs more nourishment," Dr. Kindle suggested.

"Thanks, I'll try that," Patricia agreed.

"Amelia, how are you feeling?" Dr. Kindle asked.

"I'm exhausted," Amelia confessed. "How much longer?" she asked.

Dr. Kindle began the exam as she spoke, "Let's just see shall we?" she asked.

Dr. Kindle used her stethoscope to listen to the babies' heartbeats. "Amelia, is Chogan working today?" she asked.

"Yes, is something wrong?" Amelia asked.

"I think we should get you admitted and go ahead and deliver these boys," she spoke gently. "Patricia, can you call Amelia's husband to meet us at the hospital?" she asked.

Patricia had her cell phone out and moved to the hallway to talk to Chogan. She returned to the room as the paramedics arrived to move Amelia to a gurney.

Amelia's face was filled with fear. "Dr. Kindle, why can't I ride to the hospital with Patricia?" she asked fearfully.

Dr. Kindle squeezed her hand. "Amelia, your babies are sitting too low and I'm concerned that any unnecessary movement could put you into labor. I want you to be in delivery as soon as possible."

Amelia was driven in the ambulance to the hospital and Chogan was waiting when they arrived. He held her hand and smiled as she was wheeled to maternity. Patricia held Sabrina in her arms and waited for Geoff to join her.

Dr. Kindle came into the room in her scrubs. “Amelia, Chogan, I am concerned that the babies are in distress and I want to do a C-section immediately,” she explained.

Chogan agreed. “Can I stay with Amelia?” he asked.

“Yes, there will be a curtain between you and the medical team and as long as we have no issues, you will be permitted to stay.” Dr. Kindle followed them to the delivery room and talked with her staff as Chogan was gowned and Amelia was given an IV and sedation was started.

Chogan kissed her forehead and whispered encouragement, “Amelia, can you hear me?” he asked. When she nodded yes, he smiled and continued, “I’m right here Amelia, everything is going to be fine.”

Within minutes, Amelia was sedated and Dr. Kindle removed the first baby. He was passed to the nurses who resuscitated him and weighed him and wrapped him for Chogan to hold. He was beautiful. He had black hair and blue eyes and a healthy cry. The second baby was removed and again resuscitated, weighed and wrapped for Chogan to hold. He had blond hair and blue eyes and a soft cry. Chogan held them briefly before they were moved to an incubator and rolled into the pediatric care unit for further processing.

Amelia’s blood pressure began to drop quickly and an alarm sounded. “We’re losing her doctor,” the anesthesiologist stated.

Dr. Kindle called out instructions and spoke quickly, “Chogan, I’m sorry but you have to leave.”

Chogan was escorted to the hallway and as the doors closed he slumped against the wall, “God no, please God no, don’t take her from me,” he sobbed.

Geoff was walking with the baby and saw what happened. He passed Sabrina to Patricia and headed to Chogan. He didn’t say a word; he wrapped Chogan in his arms and allowed his friend to cry.

Patricia cried, she prayed as she had never prayed before. Pastor Taylor joined hands with his wife and they too began to pray in earnest.

Amelia felt the cold darkness as she slipped into a deep dark place. She was free from pain and suffering and then there was a light. The light was so bright it hurt her eyes. She heard voices praying and then there was pain. "Oh please, help me," she whispered.

"That's it, talk to me sweetie," the voice was firm and unfamiliar. "Are you in pain?" the voice asked.

"Yes," Amelia replied. She felt nauseated and opened her eyes searching for a focal point. "I'm going to be sick," she whispered.

She felt herself held up and a basin placed under her chin as she heaved until she could throw up no more. Amelia was trembling from head to foot and she was cold.

The nurse rubbed her back slowly and smiled. "You did very well. Your nausea is caused by the anesthesia, we can help with that." She injected medicine into Amelia's IV and smiled as the trembling stopped and her patient went to sleep.

Amelia was moved to recovery and was placed on monitors. She slept deeply, not knowing that Chogan was devastated.

Dr. Kindle walked into the waiting room and found Chogan surrounded by friends. "Mr. Hawk, may I speak with you please?" she asked.

Chogan turned and walked slowly to follow the doctor to the hallway.

Dr. Kindle spoke softly. "Amelia has been moved to recovery. She's been sedated and given anti-nausea medication to prevent her tearing any of the stitches in her incision."

Chogan looked up startled and interrupted the doctor, "She's alive? Amelia is alive?" he asked.

Dr. Kindle looked confused, "Of course." Realization dawned as Dr. Kindle took Chogan's hand. "Mr. Hawk, your wife had a ruptured blood vessel in her uterus caused by the weight of the babies. The excessive bleeding caused her blood pressure to fall at a rapid pace. We had to remove you so we could surgically repair the blood vessel." Dr. Kindle smiled as she continued. "Amelia is exhausted but she is doing very well. We are going to keep her sedated for a few more hours to give her body a chance to rest and to allow the nausea to pass. I suspect she'll be ready to meet her sons by tomorrow morning."

Chogan felt the tears of gratitude falling and didn't try to stop them. "Can I see her? He asked.

Dr. Kindle laughed softly. "You can follow me now to recovery and I'll let you see her for just a few minutes. Then once she's moved to a room, you can stay with her."

Chogan walked around the curtain and moved to stand at the head of Amelia's bed. He kissed her gently and whispered, "I'm here, Amelia. I love you so much and I'm so proud of you."

Chogan left recovery and headed for the waiting room to share his news.

Chapter Thirty-Three

Amelia woke up in her room, surrounded by bouquets of flowers. She laughed at the balloon bouquet of all blue balloons. The card attached simply read, “Aunt Mia—you rock! Love, Henry.”

Chogan was asleep in the chair beside the bed. He was still in his fireman’s uniform and looked exhausted. He stirred and opened his eyes to see Amelia smiling at him. Chogan stood and leaned across the bed and kissed Amelia. “Good morning Mama,” he whispered smiling.

“Good morning daddy,” Amelia stroked his face and pulled him closer to kiss him soundly. “I feel so thin,” she giggled.

Chogan laughed. “Would you like to meet our sons?” he asked.

Amelia looked around the room, “I can’t wait!”

Chogan rang the nurse button and within minutes two little bassinets were rolled into the room. Chogan picked up his firstborn son and handed him to Amelia.

Amelia cradled him and checked his fingers and toes and her eyes filled with happy tears. “My beautiful baby boy, you look like your daddy.” She kissed him gently and shifted him to her left arm. “How much did he weigh?” she asked.

Chogan smiled, “Your firstborn son weighed in at six pounds and three ounces. Chogan handed her their second son and Amelia gasped in delight.

“Oh Chogan, he looks like me,” she sighed as she kissed him. “Welcome my beautiful baby boy, you look like mama.” Amelia checked his fingers and toes and smiled as she asked. “He feels lighter, how much did he weigh?”

Chogan laughed, “Your second born son weighed in at six pounds and two ounces.”

Amelia held her babies close. “No wonder I was tired, that’s over twelve pounds of baby,” she laughed.

“So don’t you think we should name our sons?” Chogan asked.

Amelia rocked the twins gently in her arms. “I have an idea that I hope you will like,” she said.

"I'm listening," Chogan confirmed.

"I believe that God brought us together, I would like to give our sons, biblical names," Amelia paused. "However, I want their middle names to be Native American."

Chogan kissed Amelia on the forehead, "What did you have in mind," he asked.

"Nathanael Koda Hawk, and Tobias Kota Hawk," Amelia smiled, "Nathanael means the gift of God and Tobias means the Lord is good," she explained.

Chogan was thoughtful, "Did you say the same middle name?" he asked.

Amelia smiled. "Koda with a d and Kota with a t, both are Native American and they mean the allies."

Chogan took his eldest son in his arms. "What do you think about Nathanael Koda?" he asked. "He likes it, and so does his daddy," Chogan agreed.

Amelia spoke softly to her younger son, "Tobias Kota will be your name."

Chogan sat on the bed facing Amelia and gently rocking his son. "How do you feel this morning?" he asked.

Amelia touched his hand. "I'm sore but I am so grateful that the babies are healthy; I can't think about the pain," she admitted.

"Do you realize that yesterday was our first wedding anniversary?" he teased.

Amelia's eyes filled with tears. "Oh Chogan, I am so sorry, with the babies, I didn't even think about what day it was."

Chogan rushed to reassure her. "There's no need to apologize, you gave me the best present a man could ask for."

Amelia laughed. "How many children share their birthday with their parents' anniversary?"

Amelia and the twins went home three days later. Amelia settled the babies in their cribs and set the baby monitor. She tucked Topanga and Lovella in bed that night and rejoiced in being able to hold them close again.

"Mama, do you still love me?" Lovella asked as Amelia tucked the blanket around her.

"I will always love you my sweet daughter; why would you ask me that question?" Amelia asked.

"You have two new babies to love, will you have enough love for me and sissy?" she asked.

Amelia pulled Lovella into her lap and held her close for a hug. She spoke very carefully to reassure her daughter. "Lovella, you and Topanga are big sisters now. You will always be my special girls and I will always have enough love for all my children," she promised.

Lovella hugged her tight and kissed her on the cheek. "I love you mama," she whispered.

Amelia tucked her back under the blankets and kissed her, "I love you too my sweet baby girl."

Topanga was waiting for Amelia. "Are you gonna tuck me in too, mama?" she asked.

Amelia pushed her gently into the bed and tickled her until she giggled uncontrollably. "I've missed being able to tuck my girls in," she admitted.

Topanga reached up and touched Amelia's face. "I love you, mama."

"I love you too, Topanga. You and Lovella are my precious, priceless daughters and I am so glad I get to be your mama," she assured her.

Chogan checked the twins and made sure they were sleeping. He met Amelia in the living room and laughed as Amber guarded the Christmas tree from the cats. He growled softly and they both ran for their rooms to curl up with the girls for the night. "I underestimated that dog," Chogan teased.

Amelia took Chogan by the hand and sat down on the couch slowly.

"Are you ok?" Chogan asked.

"I'm just tired, but that's to be expected," Amelia acknowledged. "Chogan, I haven't done much Christmas shopping and today is December twentieth."

Chogan smiled. "Not to worry, it's done."

"How?" Amelia asked surprised.

"I took your list and ordered it online. The gifts arrived, are wrapped and tucked away safely for the holiday." Chogan sat back pleased with his success.

Amelia breathed a sigh of relief. "Thank you, Chogan. I appreciate you so much."

Chogan stood and pulled Amelia to her feet. "I believe you told me a few weeks ago that you missed holding me close," Chogan pulled her close and held her gently in his arms.

Amelia cuddled close, "Now this feels nice."

Amelia was in the kitchen decorating Christmas cookies on Christmas Eve with Topanga and Lovella. The twins were napping in their cribs and the snow was gently falling outside.

Chogan arrived home and walked to the kitchen doorway, loving the sight of his wife and daughters celebrating the holidays. "Merry Christmas family," he announced.

"Merry Christmas," they shouted together.

"Amelia, are you ready for your Christmas surprise?" Chogan asked.

"It's only Christmas Eve," she laughed, "However, if you want to give me my gift early, I'm ready."

"Follow me," Chogan winked at the girls and pulled Amelia around the counter. "Close your eyes and don't open them until I tell you," he instructed.

Amelia held Chogan's arm and felt herself move into the living room. She felt the heat of the fireplace and grinned.

"Open your eyes now," Chogan whispered from behind her.

Amelia opened her eyes and heard "Surprise!" She stood in shock; there stood her parents, Myron, Anne and the children. "I can't believe you're all here!" she cried.

Chogan stood back grinning and watching as Amelia reunited with her family and introduced them to the twins. This was his best Christmas surprise, ever.

Chogan woke at 6:30 am Christmas morning to the smell of cinnamon. He heard giggling and walked into the kitchen to find

Amelia and five children icing sticky buns around the counter. He grinned at Reggie and Cecilia sitting at the table rocking the twins. "Merry Christmas," he spoke above the noise.

"Merry Christmas!" the children shouted.

Myron sat next to Anne and fed Hannah icing from the sticky bun he held.

"Myron, you're going to make her hyper with all that sugar," Anne scolded gently.

Myron grinned, "It's Christmas, and this is a tradition."

Chogan walked over and hugged Amelia close; he smiled at Hilary, Harmon, Henry, Topanga and Lovella, with faces covered in icing and cinnamon. "Do I get one of those sticky buns?" he asked laughing.

"Here daddy," Topanga held out a sticky bun dripping with icing.

Chogan bit into the bun and rolled his eyes, "Mmmmm these are wonderful," he exclaimed.

Geoff, Patricia and Sabrina joined Amelia and her family on Christmas day. They shared stories with Chogan's family and the children swam in the indoor pool for hours; enjoying their opportunity to swim in the middle of winter.

Amelia enjoyed playing with her niece Hannah. At six months old, she was happy and lively. Amber stayed close whenever Hannah was placed on the floor, she barked softly if Hannah rolled or crawled too close to the edge.

Myron watched Amber, "Amelia that dog is amazing. She's absolutely guarding the baby," he said.

Amelia stroked Amber's fur. "She's very special to me. During the last few weeks of my pregnancy, she was wonderful company."

Anne sat back holding Nathanael in her arms. "Amelia, motherhood agrees with you."

"I have to agree," Myron said. "I never dreamed that you would have four children of your own," he laughed as he continued. "I also never dreamed that we would have four children."

Cecilia listened to their conversation. "Your daddy and I are very happy to have eight thriving grandchildren."

Amelia took her mother by the hand. “Mom, you and dad need to sit, Myron, Anne, Chogan and I have a gift for you.”

Reggie sat beside Cecilia on the couch and smiled at his sleeping grandson in Myron’s arms. “Amelia, we have more than anyone could want or need,” he assured her.

“Well, we want you to have this,” Amelia said as she handed them a box.

Cecilia lifted the lid slowly and passed the contents to Reggie. “Are you serious?” she asked.

Myron laughed. “You and dad have done so much for us that we decided it was time the four of us gave something back.”

Reggie was surprised. “This is an Alaska Cruise,” he stated.

“Not just a cruise,” Chogan explained. “We have also added a land tour with the glass top train from Anchorage to Fairbanks.”

Cecilia hugged each one of them. “I couldn’t have been blessed with better children,” she exclaimed.

Onawa and Talise pulled another box from beneath the tree and turned to Dakota and Uda who were sitting on the love seat. “This gift is from Chogan, Amelia and Us,” Onawa stated.

Uda opened the box and laughed. “You’re kidding, we are going on a cruise too?” she asked.

Chogan laughed. “Actually the four of you are booked on the same cruise,” he explained.

Uda hugged each of her children and Amelia. “Cecilia, how did we get so blessed to have such wonderful children?” she asked.

Cecilia laughed. “I think we are just blessed.”

Chapter Thirty-Four

After the holidays, Amelia and Chogan's lives settled into a routine. Amelia was scheduled for her six-week check up with Dr. Kindle and had planned a very special dinner to celebrate. Uda and Dakota were keeping the girls overnight. Alice was sitting with the twins until Amelia returned.

Dr. Kindle completed Amelia's exam and helped her to sit up on the exam table. "So how are you feeling?" she asked.

Amelia smiled. "I feel lighter," she laughed at her own joke. "I'm tired, but that's from having two babies to care for."

"How are the babies?" Dr. Kindle asked.

"They are wonderful," Amelia said softly.

"I'm glad to hear it," Dr. Kindle replied. "Amelia, I'm pleased with your progress and there's no reason why you can't resume your normal activities."

"Thanks Dr. Kindle, I appreciate the way you've cared for me and the delivery of my sons," Amelia spoke softly.

Dr. Kindle smiled. "You are most welcome. If you need us, just call; otherwise, I'll see for your annual exam in December."

Amelia left the office and stopped by Butterhorn Bakery to pick up a special dessert. She drove home and placed the homemade chicken pot pie in the oven to bake. She tossed a salad and made sure the glass bottles of coke were chilled.

Amelia fed the twins, bathed them and placed them in the cribs. She smiled at their tiny smiles as they slept. The baby monitor was on and Amber was lying between the cribs keeping watch over the sleeping boys.

Amelia checked her watch and hurried to shower and change. She brushed her hair and clipped it up with a banana clip. Amelia smiled at her reflection in the mirror and checked the twins one more time. The table was set with candles, china and Amelia had an instrumental CD playing softly.

Chogan entered the house and walked slowly into the kitchen. "Where are the girls?" he asked.

"Your mother asked them to spend the night," Amelia responded. "Could you carry this chicken pot pie to the table?" she asked innocently.

Chogan carried the dish to the table; before he could return to the kitchen, Amelia joined him.

Amelia kissed Chogan softly and gently pushed him into his chair. She went to the kitchen and returned with the salad and their cokes. Amelia sat down and took Chogan's hand. "Would you offer the blessing?" she asked softly.

Chogan squeezed her hand and prayed over their meal. "What's the occasion?" Chogan asked not wanting to spoil the mood.

Amelia served the salad and chose her words carefully. "I saw Dr. Kindle today," she said.

"Are you okay?" he asked.

"I'm fine. Today was my six week check-up and I received a clean bill of health," Amelia assured him.

Chogan let out his breath in relief. "I'm glad," he whispered.

Amelia listened as Chogan told her about the latest events at the firehouse. They ate their meal and Chogan went to change the twins while Amelia did the dishes.

Amelia was still in the kitchen when Chogan finished with the twins. He slipped in behind her and wrapped his arms around her waist. "Dinner was great, Amelia," he whispered as he traced her neck with his fingers.

"I've got dessert," Amelia offered.

"I couldn't eat another bite," Chogan laughed. "Maybe later," he suggested. Chogan lifted the dishtowel and began to dry the dishes.

Amelia drained the sink and turned to face Chogan. "I'll be right back," she said.

Chogan whistled while he placed the clean dishes in the cabinets. He hung the towel to dry and turned to see Amelia standing in the doorway. She was wearing a satin gown and her hair was out of the clip and loose around her shoulders. Chogan stood completely still.

Amelia lifted her finger and motioned for Chogan to come to her.

Chogan swallowed and moved slowly towards Amelia. He stopped directly in front of her.

Amelia stood on her tip toes and kissed Chogan softly. She wrapped her arms around his neck and brought him closer.

Chogan pulled her close and deepened the kiss. He groaned softly as Amelia pulled away.

“Dr. Kindle said I can return to all my normal activities,” Amelia whispered.

Chogan smiled, “That’s the best news I’ve heard all day,” he spoke softly.

Chapter Thirty-Five

Mother's Day was extra special for Amelia and Patricia. This was their first Mother's day after the birth of Sabrina, Nathanael, and Tobias.

Pastor Taylor had planned a special service and gave each mother a pink rose and a satin Bible book mark with a poem and scripture printed in gold ink.

Amelia and Chogan were hosting a cookout at the ranch after church. Topanga and Lovella pulled Patricia into the family room and whispered like conspirators.

"Girls, are you ready for lunch?" Amelia asked.

"We'll be there in a minute, mama," Lovella hollered.

Amelia laughed and carried the fruit tray and the vegetable tray to the table. She checked the babies in their playpen and smiled at Amber protectively watching over the babies.

Patricia came out the door and cleared her throat to get everyone's attention. "Amelia, your precocious daughters have a Mother's Day gift they would like to present."

Patricia moved off the porch and started the CD player.

The music started Topanga and Lovella emerged dressed in bright pink boas. They had a choreographed a dance to go with the music. The song they chose was "Mama Mia."

Amelia laughed as they moved in rhythm to the music and sang and danced without missing a word. She stood and applauded loudly as they finished with a sweeping curtsey.

Patricia joined the table laughing. "Girls that was great," she encouraged.

Amelia hugged them both before they ran off to play on the swing set. "Patricia, did you teach my daughters that song?" she asked laughing.

Patricia giggled. "They begged me to help them plan a special gift for Mother's day and that song was just too appropriate."

Chogan joined the conversation. "Admit it Amelia, she couldn't have picked a more perfect song for you."

Amelia agreed. “Just wait until Sabrina gets a bit bigger; Mia will teach her lots of things,” she promised.

The alarm sounded at the fire station early Monday morning. Chogan and Geoff were on the first truck to respond to an apartment fire. The entire structure was fully engulfed when they arrived. A window from the second floor was broken from the inside and a young mother screamed from inside, “Help me, please God save my baby!”

Geoff and Chogan were the first responders as EMTs; they followed the hose team and worked their way up the stairs and into the apartment where the window had been broken. The apartment was filled with smoke and flames licked the walls making an eerie sound as the structure heaved under the heat.

Geoff found the mother collapsed at the window and quickly placed his ventilator on her face. Chogan carried her to the waiting EMTs in the hallway and she was carried down the stairs to a waiting ambulance. Geoff had located the child and passed him to Chogan to carry. Chogan placed his respirator on the child.

Chogan was half down the stairs with Geoff behind him when the second floor began to collapse. Chogan jumped the distance and rolled across the yard holding the child in his arms. The paramedics grabbed the child and headed for a waiting ambulance. Chogan turned and realized Geoff had not made it out.

Chogan raced back into the house and saw Geoff trapped under the rubble. He heard his fellow firemen screaming for him to get out, but he couldn’t leave his friend. Chogan prayed and struggled to lift the beam that was holding Geoff captive. As he prayed a second pair of hands lifted the beam allowing him to drag Geoff out of the building.

The paramedics were waiting and as Chogan helped lift Geoff to the stretcher. As he turned to say thank you, he realized the other fireman had not emerged. “Where’s the other man that was inside helping me?” he asked the team working the hose.

“Chogan, you were alone in there, how did you get Geoff out?” they asked.

Chogan felt a chill run down his spine and a small still voice, “Beware lest ye entertain angels unaware,” it said.

Chogan rode with Geoff to the hospital. He was forced to the waiting room as Geoff was moved to trauma.

Patricia arrived within minutes; she was white with fear and held Sabrina tightly in her arms. "Chogan, what happened?" she asked.

"Geoff and I were rescuing a mother and child from a second story apartment; the floor collapsed and Geoff got caught under the rubble," Chogan choked on the words, trying to stay calm for Patricia's benefits.

Patricia staggered and Chogan steadied her and helped her to a chair.

"Let me take Sabrina; go to the desk and see if they'll let you go back to be with him," Chogan suggested.

Patricia didn't say a word; she passed Sabrina to Chogan and headed for the desk. She was admitted to the trauma unit as Geoff's wife.

Chogan held Sabrina close and slowly paced the ER waiting room.

Amelia got the call and immediately called Uda to pick up Topanga from school. Alice arrived quickly and stayed with Lovella and the twins so Amelia could drive to the hospital.

"Chogan how's Geoff?" Amelia asked.

"I don't know, they won't tell me anything and Patricia hasn't come out yet," Chogan whispered. "I took Sabrina so Patricia could go back."

Amelia took Sabrina and held her close. "Chogan, go see if they'll let you go back and check on Geoff; I'll stay here with Sabrina," she offered.

Chogan kissed her gently and walked to the desk. They admitted him to the trauma unit and he walked into the curtained area.

Patricia was seated beside the bed and crying softly.

"How is he?" Chogan asked quietly.

"He's got internal injuries and is headed for surgery. They haven't been able to revive him from the smoke he inhaled; so he's on a ventilator." Patricia struggled to control the sobs that were shaking her body. "Chogan, where was his respirator? Why wasn't he wearing a respirator?"

Chogan knelt down on the floor in front of Patricia's chair to explain. "He did have a respirator; he took it off and placed it on the mother. I used mine on her child."

Patricia couldn't control the tears any longer and Chogan wrapped her in his arms and allowed her to cry.

Amelia had changed Sabrina's diaper, fed her and had rocked her back to sleep before Chogan joined her in the waiting room. "How's Geoff," she asked fearfully.

"They don't know; he's on a ventilator from the smoke inhalation and he's got internal injuries," Chogan sat beside Amelia and placed his head in his hands. "I should have gotten him out sooner," he whispered.

Amelia leaned against Chogan offering him her strength. "Pastor Taylor is on his way; let's pray;" she whispered. They prayed for Geoff and for God's divine intervention and were still praying when Pastor Taylor arrived.

Patricia walked slowly into the waiting room feeling lost and confused. She took her daughter in her arms and cuddled her close. "They've taken him to surgery," she whispered.

Three hours later, the waiting room was filled with firemen. Chogan and Amelia saw the doctor approaching and Patricia held Amelia's hand as the doctor sat down next to her.

"Mrs. Sandidge, your husband has been moved to recovery. He's still on the ventilator but hopefully he will be breathing on his own before long. We removed his spleen and had to repair a tear in his intestine. His hip was broken and his shoulder dislocated, but those will heal. He's young and he's strong."

Patricia nodded slowly, trying to absorb his words. "Can I see him?" she asked.

The doctor patted her hand soothingly. "He will be moved from recovery to ICU for the first forty-eight hours. You will be able to go to his room once he is out of recovery."

Patricia thanked the doctor and sat down slowly. "Pastor Taylor, pray with me, please?" she pleaded.

Pastor Taylor, Amelia, Chogan and the other firemen joined Patricia in prayer for Geoff's health and strength.

Patricia wiped her eyes slowly and turned to Amelia. "I need a favor," she started to say.

Amelia hugged her close. "We'll keep Sabrina until Geoff is better," she assured her.

Patricia's eyes filled with tears, "You have four children at home; how can I ask you to keep my daughter too?"

Amelia laughed softly. "Patricia, how many children do we typically have in a classroom? Five is easy," she joked.

Patricia hugged her, "Thanks Amelia, you've always been there for me," she whispered.

"No thanks necessary, that's what friends are for. Go take care of your husband and we'll be here when you need us," Amelia responded.

Chapter Thirty-Six

Geoff was moved from recovery to ICU and Patricia was admitted to the room once he was settled. Geoff's face was burned' his hips were aligned with a brace, and he was in traction.

Patricia's eyes filled with tears and she watched the ventilator breath for her husband. "God, please spare Geoff's life. He risks his life every day as a fireman; honor that faithfulness Lord, please," she pleaded in prayer.

Geoff was on the respirator and unconscious for several days. Patricia left his side only long enough to shower and change clothes. She was sitting beside him when he coughed. Patricia looked up and saw Geoff's eyes open and he reached for the tube. Before she could say anything the nurses were in the room and moved her out of the way.

"Mr. Sandidge, can you hear me?" the patient care tech asked.

Geoff nodded his head and pointed to the tube going down his throat.

"I understand, we can remove that tube but you'll have to help us, ok?" The patient care technician explained the procedure as they eased Geoff's bed into a slightly elevated position. Once the technician was sure Geoff understood, he counted to three and removed the tube as Geoff coughed.

Geoff coughed and groaned in pain as the coughs shook his body. Geoff tried to speak and started coughing again.

Patricia took the coke from the nurse and placed a straw in the can. She moved to Geoff's side and held the can for him. "Sip it slowly, sweetie, your throat will be sore and this might burn a little," Patricia explained.

Geoff took a sip and a tear slid down his face. When Patricia started to move the coke away, Geoff grabbed her hand and pulled the coke back towards him. "More," he whispered.

Patricia grinned and held the can while Geoff took slow sips at first and then drank over half the can. She laughed softly when he sighed and leaned back against the pillows.

"Where's Sabrina?" Geoff whispered hoarsely.

"Amelia and Chogan are keeping her," Patricia whispered.

Geoff smiled and reached for Patricia pulling her close. "Need a kiss," he whispered.

Patricia kissed him softly and Geoff wrapped his uninjured arm around her and pulled her as close as possible, kissing her soundly.

"Much better," Geoff teased.

Patricia sat gently on the side of the bed and took Geoff's hand in hers. "I am so glad you're back. I've missed you," tears slid down her cheeks as she spoke.

Geoff wiped the tears with his thumb and smiled. "I'm sorry I made you worry, Patricia," he apologized.

Patricia leaned forward and kissed him again. "Don't apologize for being the best fireman ever. You had two visitors earlier today," she paused and took his hand again. "The young mother and her two year old son, that you saved, came to visit you."

Geoff grinned. "I'm glad they're okay, that makes it all worthwhile."

Geoff stayed in the hospital for an additional week while he learned to walk with a walker. He was released with strict instructions for rest and rehabilitation.

Amelia and Chogan brought Sabrina home after Patricia had Geoff settled. She reached for her daddy and laughed out loud as he reached for her.

"Geoff, be careful, your shoulder," Patricia scolded gently.

"I'm fine," Geoff responded as he kissed his daughter and made her giggle. "Daddy missed his little angel so much," he told the baby.

"Lovella and Topanga are very upset that we had to bring Sabrina back; they were getting pretty attached," Amelia teased.

Patricia laughed, "Maybe you'll have to give them a sister, next time," she teased.

Chogan laughed. "Now that's what we need another baby to make our lives more interesting."

Amelia agreed.

"Chogan who was that other fireman that helped you pull me out of that house?" Geoff asked.

Chogan ran his hand through his hair. "I'm glad you saw him, too. The other firemen said I was in there alone and he never emerged from that house. If I had to guess, I'd say we had an angel in that fire with us," he admitted.

Geoff smiled, "That explains why I didn't recognize him. All I saw was a smile and felt a strong hand lifting that rubble off my body."

Patricia's eyes filled with grateful tears. "God has been so good to us, we have so much to be thankful for," she spoke softly.

Amelia hugged her friend tightly. "I agree my friend," she whispered.

Geoff's recovery was complete by the middle of July. He was back to work and life settled back into a routine.

Patricia's family was scheduled to visit in September to celebrate Geoff and Patricia's second wedding anniversary.

Amelia and Chogan hosted a barbecue during Patricia's family visit. After dinner, the adults, Topanga and Lovella swam while Amelia put the twins to bed.

Patricia joined Amelia in the nursery. "Hey, are they asleep?" Patricia asked softly.

Amelia grinned, "Finally, my boys are growing more adamant about being up longer each night," she teased.

Patricia walked with Amelia to the kitchen. "You are so comfortable raising four children, how do you find the energy?" Patricia asked.

"They keep me so busy, I don't have time to think about it," Amelia mused. "Actually, I love having four children, I feel like my life is complete."

"Amelia, I haven't told Geoff yet," Patricia paused and chewed her lower lip.

"When is the baby due?" Amelia asked knowingly.

Patricia smiled a wistful smile, "If my calculations are correct, around Mother's Day."

Amelia hugged her. "Congratulations my friend," she spoke softly.

"I've got one problem with this pregnancy," Patricia confided.

"What's the problem?" Amelia asked concerned.

"I don't want to leave my babies and go back to the classroom. I know we need the income, but I'm selfish and want to be with my children," Patricia explained.

Amelia smiled. "Can I make a suggestion?" she asked.

"I'll take any suggestions or advice you can offer," Patricia assured her.

"Why don't you start a daycare?" Amelia asked.

Patricia grinned. "You've heard that the daycare I take Sabrina to is being sold."

Amelia laughed. "Yes, and I have to admit that you're desire to be with Sabrina and the new baby fit perfectly into my plan."

Patricia liked what she was hearing. "So tell me more," she encouraged.

Amelia explained the idea of taking over the daycare. With their teaching experience, Patricia and Amelia could help preschool age children prepare for public school.

Patricia chewed her lip. "I love the idea, but we have a major stumbling block. How do I get the funds to buy the daycare?" she asked.

Amelia laughed softly. "Patricia, that's taken care of."

"You'll have to explain that statement, Amelia." Patricia had no idea what Amelia was referring to.

"After my accident, I received a settlement. I've followed God's direction on how to invest that money. This daycare is an opportunity to work together and to touch the lives of children every day." Amelia smiled as she continued. "Patricia, I truly believe God is opening a door for us and we've got to apply that Now Faith."

Patricia stood and hugged Amelia. "This is an answer to prayer. I could continue to work and still be with my babies. Are you sure you can afford to do this?" she asked.

Amelia laughed, "Trust me, I can afford this and it's a great investment!"

Patricia sat down and picked up her tea. "I stand amazed at how God works in our lives to provide for our every need."

Amelia spoke wistfully, "Did you ever think we'd be wives and mothers when you planned our vacation to Frisco?"

Patricia laughed. "I had hopes, but no, I had no idea. Are you happy that we took that trip, Amelia?" she asked.

Amelia leaned against the counter and smiled. "Patricia, you gave me a priceless gift by bringing me to Frisco. I found my faith in Frisco and with it I gained a wonderful husband, two beautiful daughters and two precious sons. I also get to live close to my best friend and watch her beautiful daughter grow. Happy doesn't begin to express how I feel."

Patricia sighed, "I will forever be grateful that God led me to Frisco," she agreed.

CPSIA information can be obtained at www.ICGtesting.com
Printed in the USA
240863LV00002B/346-393/P